Meryl Wilsner writes happily ever afters for queer folks who love women. They are the *USA Today* best-selling author of *Something to Talk About, Mistakes Were Made,* and *Cleat Cute.* Born in Michigan, Meryl lived in Portland, Oregon, and Jackson, Mississippi, before returning to the Mitten State. Some of Meryl's favorite things include: all four seasons, button-down shirts, the way giraffes run, and their wife.

T0385180

ALSO BY MERYL WILSNER

Cleat Cute
Mistakes Were Made
Something to Talk About

MY BEST FRIEND'S HONEYMOON

MERYL WILSNER

PIATKUS

PIATKUS

First published in the US in 2025 by St Martin's Griffin,
An imprint of St Martin's Publishing Group
Published in Great Britain in 2025 by Piatkus

1 3 5 7 9 10 8 6 4 2

A CIP catalogue record for this book
is available from the British Library.

ISBN 978-0-349-43411-7

Printed and bound in Great Britain by Clays Ltd, Elcograf S.p.A.

Papers used by Piatkus are from well-managed forests
and other responsible sources.

Piatkus
An imprint of
Little, Brown Book Group
Carmelite House
50 Victoria Embankment
London EC4Y 0DZ

The authorised representative
in the EEA is
Hachette Ireland
8 Castlecourt Centre, Dublin 15, D15
XTP3, Ireland
(email: info@hbgi.ie)

An Hachette UK Company
www.hachette.co.uk

www.littlebrown.co.uk

To Trinica,
for never letting anything slip through the cracks

MY BEST

FRIEND'S

HONEYMOON

1

GOD, THIS MAN IS TRULY NOT VERY BRIGHT.

Ginny has spent the past three years trying to give him the benefit of the doubt—Derrick is Elsie's partner, not theirs, and they want Elsie to be happy, so they've always tried not to think about his flaws—but this proves it. Incontrovertibly.

"What do you think?" Derrick asks with a grin.

Ginny thinks a lot of things. They think the old train depot is a lovely venue, all creamy painted brick and tall ceilings and an old train schedule board that currently reads CONGRATULA- TIONS, ARMIN AND SASSY! There's plenty of room for tables, and Ginny can imagine the space would be magical all done up with flowers and twinkle lights. They think Elsie might even like it, in another situation. They just also think that planning the entire wedding without consulting her is not the way to go.

"I think Elsie will probably want some say in the wedding planning," Ginny says slowly.

Derrick grins even wider. "I used her Pinterest board!"

Elsie created that Pinterest board six months into the engagement, when her mom complained about how she didn't seem to want to plan anything. It placated Mrs. Hoffman at the time, but Ginny is pretty sure Elsie hasn't added to it since. In fact, Ginny's pretty sure Elsie hasn't thought about the wedding unprompted very often, if at all, the entire engagement. They've had lunch together almost every single workday during that time, and Elsie has never said a single thing about the wedding. Her ring sits unremarkably on her third finger, not like she's accustomed to it so much as like she's forgotten about it.

"Plus," Derrick continues, "she always says she's too busy with the store to plan. She gets overwhelmed. So I took care of it for her."

It's so close to romantic, except for the part where maybe one member of a couple being "too busy" to make a single decision about wedding planning for an entire year and a half is indicative of more than their workload.

"I just don't want you to go to all this trouble for her to be upset at you," Ginny says, like their lack of enthusiasm is due to worry about *Derrick*.

"It was no trouble," he says. "Any annoyance she has about not having a say is gonna be offset by how glad she'll be that I took it off her plate." He's been standing in the middle of the giant room, but now he walks to the opposite wall and looks out the paned-glass windows. "They've even got space heaters so we can be outside if we want, though obviously Minnesota in January isn't exactly outdoor weather."

Wait, what?

"What do you mean, *January*?"

"Oh yeah, I haven't even told you the best part," Derrick says. "This is all going down a week from tomorrow."

Ginny rubs their temples. He didn't just plan the entire wedding without talking to Elsie; he planned the entire wedding *for next week* without talking to her.

Derrick isn't mean-spirited. He's just not particularly smart. And it's not that Ginny wants him to be in Mensa; they simply want him to think through the consequences of his actions. Especially when those consequences will land on their best friend.

"I'm gonna bring her here after her shift at the store tomorrow, and they're gonna have changed the sign so it's for us, and I'll tell her the whole plan. But I wanted to check with you first. You know her better than anyone, so you'll know if there's anything else I need to do to make this the perfect day for her."

"Derrick." Ginny swallows. Lets out a slow breath. "I really think it's important you ask *her* what would make the day perfect for her."

"Oh, I'm going to," Derrick says, all blonde hair and big grin. "Of course I'm going to. I just want as much taken care of as possible. And you know she's not always good at asking for what she wants."

Understatement of the year. Elsie has no problem standing up for her siblings, or Ginny, or someone she barely knows, just never for herself. The first time Derrick learned Ginny's pronouns, it was Els who put him in his place.

"If you're okay with they *and* she, why not just use she?" he asked. "That'd be so much easier."

Ginny didn't get into the complexities of her identity with him, and she didn't have to. Elsie told him not to be an idiot, and that was that.

But as for what Elsie herself wants? Never.

The fourth of five children, all of whom still live in the Twin Cities and work at the hardware store their parents own, Elsie tends to go along with whatever her family does. Ginny goes with the flow, too, but there's a difference between being chill and being used to being overlooked. Since they first met, Ginny has been trying to teach Elsie that what she wants matters. Ginny has never known anyone else who had to be peer-pressured into doing what makes them happy.

And Derrick is *so close* to getting the point here. Elsie *isn't* great at asking for what she wants—that's why he shouldn't be planning the entire wedding without talking to her.

Truthfully, Ginny can't help him create the perfect wedding for Elsie because Ginny doesn't even know if Elsie wants to marry him. She said yes when he proposed, sure, but Derrick is the one thing she and Ginny don't talk about.

Ginny's never asked her why she hasn't even so much as picked a season to get married in. For most of their friendship, they've never asked Elsie much about any of her relationships. Ginny knows what *they* want: as much of Elsie as they can have, for as long as they can have her.

It's hard to give relationship advice to someone you're in love with.

"I won't have time to make a chuppah," Ginny says.

It seems like a non sequitur, but it isn't.

"A what?"

"A canopy thing for y'all to stand under."

Derrick stares at her blankly.

"It's Jewish," Ginny says.

That makes Derrick laugh, and he waves a hand. "Come on, you know she's not even really that Jewish."

So what if Elsie's family doesn't go to temple except on the High Holidays? Ginny promised they'd make her a chuppah when they took their first woodworking class, back in high school.

Engaged for a year and a half and Derrick doesn't even know what a chuppah is.

"Hey!" Derrick's eyes light up like he has an idea. Ginny doesn't want to know what it is. "Do you think it'd be better if *you* brought her here tomorrow? She'd never be expecting it then."

Ginny is quite sure Elsie isn't going to be expecting it, regardless.

"I can't," they say. "I'll be at the farmers' market."

The farmers' market ends at one, and even after packing up their stuff—mostly cutting boards and other small handcrafted wooden ware, though they always bring a couple of furniture pieces, too—they'll be done before Elsie's shift finishes. But Derrick doesn't need to know that.

"That's cool. I still think she'll be surprised," he says.

"Yeah," Ginny says. "Me too."

"Is there anything you can think of that she wants that I missed?"

Maybe she wants to break up.

Or maybe that's Ginny's lovesick heart. Maybe Elsie really does want to marry Derrick. Maybe her refusal to plan actually *is* because she's too busy—though she has time to plan an entire weekend for Ginny's birthday every year. Maybe Elsie will think this is romantic.

Just because Ginny thinks Derrick's actions are myopic and even selfish doesn't mean Elsie will. They have to let Elsie decide what she thinks about this absurd plan herself.

But they *cannot* be a party to it.

2

BACK WHEN THEY WERE KIDS, GINNY THOUGHT ROMANTIC RELATION-
SHIPS WERE SOMEHOW A STEP UP FROM FRIENDSHIPS. That was what
everyone said. Magazines and movies and all the kids in their school.
The way Ginny longed for Elsie seemed to confirm it. If friendship
were enough, then why did Ginny want to kiss her so bad?

If friendship were enough, why did Ginny want *more*?

Sophomore year, they decided to do something about it. They
were at the mall, sitting on the bench in the accessible dressing
room while Elsie examined herself in the mirror in the sixth
dress of the day.

"I feel like the color makes my skin look green," Elsie said.

"I like the blue one better."

"Yeah. Unzip me?"

It took Ginny two tries to unzip, their fingers thick and
clumsy. Elsie didn't seem to notice, just shimmied out of the
dress and reached for the next one on the hanger.

Ginny's stomach was in knots, but they were doing this. They had to do it before they puked right there in the dressing room.

"So, uh, the dance." They looked at the floor. "Do you wanna go with me?"

Ginny should've listened to their gut. Because Elsie didn't say no—oh no, it was worse.

"Obviously," Elsie said, presenting her back to Ginny to zip up the next dress. "Even if there was someone I wanted to go with—like as a date—we'd still be going together."

If Elsie hadn't known them so well, Ginny could've played it off like that's how she meant it: going as friends. Instead, Ginny flinched, the tiniest reaction they could manage to what felt like a knife to the chest, and even though she was only looking at them in the mirror, Elsie *knew.*

"Oh," she said.

"It's fine."

Ginny went to zip her in, but Elsie stepped out of reach and turned around, holding the open strapless dress to her chest. "No, Gin, I—"

"Don't worry about it."

"I didn't realize you meant it like that."

Ginny should've moved on, but they had to be sure. "Now that you do . . ."

It took Elsie a moment to reply, and her voice was quiet when she did.

"I don't want anything to mess up our friendship, Gin."

"Right, of course," Ginny said. "No worries."

They wanted to melt into the wall, or for a sinkhole to open beneath them, or to move across the country. Elsie pretended it wasn't a big deal.

"We'll still go, though, obviously," she said. "You and me and Claire and Jake and Amrit. See who else wants to come. My mom will wanna buy you a corsage like last year. Or maybe a boutonniere? It'd be so cool if you wore a suit."

"For sure," Ginny said instead of crying. "Let me zip you up. I like this one."

~~~

THEY WENT TO THE DANCE IN A GROUP. Everyone came to Ginny's house for pictures beforehand. Ginny had seen Elsie in the ice-blue gown in the dressing room—one of the dresses she tried on *before* Ginny had made a fool of themselves—but it was different with makeup and hair, all glossed lips and a braided updo with a few perfect blonde waves loose and framing her face. Her dress shimmered every time she moved.

Ginny had found a dark-gray suit at Goodwill and their mom had hemmed the pants and sleeves to fit. They picked a bright-red tie so they wouldn't be anywhere close to matching Elsie. Their tongue was too heavy in their mouth to tell her how amazing she looked. They didn't want to make her uncomfortable.

Elsie avoided eye contact while she attached a boutonniere to the lapel of Ginny's suit jacket. Ginny's face felt like it was the color of their tie.

"You look great," Elsie murmured.

Ginny swallowed. "Thanks." Swallowed again. "Same."

They made sure not to sit next to Elsie at dinner. At the dance, every time a slow song played, Ginny went to the bathroom or to get a drink or outside to get some air, since it was so hot in the gymnasium. Elsie never came with.

～～

EVEN AFTER THE DANCE, NOTHING WAS THE SAME.

Elsie was always a popular kid—skinny and blonde and pretty, even when they were awkward teenagers. She could've dropped Ginny, could've told someone, anyone, that Ginny had an embarrassing crush on her and made them an outcast. Ginny hadn't quite figured out the gender stuff by then. To most of her classmates, she was the chubby weird girl. It wouldn't have been hard for Elsie to leave her behind.

It was harder to stay friends, to push through the awkwardness, to relearn how to interact—how to compliment each other and sit together on the couch watching movies and hug hello and goodbye without it all feeling too heavy. But Elsie never let Ginny quit. She texted first, and often; invited Ginny any place she went. Elsie was perfect, determined, faking it until they made it. Like if she could pretend it wasn't awkward for long enough, someday it wouldn't be.

Ginny wanted so much for that to be true, but they didn't believe it. How could anything ever be normal again, when they kept catching Elsie with this *look* on her face—concern and pity.

They got through it somehow. Ginny wasn't sure how, really, but eventually things evened out between them. Elsie stopped looking at them like that, and they stopped second-guessing everything they wanted to do or say to Elsie, and it all worked out.

Ginny knows now: what they'd wanted wasn't *more*, it was just *different*.

None of their romantic relationships have come close to their relationship with Elsie, much less been somehow *more* just because they were romantic. Elsie is always going to be the most important person in Ginny's life. To this day, they're so fucking grateful that Elsie didn't let fifteen-year-old Ginny mess that up.

Do they still ache for something different sometimes? Sure. Even with how often they're together, Ginny would gladly take more. There's no such thing as too much time with Elsie. Beyond that, they'd like to kiss her sometimes. They'd like to plan a life together that's more concrete than *we should start a queer commune* and *we're gonna be roommates in the retirement home, right?* But overall, "something different" wouldn't actually *be* that much different from what they already have.

So that occasional ache doesn't matter. It's not going to mess anything up. It just means Ginny's not very good at relationship advice.

3

IN THE THREE YEARS THEY'VE BEEN TOGETHER, DERRICK HAS NEVER ONCE SURPRISED ELSIE. There have been no flowers *just because,* no errand that was secretly a birthday party. That he's a Vikings fan was obvious, that his favorite movie is *Fight Club* wasn't shocking. Even the proposal—he'd hinted at marriage so much by then, Elsie was expecting it. Maybe she wasn't expecting him to hop onstage as she got handed her associate's degree and get down on one knee right there, the public spectacle of her nightmares, but the proposal itself wasn't shocking.

So when Derrick says, "I wanna show you something, but it's a surprise," after picking her up from her shift at the store on Saturday afternoon, Elsie really has no idea what's about to happen.

She closes her eyes, as instructed, while he drives. "Where are we going?"

"I just told you it's a surprise!"

"Can I have a hint?"

"No, ma'am." Elsie's eyes may be closed, but she can tell Derrick is grinning.

Elsie doesn't like surprises, is the thing. Her relationship with Derrick works just fine with no surprises—they live together in their quiet one-bedroom apartment in Minneapolis, she spends six days a week at her parents' hardware store while he works selling vacuum cleaners. Their life is simple, and predictable, and she likes that.

She doesn't like surprises and she doesn't like driving around with her eyes closed. Is her perception off with only four senses, or are they going in circles? Elsie leans forward and adjusts the heat vents to point at her instead of trying to keep track of every turn.

After what feels like half an hour, Derrick pulls into what Elsie assumes is a parking spot and puts the truck in park.

"Just stay there a second," Derrick says.

His seat belt unbuckles; his door opens, letting in a *whoosh* of cold air, then closes again. His footsteps round the front of the truck toward Elsie's side, then her door opens.

"Keep 'em closed," he instructs, and helps her out of the truck.

Aren't your other senses supposed to pick up when you lose one? Elsie's don't seem to. Derrick's hand on her arm is just his hand. The air is just cold, and smells like . . . nothing. Like the city. It sounds that way, too—nothing particularly standing out to give Elsie a hint to where they are. If anything, she's lost more than just her vision; her legs wobble like she's forgotten how to walk.

Derrick leads her a few steps forward, then says, finally, "Okay. Open your eyes."

Elsie keeps one eye squinched closed, too apprehensive about what she might find.

They're at . . . some brick building? She opens her other eye. That doesn't help her understand where they are, or why Derrick insisted it be a surprise. The building is long, one story, its bricks painted a creamy off-white. The roof hangs over the sides far enough to be more like an awning than an eave, and on top is a cupola—Elsie is pretty sure that's what it's called—square-paned windows on each side and topped with bronze or copper or some other reddish-brown metal. There's an old wagon down a ways against the side of the building, along with some planters— snowed over months ago by this point—made of railroad ties, which is the only reason Elsie is able to guess:

"We're at . . . an old train station?"

Derrick grins. "Wait until you see inside."

Inside is mostly just open space—like a banquet hall or concert venue, though there's not really a stage. The walls are the same creamy off-white as the exterior, the trim painted dark green. It still says TICKETS over a window off to the side.

There is an old-school train schedule board above the doors they came through. Instead of departure and arrival times, it reads CONGRATULATIONS, MR. AND MRS. BAUER! TODAY IS THE FIRST DAY OF THE REST OF YOUR LIFE! Elsie doesn't roll her eyes, but it's close. The phrase is both trite and meaningless—*every day* is the first day of the rest of your life.

It takes her a second to process: "*Mr. and Mrs. Bauer?*"

Derrick's grin grows even wider. "Pretty good venue, don't you think? I couldn't get them to put up the twinkle lights in advance because they have another event here tomorrow, but they'll be up for us."

Another second of processing. "Wait. You want us to get married here?"

Her first issue is that she has never said she would take his last name.

"I don't just *want*. We *are* getting married here."

"We are?"

Derrick takes her hands in his. "You know how you're always too busy to talk about the wedding? How even the idea of picking a date is overwhelming to you because of everything you want to do at the store?"

Elsie nods, though none of that helps her understand why he said they're getting married here.

"I took it all off your plate, baby," Derrick says. "The venue, the caterer, the photographer, the honeymoon. We're gonna have white tablecloths and royal-blue accents. I picked the flowers and the silverware and everything. You don't have to do a single thing but get a dress."

Elsie can't feel her feet. They could've turned into tree trunks, rooting her to the ground, and she would have no idea. It's like they're not there.

"What?" she manages to say.

"We're getting married. Here. A week from today."

The *not-there* feeling is moving up past Elsie's knees. She's losing her entire bottom half.

"A week from today?"

"I know it's fast, but that's good. This time next week—" He lets go of one of her hands to check his watch. "Well, actually, like four hours from now next week, we'll be married, and you won't have to think about wedding planning ever again."

"You know the exact time?"

"Well, yeah, I had to know what to put on the invitations."

Elsie drops his other hand, presses her fingertips to her forehead. "Okay. So, like—people are already invited. Other people already know this is happening, but I don't."

"Well, I only sent them out yesterday, so people probably don't have them yet," Derrick says. "And it's not that many other people—I know that's like the one thing you knew you wanted, a pretty small wedding. Fifty guests, tops. And that also kept costs down, which meant I could do another surprise."

"Another," Elsie says, not so much a question as a dread.

Derrick's smile is so damn cute it almost makes Elsie forget she's about to have a panic attack.

"We're going to Santa Lupita for the honeymoon," he says. "A whole week, all-inclusive, with our own private over-water bungalow. It's going to be *amazing*."

The high today in Minneapolis is seven degrees. The Caribbean sounds like heaven. It also sounds impossible.

"Derrick, how am I supposed to go on a honeymoon? You know I can't take a week off from the store."

"No, babe, I talked to your dad already. He loved the idea. He's already approved it all."

Is there *anyone* besides her who doesn't know about this?

Elsie didn't like to think about wedding planning because she didn't know what she *wanted*. Now there's a venue and a caterer, place settings and decorations and invitations already sent out. Her parents know. It doesn't feel like what she wants matters anymore.

Derrick has never been particularly talented at figuring out Elsie's mood, and today is no different: he's grinning just as big as when they first came inside, seemingly unaware of the way Elsie's feet have cemented to the ground and her stomach has dropped out of her body and all the blood has drained from her face. All that, and still Derrick's excitement hasn't lessened one iota. He's like a golden retriever, too simple to be anything but happy.

Jesus, she cannot think about someone she's supposed to *marry* like that.

It's a good thing, most of the time—Derrick's inability to be in anything but a good mood. He's kind, and an optimist, and prevents Elsie from wallowing in her lows. But it also makes Elsie feel like a monster any time she makes him sad.

So she doesn't say *what were you thinking?* or *I don't want this* or even *I'm sorry.*

She says, "I guess I'd better go dress shopping," and Derrick grins even bigger.

Elsie feels like she might puke.

4

GINNY IS PUTTING ENCHILADAS IN THE OVEN WHEN BONNIE, THE
SHETLAND SHEEPDOG THEY'RE FOSTERING, STARTS BARKING WILDLY
AT THE FRONT WINDOW.

"Who's here?" Ginny asks, though she's pretty sure she
knows the answer.

Took longer than they'd expected, honestly. There's been a
rock in their stomach all day that only got bigger when Elsie went
hours without texting this afternoon.

Elsie comes in without knocking, like she's been doing anywhere Ginny has lived since they were nine years old.

"I need your honest opinion about something," she says from
the door.

Her snow boots clunk against the floor as she takes them off.

"What's up?" Ginny asks.

They come out of the kitchen because Elsie hasn't made it
past the living room, where Bonnie has turned from fierce guard
dog to a wriggly mess of excitement.

"Who's a good girl?" Elsie's voice is sweet and high-pitched. "Who's the best girl?"

She goes down on one knee to rub Bonnie's belly, shaking her head along with the dog's wiggles, so her blonde ponytail flicks back and forth.

Ginny can't help but smile. "Why do my dogs always like you more than me?"

"Because I'm the cool aunt who can spoil them instead of making them follow rules."

"Following my rules means they're more likely to get adopted by a lovely *family* who can spoil them."

Elsie's engagement ring catches on Bonnie's blue merle coat and she has to untangle it. So the engagement is still on. Not that Ginny expected Elsie to break it off after Derrick's stunt this afternoon, but the possibility did cross their mind.

Ginny counts to ten. That's as long as they can last with Elsie not saying anything beyond telling Bonnie she's perfect.

"So what do you need my opinion on?" Ginny asks, like they don't know.

Elsie finally stops petting the dog, who leaps to her feet and races around the living room, barking. Elsie laughs, and when she sits on the couch, Bonnie boomerangs over, but after glancing at Ginny, she keeps all four feet on the living room floor. Ginny opens the treat container on the coffee table rather than analyzing Elsie's face. The moment the container is opened, Bonnie sits.

"Good girl," Ginny says, and tosses a treat her way. Then they sit beside their best friend.

Elsie reaches down to pet Bonnie, but when she talks, it's no longer in the *who's a good girl* voice.

"Derrick wants to get married next week."

Ginny lets out a breath.

They try to stay neutral—not to focus on how the flatness in Elsie's voice means she's not happy about the whole surprise wedding thing. It shouldn't matter—Elsie's relationship status is not about Ginny—but a weight has lifted off their shoulders.

"I know," they say quietly.

Elsie leans back into the couch and sighs. "Your invitation already arrived?"

"He sent out invitations?!"

"Yesterday, he said." Elsie squints at them. "If you didn't know that, how did you know he planned it for next week?"

Ginny grimaces. Elsie isn't going to like this. "He asked for my help getting you to the venue, but I had the farmers' market."

Elsie knows how long the market takes, but whether she doesn't think about it or just lets Ginny off the hook, she doesn't call them out.

Maybe because there's a bigger issue.

"You knew and didn't tell me?" Her voice is stone. Harder than it's ever been when directed at Ginny. They don't fight, not over anything serious.

Ginny's shoulders creep toward their ears. "I didn't want to ruin the surprise."

"I don't even like surprises!"

Ginny knows that. They know that Elsie doesn't like surprises and that her favorite color is yellow and that she wants to get married under a chuppah. They know her better than Derrick does.

"I know you don't usually"—they shrug, trying for nonchalant—"but he seemed so excited, and I thought you might be, too."

"You thought I'd be excited that he planned an entire wedding and gave me a week's notice? I'm just supposed to be ready to marry him in seven days?"

Since yesterday, Ginny themself has been trying to come to terms with the idea of Elsie getting married next week. It hasn't come close to working, even though: "Well, you *have* been engaged for a year and a half."

"Engaged!" Elsie slaps her palms on her thighs. "*Engaged* is not married. *Engaged* is not getting married in seven days. *Engaged* I still have time to—to—to . . ."

Ginny gives her time to finish the sentence, but Elsie flounders, her mouth opening and closing a couple of times.

"To what?" Ginny prompts gently.

"To figure out whether I want to marry him."

"Els."

Ginny's voice is too soft. Not quiet, but *soft*. It gets that way around Elsie sometimes. They can't help it.

Elsie's voice, meanwhile, is sharp. "You don't think I should marry him next week, do you?"

They don't think she should marry him at all, but they can't say that. They didn't think Elsie should date him, either, always knew she was too good for him. But it's never been about what Ginny thinks. What Elsie wants is all that matters.

"I want you to be happy," they say. "If marrying him next week will make you happy, then I think you should. If it won't, then you shouldn't."

Elsie stands up. Bonnie leaps to her feet as well, ready for wherever they're going to go. When Elsie paces back and forth across the living room, Bonnie follows her, leaping from one side of the room to the other.

"He's already done all the planning," Elsie says, still pacing. There's a chaotic edge to her tone now. "Paid for everything."

"So?"

"What do you mean, so? He's already sent out invitations."

"That doesn't matter," Ginny says.

Elsie stops and pivots to face Ginny. "Of course it matters. We'd have to let everyone know it wasn't happening. He'd be so embarrassed."

"You can't marry someone just because they'd be embarrassed if you didn't."

"I know." She starts pacing again. "Obviously that wouldn't be why I'd do it, if I do it."

Ginny asks the question they've never been able to answer. "Why would you, then?"

"He's nice. He's sweet. And really cute."

Ginny's pretty sure none of those are good enough reasons to marry someone.

"And he's good to me," Elsie continues. "Or he tries to be anyway. Like when I told him I was pan, he's always said he'd support me doing whatever I want in terms of feeling connected to my queer identity."

Ginny tries not to react, but must not keep their face in check.

"What?" Elsie asks.

"Nothing."

"No, what?"

She returns to the couch. Bonnie sits at her feet, then looks at

Ginny like she thinks she deserves a treat every time she doesn't get on the sofa. Ginny gets her one just to avoid looking at Elsie.

"Els, you made it sound like a reason to marry the guy is he'd let you eat someone out."

"Oh my gosh, that is not what I meant. Obviously that's not what I meant. I just mean—he tries to be good to me. Even planning the wedding without telling me is him trying to be good to me."

"Right." Ginny knows it's true. Derrick loves Elsie. Of course he does. "So that's why you *would* marry him. If you didn't, why wouldn't you?"

Elsie pets Bonnie some more. Sometimes it's like this, trying to get her to talk about her feelings. But Ginny is patient.

"Marriage is supposed to be forever," Elsie says finally. "And forever feels like a really long time. I'm only twenty-three. Marriage just seems so, like, *final*. It's not the committing-to-one-person thing—it's that it feels like that means committing to *being* one person. Like saying I'm forever going to stay someone Derrick wants to be married to."

There's so much wrong with that, Ginny doesn't know where to begin. Elsie framed the question of marriage around whether she'll stay someone Derrick wants to be married to, not whether *he's* someone *she* wants to be married to.

"It's like—do you remember in middle school when Emileigh Brown signed yearbooks *Don't ever change*?" She doesn't wait for Ginny to respond. "Like, I'm thirteen years old, I sure hope I'm gonna change!"

"I don't think marriage is saying you're never gonna change,"

Ginny says. "It's more about changing together. Growing together."

Like how she and Elsie are completely different people than they were in middle school, but they're still best friends.

Elsie is quiet for a moment before responding. "What if I wanna grow on my own?"

Ginny takes it as a rhetorical question—mostly because they want to shout *good* and *finally* and *yes, please*. Elsie has been defining herself based on the people around her for as long as they've known each other. Her siblings. Her parents. Her boyfriend. Even Ginny, sometimes. It'd be *great* if Elsie wanted to grow on her own.

"He's already sent invitations," Elsie says quietly.

"Els."

Ginny can see where Elsie is going, can feel what decision she wants to make, but they refuse to lead her there. This is her life. Her choice.

"I kind of thought when he got tired of me putting off wedding planning, he'd call off the engagement, not plan the wedding."

"You've been hoping he'd do it so you wouldn't have to?"

"Well, when you put it like that, I sound pathetic."

"You're not pathetic," Ginny says immediately.

Elsie's not, but Ginny might be, the way some white knight rears inside them at Elsie talking about herself like that.

"I am," Elsie says. "If I wasn't pathetic, I would've said no when he proposed, and we wouldn't be in this situation at all."

That's new.

"You didn't want to get engaged?"

"I was barely old enough to drink, Ginny." Elsie says it like she's mad at them. "And suddenly my boyfriend makes this moment that is supposed to be about me, about me graduating—I know it was just an associate's, but it's still a degree. It was still *my* graduation day. And instead, it became about us. I had no idea what I wanted—I still have no idea what I want—but how was I supposed to say no when he proposed in front of the entire graduating class?"

Elsie has never before said a single word of this to Ginny. They don't disagree, but they also don't know how to react.

"Come on," Elsie says. "I *know* you don't like him anyway."

"I've never said that."

It wasn't that she didn't *like* Derrick. He just wasn't good enough for Elsie. Ginny's never met anyone good enough for Elsie.

Elsie sighs. "He's not a bad guy, you know?"

"I know."

He really isn't. Ginny does know that.

"I think if he'd just talked to me about this, maybe we could've figured it out," Elsie says. "But the way he went about it just makes it really not what I want. Invitations sent out before he told me. Talking to my dad to get me time off work for the honeymoon."

Ginny's eyes go wide. "He didn't."

"He did. Which, to be fair—it sounds amazing. Santa Lupita for a week in an over-water bungalow. All-inclusive."

"Holy shit, *I* might marry him for that."

Elsie giggles, then sobers. "I can't . . ." She goes quiet, and finally, she says, "I can't believe I'm not gonna marry him."

Thank god.

Ginny immediately feels bad for thinking it, but they can't take it back. They would've supported whatever Elsie decided, of course. But this is the only solution that doesn't make their chest hurt.

Elsie puts her head on their shoulder, and Ginny's breath comes easily for the first time since talking to Derrick yesterday.

"This is gonna break his heart," Elsie says, her voice soft.

Ginny presses a kiss to the top of her head. "It's better than breaking yours."

5

ELSIE GETS MOST MORNINGS TO HERSELF, BUT SUNDAYS ARE HER
FAVORITE. Derrick's runs are longer on the weekends, and on Sundays, the store is closed. Lately, Elsie's been thinking of getting a cat. It's the only thing that could make spending the morning snuggled up in the living room recliner with a book any better.

Elsie doesn't look up when Derrick returns from his run—the estranged sisters in the thriller she's reading are having a heart-to-heart.

"Babe, have you even talked to your parents yet?" Derrick calls from the kitchen, pulling her out of the story. "They're so excited, you should call them."

Right. They're excited about the wedding. And he knows that because he's already talked to them. Long before he talked to her.

Last night, after making the decision, Elsie stayed at Ginny's through dinner. They'd eaten enchiladas before moving to the garage, where Ginny worked on their latest commission and

Elsie made fun of their taste in music, a folksy twang playing over the Bluetooth speaker. It had been a pretty typical Saturday night, if Elsie ignored the fact that she came home and told Derrick she had a migraine before he had a chance to ask what Ginny thought of the whole situation.

This morning, she stayed in bed with her eyes closed while Derrick tiptoed around getting ready for his run. His touch was gentle as he brushed her hair off her forehead and pressed a kiss there.

"Love you, babe," he whispered, and Elsie tried not to cry.

After he left, she decided she was going to have a normal morning for as long as she could. Who knew what her Sundays would look like after today?

But the time for business as usual is officially up.

"Do you have a minute to talk?" she asks.

Derrick emerges from the kitchen grinning. "For you? Always."

Why does he have to be so sweet? It'd be easier if he were an asshole. Easier to hurt his feelings, easier to feel good about leaving the relationship behind. Because that's what she's doing, that's what's going to happen after this conversation. This is ending the relationship. Which—does she even want that? The relationship itself is fine, right? He's fine. Elsie's content. Is it that big of a deal that he doesn't light her up inside? She likes him, and he's nice, if occasionally misguided.

It'd be easier if he meant to be selfish. If he'd planned this wedding because *he* wanted to get married and all that mattered was what he wanted. But he did this for her—Elsie knows that. It's not what she wants and she'd rather he hadn't done it, but he did do it for her.

He sits on the couch in his Under Armour, cheeks like apples—in shape and color both—and hair like a ski jump over his forehead thanks to the fuzzy winter headband he wears when he runs. Elsie looks at her hands, at the two-carat diamond on her third finger. She looks at Derrick's face, open and affable.

She can't do this.

She can't.

She has to do this.

"Derrick," she says, her hands in fists in her lap. "I love you."

He beams. "I love you, babe."

"You're probably the nicest person I know. You always have good intentions. And I do love you." She pauses, her stomach twisting. Time to rip off the Band-Aid. "But I can't marry you."

Derrick reacts in stages. First his brow furrows. Next, he tilts his head like maybe he didn't hear her right. Only then, as he searches her face, does he lose his smile, his lips dropping to a flat line.

"You can't marry me?"

Elsie shakes her head.

"Why not?"

"I don't know what I want," she admits.

He swallows. "But you know it's not me."

Elsie opens her mouth. Closes it again. She *doesn't* know it's not Derrick. Does she?

It was easy, with Ginny, to be sure. Everything's easy with Ginny. They're like family, but the kind Elsie chose, not the kind that ignores her ideas for the store and still makes fun of her for an embarrassing thing she did when she was six. Elsie never feels more herself than with Ginny. Never feels more sure of herself than with Ginny.

But seeing Derrick, constantly cheerful Derrick, looking sad and confused, Elsie isn't certain anymore. Then again—that's the issue, isn't it? Not being certain.

"I know I can't get married when I don't know what I want."

She needs *time*. Not that she hasn't had that—a year-and-a-half engagement without that much pressure about planning the wedding should have been enough. But she needs to actually *use* it. To figure out what it is she wants.

"I thought wedding planning just overwhelmed you."

"It did," Elsie says. "It did, honestly. But I'm not sure I realized exactly *why* it overwhelmed me, until now."

"And the *why* is 'cause . . . you don't want to get married?"

"I feel like I'm still a kid," Elsie admits. "Maybe it's that I work for my parents or maybe it's that I've basically never been an adult by myself. I've never lived alone. I have to figure out who I am before I commit myself to something like *marriage*."

Derrick looks like he did whenever he had to study for a trig exam in college: completely lost. He stays quiet for a minute. Elsie resists the urge to fill the silence with patronizing excuses about how *it's not you, it's me*.

"How am I supposed to tell everybody?"

"I'll take care of that," Elsie says, though she'd rather pluck out her eyelashes. "If you give me a guest list, I can let everyone know. I don't want you to have to do that."

"Okay. Yeah." Another beat. Elsie swallows anything she might say and tries to let him process however he needs to. He runs a hand over his face. "And you should go on the honeymoon."

"What?"

"It's nonrefundable, and your parents are already planning for you to be away from the store," Derrick says. "You deserve a vacation, bab—Elsie. Even if the store wasn't the real reason you didn't want to plan the wedding, you work too hard."

Who gets dumped, basically at the altar, and then tells his ex-fiancée she works too hard and should still go on the honeymoon? He's obviously hurt. *She* hurt him. And yet he's telling her to go on the honeymoon.

What is she doing? She could marry Derrick. It'd be fine.

"You could take Ginny," he says, "if they can get the time off work."

Every time he uses *they* for Ginny feels like a win, but still— that's ridiculous.

"Derrick, c'mon." She could tell him she was kidding. "You planned it." She could say they should go together. "You did so much. You take it." He did so much, and she's being horrible.

He shakes his head. "I think it will just make me sad."

Elsie wants to puke. "I'm so sorry."

She wills herself not to cry. It doesn't seem fair to be the dumper and cry.

"Yeah," Derrick says blankly. "So if you don't want to marry me . . ." He takes a breath. "We're breaking up, right? Like, that's what's happening right now?"

It has to be what's happening. She can't call off the wedding but let herself stay in this relationship. It'd be easy to, but she can't.

Still, she doesn't commit one way or the other. "If that's what you want."

"I mean, I want to get married," Derrick says. He rubs at his eyes. "So if you don't, then we should break up. I want, like, kids and stuff. I want to be with someone who wants that stuff."

Elsie is twenty-three years old. Last month, when she picked her nephew up from school, one of his friends had asked, "Who's that lady?" She wasn't sure who the kid was talking about at first. She's not old enough to be *that lady,* is she? She's the cool aunt, not anyone's *mom.*

Derrick sighs. "I think I'm gonna go for a run. Or maybe to Chad's."

"Of course," Elsie says, like he didn't just come in from a run. "Whatever you want."

"I'll, uh, send you the guest list."

~~~

AN HOUR LATER, ELSIE SITS AT THE KITCHEN TABLE ALONE, SCROLLING THROUGH THE—THANKFULLY SMALL—GUEST LIST DERRICK SENT HER.

Who to call first?

In an ideal world, she'd only have to talk to Brandon. In an ideal world, her own brain clarifies, she wouldn't have to talk to anyone. Her fiancé wouldn't have planned the wedding without her, or if he did, it would've made her happy.

But Elsie's clearly not in an ideal world.

And even though her middle brother wouldn't ask questions she doesn't know the answers to, he also isn't necessarily the most reliable choice to start the family phone tree. If she tells him first, there's no guarantee anyone else in the family would ever find out.

It's tempting to call Danielle. She'd handle everything, she always does. She'd probably offer to call the guests on Elsie's behalf, and then show up with vegetarian lasagna that she somehow made at the same time.

But Elsie knows better. There was never really a choice, because she doesn't even want to imagine the guilt trip she'd get if her mom weren't her first call.

"Darling!" Her mother picks up the phone with something between a shriek and a bellow.

"Hi, Mom," Elsie says sullenly.

"Isn't it *wonderful*? I could hardly keep it a secret when your father told me. We had to adjust the schedule to cover the register, of course, but goodness, when Derrick shared pictures of that resort he's taking you to? How could we say no?"

For the first time, Elsie wonders how long ago Derrick started planning this. Surely he didn't make the plans last week—the price of plane tickets would've been astronomical. Did he ask her parents for forgiveness or permission? How long have they known?

That's not a spiral she wants to deal with currently, especially not while her mom is still babbling about how exciting this is.

"I know Derrick said you wanted a small wedding, but I was thinking of inviting the Greenblatts. They've known you since you were a baby and—"

"You can't invite anyone," Elsie cuts in, because she's not going to have a chance to speak if she doesn't.

"I'll call the caterer," her mom says, like that's the issue. "Two more guests shouldn't be a problem. Finger foods are easy to scale, if an extra two people even counts as scaling."

Apparently, they were supposed to have finger foods at the reception. Who knew? Not Elsie. Her mom is still talking, carrying on a one-sided debate about the merits of not serving a sit-down meal.

"You can't invite anyone because we're not getting married."

For the first time, the line is silent.

"What?"

"We're not getting married."

"That doesn't make any sense," her mom says. "He wouldn't have changed his mind after he planned everything."

Elsie should've just called Danielle. She should've planned this conversation better.

"It wasn't him," she says. "I'm the one not ready to get married."

Her mom scoffs. "What do you mean you're not ready? You've been engaged for almost two years. You know, your father and I were only engaged for six months."

They were also high school sweethearts. As far as Elsie knows, they've never kissed another person in their lives.

"I don't feel like a real adult yet," Elsie admits.

"I had already had Alec by the time I was your age."

"Well, I'm certainly not ready for a *kid*, Mom." She tries not to snap. This is about *her*, not her parents. "I know you and Dad have a great love story. But it's not mine. And I'm not ready for this."

There's a beat of silence, and then her mom says, "Of course," like she realizes she should be supporting her kid instead of pressuring her to get married. "That's okay, darling. How can I help? What do you need right now?"

Elsie takes what feels like her first breath since the conversation began.

"I'm letting guests know," she says. "Could you tell the family?"

Thankfully her mom simply agrees rather than asking what to say. Elsie's having a hard enough time figuring that out herself.

"And the apartment," her mom says. "Do you need to come home?"

Home. To her parents' house. Across the street from Ginny's parents. Elsie's childhood bedroom still has two twin beds pushed against opposite walls, though the tape that divided her side from her sister's is long gone.

"I'll let you know," Elsie says. It's too much to think about right now, when she's only at the top of the guest list.

"You know you can always come home," her mom says. There's another beat of silence before she adds, "And Elsbeth, I want to make sure: it's not just cold feet? Of course I understand the rest of your life feels like forever, and *forever* can seem scary, even when it's with a good man."

It quite literally *is* forever. That's what marriage is supposed to be.

"But if you love each other, you can get through anything."

There it is.

Does she love Derrick? He's gorgeous and sweet. She loves his smile. She loves that he'll snuggle with her on the couch even if she's watching *Real Housewives*. She loves their inside jokes, the way they decide what to have for dinner. He gives her five options, she narrows it to three, and he makes the final choice. She loves that he never begrudges her time with Ginny—some of her best friends from college completely disappeared when they got boyfriends, but even though Elsie goes to lunch with Ginny every day, Derrick never complains if she wants to hang out with them after work, too.

But does she love *him*? Is she *in love* with him?

If she can't answer that, how could she possibly marry him?

"Thank you for telling the family," Elsie says instead of talking to her mom about this. "I have to get to calling everyone."

"If you're certain, darling," her mom says, like she thinks Elsie is making the wrong choice. "I love you."

"Love you."

Elsie hangs up.

It's the opposite of what her mom said, though. She doesn't have to be certain to *not* marry Derrick, she has to be certain to do it.

Life has never made Elsie ask herself big questions like this before. Sure, no one can know the future, but hers has never felt particularly unclear. She was always going to work at the store. Even when she was a kid, when she and Ginny used to daydream about the future, it was never some grand adventure. It felt like it, at the time, but the big dreams weren't about travel or fame or love; they were about which neighborhood of Minneapolis they'd live in, houses side by side. Ginny hadn't known what their job would be—*something where I don't have to sit at a desk all day*—but Elsie always knew she'd work at the store.

That's what everyone in her family does. It's what her dad did when he was a kid. Hoffman Hardware opened in 1954. A mom-and-pop shop. Elsie's dad started working there in the 1980s, took it over from her grandpa before Elsie was born. He's never had another job. None of his children have, either; they've been working there since before it was legal. The kids joke it's why their parents had five of them: free child labor. The older ones each got their own specialty. Alec learned *everything*, since he's the one who will take over when their parents retire. Danielle shadowed their mom to learn the financial side of things. Brandon knows every tool in the store. By the time they got to Elsie and Claire, they'd run out of specialties. Elsie, tall and skinny with long blonde hair, got put on the cash register.

She's still there, even after a degree in business that feels worthless. Or—it isn't worthless itself, but given how her family is always too busy to listen to her ideas, she can't put anything she's learned to use.

~~~~

KNOW WHAT'S REALLY FUN? Going down a list of your closest friends to tell them your wedding later this week is canceled.

Even better, most of them haven't even gotten the invitations yet, so Elsie is starting from scratch. Everyone has questions, and her answers vary from hedges to outright lies: *we're just not ready* and *it was a mutual decision*. Once she even goes with *the invitations went out by mistake*.

Derrick texts that he's gonna stay at Chad's for a few days. He didn't leave with any clothes, but he and Chad have cookie-cutter versions of each other's bodies, so he can probably borrow some. Or come get them when Elsie is at work. Or something. It's not Elsie's business anymore.

Elsie's exhausted by the time she gets through the guest list, no matter how short it was. She retreats to the living room recliner, curls into a ball, and texts Ginny.

> Everyone now knows the wedding is off, even though most of them didn't know it was on to begin with, so that was an extra treat for me

> You're so powerful

Elsie rolls her eyes, but the comment nestles warm in her chest.

Ginny doesn't ask how the conversation went, how Derrick took the news. Elsie tells them anyway, of course, but it's nice not to be asked. Not to be pressured.

> Why is Derrick texting me?

> Ummmm, what?

> He's asking my full legal name and birthday?????

Elsie doesn't even bother to sit up so her front-facing camera won't make her look like a gremlin before video calling Ginny.

Just seeing their face, that comforting expression and their round pink cheeks, makes Elsie's teeth unclench. She even smiles.

"Okay, so actually, this is the only good thing that's come out of all this," she says.

Ginny raises their eyebrows. "Except the whole you-not-being-trapped-in-a-marriage-you-don't-want-to-be-in thing?"

"Yeah, except that." Elsie waves her hand like it's nothing, and Ginny gives her a look that makes her smile want to grow even bigger. She doesn't let it. "The honeymoon is nonrefundable, and Derrick wants me to go."

"What?"

"I told him *he* should, but he said it would just make him sad."

Ginny grimaces. "Oh, that's really . . ."

"I know. I'm not thinking about it."

If Elsie thinks too hard about how much she's hurt Derrick, she's afraid she'll change her mind about getting married. But like Ginny said, that's not enough of a reason to marry someone. She focuses on Ginny on her screen, in their living room with a Twins hat on backward.

"So the good thing, though," she says, "is he told me I should take you."

"What?" Ginny says again.

"We would leave literally a week from tomorrow, so I know Karl might not give you the time off, but please please please."

"You want me to come to Santa Lupita with you?"

"I mean, duh, who else would I want to come?" When Ginny doesn't immediately say yes, Elsie continues. "C'mon, you said you might marry him for it! I'm gonna send you pics of the resort until you say yes."

"Oh my god, I'm not saying no." Ginny rolls their eyes, but in that way where they're actually charmed. Elsie lets her grin grow this time. "I'll ask for the time off tomorrow."

And like that, Elsie's mood plummets. *Tomorrow.* Ugh. She has to work, with her entire family hovering.

"We're going to lunch tomorrow, right?" she asks suddenly.

They get lunch together every day as a matter of course, but Ginny could have a doctor's appointment or something. If they do, Elsie might have to beg them to cancel. Tomorrow Elsie *needs* lunch with Ginny. Not as a routine but as a necessity. She always needs Ginny, but especially tomorrow. Especially after she just blew up her life. The future feels scary and uncertain for the first time, but she can do anything with Ginny beside her.

She doesn't have to beg, though, because on her screen, Ginny nods. "I'll take you anywhere you want, Els Bells."

6

GINNY HAS BEEN IN THE CEO'S OFFICE EXACTLY ONCE. When he was first hired, he held one-on-ones with every member of the staff. The room was large enough that the giant oak desk with craftmanship Ginny admired barely took up a third of it. Four plush armchairs looked out of place around a low coffee table, until the CEO explained they were about making the space inviting instead of intimidating.

Ginny's immediate supervisor Karl's office, on the other hand, is too nondescript to be either. The furniture is standard-issue, manufactured en masse, all various shades of gray. The chair Ginny sits in across from his desk has metal arms she'd think were torture devices for fat people, except she's sure whoever made it doesn't bother to spare fat folks like her a second thought. Probably not even a first thought.

"What can I do for you, Ms. Holtz?"

Karl claims calling people by their last names establishes a professional atmosphere while also showing respect, but in two years of Ginny working here, he's never once used a gender-neutral honorific. It's not even that Ginny has a problem with *Ms.* They don't identify with gender itself, so much as with loving women in a gay way. They/them pronouns mean no one can accuse them of being straight, but Ginny uses she/her, too, especially with other queers. When you use multiple pronouns, you notice the people who only use the one that doesn't make them think beyond the binary. Karl is one of those people who takes the fact that Ginny doesn't mind gendered terms as an excuse to ignore their identity.

The lack of respect is mutual.

But Ginny knows how to play nice when necessary.

"My best friend's engagement fell apart this weekend," they say, intentionally making it seem sad instead of like a good thing. "The wedding was supposed to be next weekend."

"Oh, how terrible." Karl's hand is on the computer mouse, his eyes on the monitor.

"I know, right? It's such a mess," Ginny says. They would prefer to avoid all the bullshit and just say they need time off, but, you know, capitalism. And white men's egos. "I know it's short notice, but the honeymoon is nonrefundable, and she's asked me to go with her. I really want to be there to support my friend. Would it be possible to get next week off?"

They have the time available; they don't take vacation as often as they should.

Karl doesn't even look at her. "How am I supposed to get someone to fill in next week?"

"I don't have any time-sensitive projects right now," Ginny says. "Just the regular stuff. I'll work to get ahead this week and catch up the week I get back. It'd just be a blip."

Karl's lips move as he reads an email instead of responding.

"Again, the trip is nonrefundable. The tickets are already bought."

"It was supposed to be a honeymoon, right? So, they weren't bought for *you*. She can take someone else."

Last night, Derrick asked for their birthday and full government name, no other context. When Elsie explained, Ginny told Derrick to go ahead and switch the tickets, rather than wait to ensure she could get the time off. Elsie is not taking anyone else. And Ginny is not taking no for an answer.

"Look, I just can't justify forcing people to pick up your slack so you can go on a surprise vacation," Karl says. "We're a family here, and we work together."

Ginny tunes out as Karl goes into his usual spiel. Once he gets going about the company being a family, there's no reason to pay attention.

Ginny's actual family has never stopped her from going on vacation. Even when they were a kid, their parents gave them more freedom than this job ever has. *Eighties parenting,* her mom used to call it, even though it was a new millennium. For Elsie, it was more *we have five kids* parenting. The two of them could do whatever they wanted as long as they didn't get into too much trouble. Meanwhile, this company's dress code is still gendered. Ginny's haircut is supposedly only allowed for men, their nose piercing only allowed for women.

Karl concludes his lecture with "I'm sure you understand."

"Okay, Karl." Ginny never calls him Mr. Schwartz. "Consider this my week's notice, then. Sorry I can't make it two—I've got a trip. I'm sure you understand."

He finally looks away from the computer. "What?"

Adrenaline courses through Ginny's veins.

"I quit."

The words sound amazing.

"You're quitting because I won't give you time off for this trip that isn't even yours to begin with?"

Ginny could take it back. They could say they weren't thinking, or that it was a joke maybe—that would save them some dignity at least. But they don't.

They don't take it back, and they don't explain that it's about more than this moment. They're not quitting because Karl won't give them time off; they're quitting because they hate this job. They hate the sea of cubicles. It's meaningless website design. Ginny is only here because it's the first place that interviewed her after graduation. She never wanted this particular job, she only wanted to get paid.

Ginny doesn't explain any of that to Karl, though. They don't have to explain themself at all anymore. They bite back the grin that tries to take over their face.

"I'll reach out to HR this week and see what end-of-employment procedures I need to do before—"

"No," Karl says. "Go to your desk and clear it now."

He's back to looking at the computer, clicking the mouse aggressively, but Ginny would bet he's not actually reading anything on the screen. His brows, slanted and angry, make him look like a cartoon villain.

"Are you firing me?"

"I'm not firing you, you quit," he snaps. "We don't need a week's notice. Leave now. I don't want to see you again."

Ginny chuckles. Now that they don't have to work for him, Karl's petulance is amusing rather than frustrating. She considers mentioning that if this is how he treats *family,* it's no wonder he can't hold down a girlfriend, but honestly, he's not worth the parting shot.

~~~

THE BOX IN THE PASSENGER SEAT OF GINNY'S TRUCK IS MOSTLY FILLED WITH THE CONTENTS OF THEIR SNACK DRAWER. Nestled among the granola bars and individual-serving bags of Cheez-Its is Ginny's favorite picture of them and Elsie, a shot from Ginny's birthday a few years ago. They were supposed to spend the weekend in Chicago, but they got a flat tire and had to stay in bumfuck nowhere. Elsie's laughing so hard you can see all her teeth, her eyes scrunched closed and Ginny's head turned away as they try to hide their own laughter. It's how Elsie always makes Ginny feel—even when things are going wrong, they're really fucking good.

It's not even 10 A.M. by the time Ginny gets home. Bonnie's whole body wags along with her tail at the surprise return.

"That's a good girl," Ginny says, crouching to give Bonnie the chest scritches that are her favorite. "What do you say we go to the dog park?"

The magic words are too thrilling for Bonnie to stay still—she bounds to the door and back, starts herding Ginny in that direction.

In the negative two wind chill, four other brave souls are at the park with their dogs. Ginny doesn't even mind the cold. They're still running on adrenaline.

They quit their job.

They *quit* their *job*.

It's exhilarating, even if they have no clue what they're going to do now. They can survive without income for a few months, maybe half the year. Ginny's grandpa spent thirty years as a financial advisor; he instilled the importance of an emergency fund in them from a young age. Beyond that, though, who knows? Surely they can get some other worthless pencil-pushing job, but the idea is too much of a damper on their mood to think about. Instead, they watch Bonnie befriend a Husky midmorning, no responsibilities but lunch with Elsie and a bathroom vanity to finish up for a client—neither of which actually count as responsibilities, because Ginny loves doing them. Things are good.

~~~~~

GINNY IDLES AT THE BACK ENTRANCE OF HOFFMAN HARDWARE AT NOON. Elsie bursts through the employees-only door before they have a moment to text that they've arrived. Her breath billows around her as she hustles to the passenger side.

"It's *freezing*," she says as she gets in.

She reaches to adjust the vents to aim at her, but Ginny has already done that. Elsie tugs off her wool mittens and holds her fingers in front of the warm air. Her messy blonde braids hang out from her bright red beanie.

"I'm going to kill my parents," she says. "I swear my mom *teared up* talking about me not marrying Derrick."

"Where to today?"

"Uncle Cheetah's," Elsie says. "I need soup."

"Good call." Ginny shifts into drive.

Elsie keeps complaining. "They're acting like they've lost a son—like they don't already have two of their own, plus Matthew."

"Matthew is the best of the lot," Ginny says about Elsie's brother-in-law. "No offense to your own bloodline."

"Obviously he's the best of the lot, but that's my point. Like, let's be honest, they're all smarter than Derrick."

Ginny's eyes cut to Elsie. Less than a day since the engagement ended and already she's okay saying negative things about him.

"I mean, Derrick is great," Elsie amends. "But you have to recognize it's not super smart to plan our entire wedding without asking me."

"There is that."

"They just kept bringing up Derrick, asking so many questions. What are we going to do now? Where am I going to live? And I don't know yet, okay?" She blows on her hands, puts them back in front of the vents. "We broke up, yeah, but it's barely been twenty-four hours. Could you give me, like, a day to process? I swear I had barely finished checking out a customer and my mom was asking me about canceling the caterer. My parents give us shit for doing personal stuff at work but when they want to, suddenly it's fine." She turns fully sideways in the passenger seat to look at Ginny. "Wait, did you get the time off for the trip? Can you come with me? Please say yes."

Elsie had texted to ask the same thing this morning, but Ginny hadn't answered.

Telling Elsie that they quit their job would lead to questions they're not ready for. It's the same as Elsie not wanting to talk to her parents about Derrick—Ginny doesn't know anything yet. They need a little time to process.

Plus, Elsie's engagement just ended. Ginny wants to support her, not burden her with their own issues.

"Yeah," they answer. "I can come with."

It's not lying.

"Oh, thank fuck," Elsie says. "I don't know what I would've done if you couldn't."

"I don't think it'd be hard to find someone else who wants a free all-inclusive vacation to the Caribbean."

"Another person I'm willing to spend a week in the same bed with?"

"Admittedly more difficult."

"But it doesn't matter because you can co-o-o-ome!" She drags out the last word, happiness obvious and infectious, and Ginny can't help but grin.

7

This morning, she tried to act normal. Mondays are full of contractors starting their workweeks and DIY home improvers who realized they needed something for what was supposed to be a weekend project. The register isn't terrible. Elsie is a friendly face. She's a professional at small talk, makes the same jokes to different people all day. A hardware store isn't saving the world or anything, but they do help people, and it feels good to work at her family's business. She likes the tradition of it.

She likes her family, too, for the most part, even if they annoy the hell out of her sometimes, today included.

Her mom had some kind of sixth sense, appearing every time Elsie's line died down. "How are you doing, sweetie?"

A lot better when not being asked that question in such a pitying voice. It didn't matter how many times Elsie told her parents the breakup was her idea, her mom clearly thought she'd been dumped.

Lunch with Ginny was a respite. The not-honeymoon next week with Ginny will be even more of one. Almost a full week in fucking paradise. The thought buoys Elsie as she takes a deep breath and yanks the staff door open. The employee break room is the first door off the hallway, but she slides silently past it rather than deal with whatever combination of her siblings is in there finishing up lunch. As for her dad's office door, there's no need to sneak past, because—like always—he doesn't look up from whatever *absolutely critical* work he's in the middle of.

Elsie's mom is checking someone out when Elsie gets to the registers. She's standing, even though there's a stool right next to her. It took years to convince Elsie's dad that stools were acceptable at the register, that cashiers weren't lazy if they didn't want to stand in place for eight hours a day. Every time Elsie's mom covers the register, she never sits.

As soon as the customer leaves, Mrs. Hoffman turns a pitying eye to her daughter.

"How was Ginny? Did they make you feel better?"

Of course they did. They always do. Nothing is ever too terrible as long as she has Ginny. But the question from her mom puts Elsie right back into a bad mood.

"I feel *fine*, Mom," she snaps. Very convincing.

"Are you sure you want to work a full day? It's quiet this afternoon, I could stay on the register."

Elsie has an idea. "Actually, could you? I've been wanting to talk to Dad about rebranding again."

"Oh, Elsie, he's very busy today," her mom says, like she didn't *just* say it was a quiet afternoon. "Don't bother him with that."

"He's always busy," Elsie says. "Besides, it'll be my own project. He won't have to do anything."

Her mom clocks out at the register. "Let me talk to him first. You take over here."

Elsie knew that would work. Distract her mom from the breakup with talk of a rebrand her dad's never gonna go for.

Elsie hasn't talked about rebranding in years, not since she took Principles of Marketing her second semester at Minneapolis College. In her highlighted, color-coded notes were the seven Ps of marketing, the last of which is physical evidence, aka packaging. It's the brand.

Hoffman Hardware doesn't have a logo. It has a signature font, swooping script in navy blue. Kids aren't even taught to read cursive anymore, and somehow her dad still doesn't think it's outdated. Elsie had never particularly liked the sign, but once she took Principles of Marketing, she had more reasons than *navy blue is boring.*

She brought it up at their once-monthly family dinner—that way, her dad couldn't claim he was too busy with work to talk about it. Though family dinner with five kids, plus their partners and children, was rather busy in and of itself.

Elsie had a plan. She printed out an article her professor had had them read for class. It was about the difference between a rebrand and a brand refresh. Her dad always says, *Hoffman Hardware is an institution,* and honestly, Elsie agrees. She's proud of the store, always has been. She's proud of their values. She doesn't want to change everything. But a refresh would breathe life into their history. Her plan was to bring it up when someone asked her how school was going.

Except no one did.

It was all fawning over grandchildren and waiting on Danielle, who was due with her first kid the following month, and their mom, ever the hostess, rushing around making sure drinks were full and all the food would be ready at the same time.

In the middle of dinner, everyone having different conversations, one on top of another, Elsie abandoned the plan.

"I think we should get a new sign."

The chatter stopped. Elsie focused on her plate instead of how the entire family turned to stare at her.

After a too-long stretch of silence, her dad's gruff voice said, "The sign's fine."

"The sign is like twenty years old."

"What's wrong with it?"

"There's nothing *wrong* with it," Elsie said, though that wasn't exactly true. It was busy and absurdly outdated. "But we can make it better. Our visual brand needs to be modern, memorable, and versatile. Updating our sign would be the first step in—"

"That sounds like a lot of unnecessary trouble," her dad cut in. "The sign is fine. The store is fine. If it ain't broke, don't fix it. And this is family dinner, not work dinner."

Her dad talked about work constantly, family dinner or otherwise. Elsie didn't point that out. Neither did any of her siblings. She still didn't give up.

"This isn't me being annoying. It isn't just some wild idea I have. I printed out this article from class—it's in my bag."

She started to stand to get it, but her dad waved at her to stay seated.

"Not now, Elsbeth," he said. "Leave it on my desk tomorrow morning and I'll get to it. Now, Danielle, are you still refusing to tell us what you're going to name our newest grandchild?"

The conversation moved on.

Elsie left early, claiming she had homework.

On Monday morning, she left the article in her dad's office chair. His desk had so many piles of paper on it, she couldn't even see the desktop. At least on his chair, he'd have to look at it to move it when he sat down.

The next week, she asked if he had time to chat.

"Not much," he said, gesturing to the disaster of his desk.

"I want to talk about the article I gave you last week," she said.

"Oh, Elsie, I haven't gotten to it yet." Her dad squeezed his eyes closed like she'd hurt him. "Now's really not a good time, okay? We've got inventory next week and your sister is about to have her baby. Let's not get mixed up in this mumbo jumbo."

Her nephew was three months old when Elsie snuck onto her dad's computer and added herself to his calendar.

"Hey." He stopped by her register Saturday morning. "Any idea why I've got a half-hour meeting with you at noon today?"

"You've been too busy lately," she said. "I'm making sure you eat lunch."

His grin was so soft there was a pang in her chest over lying to him. She normally didn't take lunch on Saturdays—Ginny was at the market, and Elsie's shift ended early enough that there was no reason for the break—but if pastrami on rye was the only way to get her dad to listen to her, so be it.

But he didn't listen to her then, either.

She presented it well, she knew she did. Powered through the argument she'd memorized, only had to look at the outline in front of her twice. Her dad was hard to read, chewing his sandwich passively, but Elsie made good points. She didn't even stumble over her words. As she finished her conclusion, she felt strong. Confident.

Her dad stayed quiet when she was done, the only sound in the office Elsie's slightly labored breathing, like she'd run a marathon rather than presented a business idea.

Finally, her dad shook his head and scoffed. Elsie's stomach dropped.

"A couple of classes and you think you know everything about running a business."

"Obviously I don't know everything, Dad," she said. "But why am I going to school if we're not going to use anything I learn?"

"You're going to school because you wanted to feel special."

Elsie blinked. It had been a rhetorical question, really, but even if she had wanted an answer, she never would've expected *that*. "What?"

"I've run this store for twenty-two years without going to college. My dad did it before me. You're not even going to be the one in charge when I retire. I can only assume you decided to go to school because you wanted to feel smarter than us."

You know what you do when you assume.

She didn't say that. He clearly wasn't listening to her anyway, so why bother? She'd put together this whole argument, and for what? Her dad was right; she wouldn't be the one running this place when he retired. What she thought was best for it didn't matter.

Elsie's mom found her soon thereafter.

"I'm sure he was just feeling sensitive," Mrs. Hoffman said. "This is our life and our livelihood, Elsbeth. He's never done anything but love this store. It's not easy to be told you're doing it wrong."

"I didn't say he's doing it wrong." She loved this place, too. She was trying to *help*.

"And I know you don't know the finances like your sister, but everything is more expensive than you expect."

Of course her mom wasn't listening to her, either. Why fucking bother?

Elsie's dad apologized before the end of her shift. Well—he didn't say he was sorry, but he at least admitted he was out of line. He claimed he was glad she shared her ideas even if that didn't mean he was going to implement them. He claimed he wanted to hear what she thought.

She appreciated the non-apology, but she didn't believe it. No one in her family had ever been interested in her opinions. It was more exhausting to share them and be dismissed than to keep them to herself.

So no, Elsie never had plans to talk to her dad about re-branding again. But this afternoon, it gets her mom to stop hovering and leave her alone. It's easier to handle the brush-off about rebranding than the pity over Derrick. At least her ideas for the store being ignored is disappointment she's used to.

She picks up a pen and marks the calendar next to the register with a giant red star on Monday. Five more shifts and she'll be in the Caribbean with her best friend. That thought will sustain her through anything.

8

NOTHING LIKE RACING THROUGH THE ATLANTA AIRPORT TO WAKE YOU UP AFTER A 5:30 A.M. FLIGHT. Their layover is barely an hour, but after speed-walking down moving walkways, they make it through international security and into the boarding line for their flight to Santa Lupita.

"I'm so glad you could come with," Elsie says. "I really didn't think you'd get the time off on such short notice, but I couldn't do this without you."

"You could," Ginny says.

They don't correct Elsie's understanding of the events that got them here. Telling her at this point that they quit their job makes no sense. Elsie's the one in—well, *crisis* seems a bit excessive, but—in crisis right now. Ginny doesn't need to make it about them.

It did feel a bit like lying last week, though, when they would pick Elsie up for lunch every day like nothing had changed. It felt calculated—it *was* calculated, the way Ginny never started woodworking in the morning because otherwise she'd have to shower before lunch so Elsie wouldn't know. They've never lied to each other before. But it wasn't lying, really—just omitting something, and for a good reason—so Ginny tries not to feel too guilty.

Now that they're past the calculating part of it, though, there's really no need to tell Elsie until after the trip.

Ginny has only been out of the country once, on an eighth-grade trip to Winnipeg. In high school, Elsie did a spring break trip to France, but Ginny stayed home. The farthest south they've ever been is Gulf Shores, Alabama. They've certainly never been in first class.

The first leg of the trip was in coach, but Ginny managed to sleep through it anyway, the armrest up between them and Elsie so their hips weren't squeezed to the point of torture. Now that they're in first class, the seats are big enough to be comfortable. They don't even have to use the seat belt extender they bring on every flight.

The rest of the plane has yet to finish boarding when a flight attendant asks what they'd like to drink.

"I feel like we should take advantage of being in first class," Elsie says, "but it's too early to get alcohol, right?"

"She'll have a Fuzzy Navel," Ginny tells the flight attendant. It's been Elsie's favorite drink since before they were legal. "And I'll have a Bloody Mary."

"So you don't think it's too early, I guess." Elsie giggles as the flight attendant goes to make their drinks.

"I think for this trip you should do whatever the hell you want."

"What happens in Santa Lupita stays in Santa Lupita?"

"Not even that," Ginny says. "Unless that's what you want. But Els, you almost ended up *married* because you didn't speak up about what you wanted. So this trip, you get to do anything you want."

"Anything?"

"As long as you ask for it."

"You'll do whatever I want as long as I ask?" Elsie sounds skeptical.

"Yep."

"Gimme five dollars."

Ginny gets out their phone and sends Elsie five bucks through their banking app. Elsie grins mischievously.

For the entire four-and-a-half-hour flight, she uses the rules like a superpower. She makes Ginny play tic-tac-toe and read the safety pamphlet in increasingly silly voices and ask the flight attendant if they've ever caught anyone joining the Mile High Club. She has two more drinks, and as they begin their descent, she tells Ginny to switch seats so she can look out the window. Ginny makes no complaint, though the view is incredible: an endless expanse of blue—water and sky smoothing into ombré, almost, cobalt and royal and cerulean fading to turquoise around groups of islands.

Once they land, Ginny barely processes anything but the *weather*. Eighty degrees, and what's that thing in the sky? The *sun*? Minnesota hasn't seen that for months.

Ginny holds doors and carries luggage and handles check-in, all without Elsie asking. It's habit, taking care of things. This trip is about taking care of Elsie. A lot of their life is about taking care of Elsie. They wouldn't have it any other way.

The person at the front desk lists too many amenities for Ginny to remember them all. Horseback riding and snorkeling and couples' massages. Neither Ginny nor Elsie mentions that they're not actually a couple. *Everything* is included—Ginny's gotta give Derrick credit for that. It doesn't feel like real life.

That feeling is compounded by being taken by sea to their bungalow. Their luggage already went in one boat, and they climb into another, a wooden dinghy with an outboard motor attached. The dinghy seems unassuming, but Ginny can tell that's intentional—they may not build boats, but they know enough about woodworking to recognize this boat was put together with care and skill.

Both Ginny and Elsie have been practically silent since walking out of the airport into a new world. The color palette around them has completely changed. Minneapolis was white and gray and darker gray, that brown slush of snow in the streets that too many cars have driven over. The island is all blue sky and bluer water, green plants and tan sandy beaches.

Their boat hugs the curve of the beach, and just around a bend, the bungalows appear. Elsie gasps. A long straight dock extends from the shore, ending in an upside-down triangle with one bungalow off each side, facing different directions. The roofs are thatched and the walls are another new color: warm brown, baking in the sun. Ginny wonders what type of wood they're built out of.

"That's really where we're staying?" Elsie asks.

"In my favorite one," the boat captain says as they pull up to the bungalow farthest from shore. "The other two face east and west, but your deck faces south. Best view of sunrise and sunset, both."

The captain ties the boat off at the corner of the deck. Along one side of the bungalow—the west, Ginny thinks, if they've got their bearings—are two hammocks, strung directly over open water. The south-facing deck has a small table with two chairs beside a staircase that leads directly into the water. Past the staircase, a wide umbrella casts shade over two patio loungers. There is no clear demarcation of indoors or out, because everything is open—window shutters and folding doors, wide-open to the ocean on three sides. Two wicker chairs face each other; their white pillows look cloud soft, but the main attraction inside is the extravagant four-poster bed. Rationally Ginny knows it's mosquito netting tied up at each corner, but it looks like tulle, like the bed itself is a princess gown. There's a mini-split above the bedframe, because they may want *air conditioning*. In *January*.

Their luggage sits beside the bed, whoever delivered it having disappeared already. The captain of the boat they just disembarked does the same, wishing them a great stay and adamantly refusing the tip Ginny offers. When the resort says *all-inclusive*, it means *all-inclusive*, though it tests Ginny's chivalry not to tip.

On the opposite side of the bed from their luggage is a doorway that must be to the bathroom. Ginny first thinks there's a turquoise floor runner leading that way, but it's actually a *glass floor*, see-through to the lagoon waters below.

Ginny looks at Elsie, who is wide-eyed and grinning.

"Dude," Ginny says.

"*Dude,*" Elsie says.

The bathroom itself begets another round of fawning. There's a rain showerhead and a tub big enough for two—and not just two skinny people—with an open window beside it. The way the bungalows are positioned, it's like Elsie and Ginny are completely alone, water as far as the horizon.

"This is *wild,*" Ginny says.

Elsie nods. "It doesn't feel real." She grins. "I'm going swimming."

At the airport this morning, Ginny dropped Elsie off at the door so she wouldn't need to travel in her winter coat. They themself shivered in a hoodie on the walk from long-term parking.

Now they stand on opposite sides of the bed to change into their bathing suits. Ginny bought a new one for this trip so they would have two—one to wear while the other was still drying out. For this first swim, they put on their favorite, a one-piece that ends in shorts instead of a bikini-cut bottom. The suit is navy blue with a rainbow running from one shoulder straight across the chest then down to the opposite thigh. They look good and gay; of course it's their favorite.

Once fully suited, Ginny takes a breath and turns to find that Elsie brought her bright-yellow string bikini.

Elsie grins. "Ready?"

Ginny nods, not sure they trust their voice in the face of all that skin.

They're never prepared for the first time they see Elsie in a bathing suit each year. Minnesota weather means everyone has spent months covering up—all flannels and cozy sweaters. Ginny wears fleece-lined Carhartts while she makes furniture in her heated-but-not-that-well garage. Elsie loves UGGs even though they're hideous.

Then summer comes and Elsie puts on a bathing suit and all Ginny can see is skin. It's disorienting to see in January, disorienting to know this week isn't enough for her to get tan; it takes all of summer for Elsie's pale skin to go even light bronze.

Ginny looks at the floor in front of them as they follow Elsie to the deck. They can't look at her back, bare but for the bikini strings and the end of her high ponytail between her shoulder blades, or her ass, barely covered, or her legs that go all the way to the floor. Elsie is a tall drink of water while Ginny is built like a teapot, short and stout. Elsie's long blonde hair is light gold even in the winter, while Ginny has to focus on their hair*cut,* because the color isn't doing them any favors: dishwater blonde at the height of summer and mousy brown right now.

"Sunscreen?" Ginny suggests, though the thought of covering Elsie's back for her makes them consider forgetting to mention it. How are they supposed to survive this trip? A week in paradise, sharing a bed in a honeymoon suite with the girl they're in love with. What have they gotten themself into?

"Later," Elsie says. "Water first."

She leaps off their deck.

9

GINNY IS SPRAWLED ON THEIR STOMACH, DROOLING ON THE PILLOW, WHEN ELSIE WAKES UP. The sight makes her heart soar. She grabs her phone from the nightstand and snaps a picture.

A little red bubble on her screen tells her she has four new messages. They're all in the family group chat. Both parents, plus Claire and Danielle—everyone but her brothers, as usual—saying they're glad she made it and to have a good week. She texts back *thanks* and a heart emoji, unable to leave them on read even though she hopes they don't respond so she can relax.

It's so early it should be unbearable, but the sun set at six last night, and they'd used that as an excuse to go to bed soon thereafter, the full day of travel having taken everything out of them. This morning, instead of tired, Elsie feels refreshed. Awake. *Present.*

Ginny, though, has never been a morning person. Elsie ducks under her side of the mosquito netting and leaves her best friend sleeping soundly.

The sand under Elsie's feet is yet to be warmed by the sun as she walks toward the open-air restaurant where they'd had dinner last night. It's a little way up the beach, through a copse of palm trees so she can't fully see it from the bungalows. That's right, Elsie is just casually walking through palm trees on the way to break-fast. She had no idea there were so many different types. There are the ones she expects, tall and skinny, all trunk with clusters of co-conuts under big pokey-looking leaves at the top. But between the restaurant and bungalows are trees with stubby trunks leading to huge leaves that fan out in an upside-down triangle. They're basi-cally a privacy fence. The rest of the resort is on the other side of the restaurant, around the bend of the beach. It makes the bungalows feel totally secluded. Like their own little world. Elsie can't think of anything better: a private world, just her and Ginny. They've always joked about starting a queer commune together, away from everything and everyone, and Ginny doesn't seem to mind that Elsie has no practical skills that would be helpful in that situation.

The restaurant is fully open, like their bungalow, except there's not even an option to close doors. The building is only half closed in, the other two sides open toward the ocean, a foot-ball field away. The buffet lines both walls, with a chef at a custom omelet station in the corner. Big fans spin lazily on the ceiling.

This early, there aren't many other guests—a couple in one corner and a lone traveler at the buffet. A worker greets Elsie in Spanish as she approaches. SHARA, a pin on her chest reads, she/her pronouns listed below her name. Elsie remembers enough of high school Spanish to return the greeting and ask the worker how she is. Beyond that, Elsie has to switch to English.

"Can I take stuff back to where I'm staying?" she asks. "In one of the bungalows?"

"If you're in the deluxe bungalows, we deliver your meals to you," Shara says.

"You don't have to do that."

"It is my job, mi amiga," Shara says. "There's a phone in your room you can use to order, rather than coming to the restaurant."

Who knew they could order room service? Or bungalow service, as the case may be. Deck service, Elsie decides, because that's where they're going to eat it, sky above them and water below.

She orders, for her and Ginny both, still half in disbelief that they'll be delivering this. For all the things Derrick did wrong, he picked a hell of a resort.

"Go back to your love," Shara says. "Food will be there soon."

Elsie doesn't correct her. She's loved Ginny for most of her life. Just because it's in a different way than Shara meant doesn't mean Ginny isn't her love. She gets iced coffee before she leaves, both because she refuses to leave the restaurant empty-handed and because she needs the caffeine as quickly as possible.

Ginny is still out when she gets back.

Elsie's chronically cold hands are worse from carrying the coffees, their sides wet, condensation collected on her fingertips. She puts said extra-cold hands to good use, one on Ginny's cheek and the other slid to the back of their neck.

Ginny jerks, giving her a confused squint as they wake. "Jesus, Els."

Elsie giggles and ignores the way their voice, thick and raspy with sleep, sends a shiver through her.

"What time is it?"

"Time to wake up," Elsie says. "Breakfast is on its way."

Ginny grunts.

"Breakfast is on its way, and I want you to get up."

At that, Ginny sighs and throws back the covers. Elsie beams. This whole getting-anything-she-wants thing is pretty great.

Ginny stretches, and their white ribbed tank top rides up to show skin above their thin plaid boxers. Elsie's stomach clenches, but she ignores that, too. She can't have *anything* she wants.

Once the food arrives, they eat on the deck, Ginny still wearing what they slept in. The sun is already bright enough that they both wear sunglasses. Elsie's lenses make the blue of the water go even more turquoise.

"So, what do you want to do today?" Elsie asks, then pops a bite of pancake, perfectly soaked through with butter and syrup, into her mouth. There's a plate with a more traditional Santa Lupita breakfast on the table, too, but Elsie can't turn down pancakes.

"Whatever you want," Ginny says.

"I can't even remember everything the concierge or receptionist or whoever they were—they said so much stuff. Like, did you know I could have ordered this from here?"

"There's a QR code on the bedside table that has a list of amenities and activities and whatever."

Elsie starts to get up to go scan it, then plops her butt back in the chair, smirking at Ginny. "Go scan it for me, please."

Ginny doesn't even sigh, just does as they're told. This is such a fun game.

Geez, this list of activities. Elsie scrolls down the page; it takes multiple thumb swipes to reach the end. There's snorkeling and scuba diving and parasailing and windsurfing and horseback riding. Various tours—about the colonial history of the island, or of a cacao or banana farm. A bike tour. There are botanical gardens and local marketplaces and golf courses. They could hike to any of six waterfalls. Go zip-lining or whale-watching or swimming with great whites.

For the less adventurous, there's the spa, with manicures and pedicures and facials and four different types of massages.

The resort has three restaurants and two nightclubs. Elsie isn't about to go to a pool when there's a staircase leading directly into the ocean off her deck, but if she wanted to, there's a water slide for kids and a swim-up bar for adults. They could rent Jet Skis or kayaks or paddleboards, go wakeboarding and waterski-ing and cliff diving.

"What do you want to do?" Ginny asks.

"C'mon, Gin, I wanna do half the fucking list."

Ginny plucks their phone back from Elsie, who watches from across the table as they highlight the whole page, copy it, and paste it in a note.

"Here's what we're gonna do," Ginny says. "I'll read these out loud and you tell me if you're interested or not."

"Okay, well, I can tell you right now I'm not interested in diving with great white sharks."

"Great. One down," Ginny says, thumb hitting the backspace button until that activity disappears.

The first attempt through the list, they barely narrow it down. Almost everything sounds incredible.

"This is a bit more manageable," Ginny says, though Elsie can see they still have to scroll a long way to get from the top to the bottom. "From this list, what do you *definitely* want to do?"

How is Elsie supposed to pick what she most wants to do? Snorkeling, whale-watching, zip-lining, a day at the spa. She wants to do it all.

"Well, what looks good to you?" she asks.

Ginny levels her with a stare.

"Okay, yes, I get it, whatever I want to do, but I want to take your opinions into consideration, too."

Ginny shakes their head. "I have no opinions," they say. "I'm getting a free vacation with my best friend in the fucking Caribbean. That's plenty for me."

"I'm not just gonna make you do whatever I want, though," Elsie says. "Like, I know you're not wild about heights, so parasailing is probably out, right? Or at least I'm not going to make you do it without asking."

"I'd do it for you," Ginny says. Elsie's breath catches for a second before they wink. "Only if you say you want to, though. We're not doing a single thing unless you speak up about it."

"Not doing a single thing in Santa Lupita still sounds like a pretty great vacation."

"That's exactly why I'm not complaining."

Okay, fine. Elsie can do this.

Ginny reads the list again, and Elsie is more discerning this time around. They've got limited time and amazing accommodations, so she doesn't particularly want to leave too often. Plus, she's with her favorite person, so group tours don't exactly grab her attention.

It turns out that while there are a lot of activities Elsie is interested in, there are only a few she *definitely* wants to do: see a waterfall, snorkel, horseback-ride, and get a massage. She makes Ginny add *do nothing* at the top of the list, and it's complete.

"That wasn't so hard, was it?"

Elsie sticks out her tongue at Ginny.

"Now you just gotta choose one for today."

Nothing sounds pretty excellent—Elsie brought a thriller that's supposed to be great, and the over-water hammock connected to their deck looks like a perfect spot to read—but she's too excited to spend the day relaxing. Still, having to make a choice paralyzes her. Getting whatever she wants sounded fun when it was just about making Ginny do ridiculous voices, or ask a flight attendant embarrassing questions, or wait on her so she can be lazy. Is she going to have to make *every* choice this whole vacation?

"Just one thing for today," Ginny says. Gentle. "We don't have to do it all right now. We've got time."

Five more days, four more nights.

Elsie makes a decision.

10

TALKING ABOUT WHAT SHE WANTS HAS NEVER GONE WELL FOR ELSIE. There's stuff with her family and the store, yeah, but it goes back earlier than that.

When she was nine years old, Elsie went to a friend's house for a birthday sleepover. They painted their nails and watched YouTube videos and ate too much pizza, then too much cake. Half an hour after they were supposed to go to sleep, they were playing truth or dare in the basement with no lights on.

Olivia had just been made to run around the room naked. There was no way of knowing if she was actually naked, lights off and all, but she definitely ran around the room, tripping over Ava's feet in her sleeping bag. It made all nine girls giggle so loud they shushed each other, which was not any quieter and didn't do anything but set them off into another round of giggles.

Once they got their laughter under control and Olivia's mom hadn't opened the door to the basement steps to yell down at them that they were supposed to be sleeping, it was Elsie's turn.

She was *not* about to run around the room naked.

"Truth," she said.

"Who do you have a crush on?" Olivia whispered.

Elsie's first crush had been the year before, in third grade. Every time her brother had Ben over, Elsie suddenly wanted to do everything they did. The only video game she normally liked was *Wii Sports,* but when Ben was over, watching the boys play *Halo* became her favorite activity. In the winter, when the boys wanted to build a snowboarding jump on the hill in their backyard, Elsie suddenly didn't care that she was always cold—she was on her knees packing down the snow for the jump.

She hadn't even known it was a crush until her brother yelled at her about it one day.

"It's so embarrassing that you have a crush on my best friend!" Brandon snarled. "You can't hang out with us anymore."

That was the end of that. Elsie had been too mortified to play with them again, even when Brandon said she could. Ben wasn't that cute anyway.

This year, Elsie had started playing basketball at recess. She wasn't any good at it and no one ever passed to her, but sometimes Kaitlyn high-fived her after a good play—not one Elsie had been involved in, but it was the high five that mattered, not the play itself. She didn't even know all the rules.

"Kaitlyn," Elsie whispered into the dark.

It was silent for a moment.

"Kaitlyn?" Olivia repeated.

"Yeah." Elsie's face grew hot, but of course no one could see her blush. "She's really good at basketball."

"Oh." Elsie didn't know who said it, but it didn't sound like a good *oh*.

~~~

AT SCHOOL ON MONDAY, EVERYONE LOOKED AWAY THE SECOND SHE GLANCED AT THEM. No one talked to her, but everyone talked *about* her. She didn't know what they were saying, but whispers followed her down the hallway. No one made eye contact.

The whole group of girls from the sleepover were huddled around a table in the cafeteria before the first bell rang. Elsie headed over to ask them if they knew what was going on, but Ava moved her backpack to the one open seat before Elsie could take it. None of them looked at her.

"Guys?"

They all pretended not to hear.

Elsie had no idea what was happening.

At recess, there was a crowd around the basketball court, which was weird. It parted when Elsie arrived. Finally, she heard some of the things people were saying.

"Oh my god, I can't believe she came."

"She must be, like, obsessed with her."

Oh, Elsie thought. It wasn't a good *oh*.

Kaitlyn was there, but unlike everyone else, she didn't even look at Elsie.

It wasn't unusual for Elsie to be picked last. She didn't care— why would anyone pick her? She was no good at basketball. She was used to hearing *I guess Elsie's on our team*. But this time, when there were only two of them left and the other girl got picked, that wasn't what Jake Corona said.

"I'm not taking the dyke."

The crowd laughed.

Elsie was made of glass, cracks branching out from her chest. She felt nothing but *broken*.

Don't cry, don't cry, don't cry.

She didn't cry. Didn't run. Said *excuse me* to the crowd and waited for people to move out of her way before she left, her head held high.

It wasn't until she was out of view, across the playground and in the woods, that she let herself shatter. Her back against a tree trunk, she slid to the ground, breath coming in hiccupping sobs she desperately hoped no one was close enough to hear.

She didn't know how long it took to get her breathing under control. Recess couldn't go on forever, no matter how much she wished it could. She didn't want to go back inside and face everyone. Didn't want anyone to look at her ever again.

"Hey."

Elsie jumped. She hadn't heard anyone approach.

"Oh," she said. At least at this point she'd stopped crying, though she had to rub her hand across her face to wipe away leftover tears and snot. Gross. "Hi."

Ashley Thompson sat in the pine needles next to her, crisscross applesauce. Her eyes were bright blue behind her wire-rimmed glasses.

"I don't know why everyone's being so stupid," Ashley said. "Being gay isn't a big deal."

"I'm not *gay*." Elsie said the word like it was a curse, even though she knew it wasn't.

Ashley rolled her eyes. "Don't be a dick. My moms are gay."

Being gay *wasn't* a big deal, Elsie knew, but just because she liked Kaitlyn didn't mean she was gay. She'd liked Ben, too.

The bell rang.

"Walk back to class with me?" Ashley asked.

At least she wasn't alone.

～～～

NO ONE BUT ASHLEY TALKED TO HER ALL WEEK.

Elsie herself barely talked. She lasted all day in school, head high and tears buried, never cried until she got home. Usually all the Hoffman kids ended up at the store, even though she and Claire were too young to be any help, but Elsie stopped going. Stayed in her room unless someone forced her to leave. If her parents noticed, they didn't talk to her about it. Her siblings didn't, either, not even Brandon, who was in the grade above her and must've heard the rumors about her by now.

What Brandon did do, though, was get suspended for breaking Jake Corona's nose.

There were only a few weeks left of school, but they went on like that—Elsie pretending not to be bothered and Brandon getting into fights.

～～～

THAT SUMMER, THE FAMILY MOVED. Her parents claimed it was to be closer to the store, but to this day Elsie wonders if it was partially her fault. The new house was closer to the store, yeah, but it was also in a new school district. One where Elsie didn't talk about her crushes and Brandon didn't start any fights.

It was easier to move away from the problem than to fix it. Easier to never trust anyone to care about what she wanted, never trust anyone to be kind about it, than to risk vulnerability. Easier not to risk anything than to lose everything.

That was why Elsie said no, years later, when Ginny asked her to the winter formal.

ANOTHER REASON ELSIE WOULD RATHER FOLLOW SOMEONE ELSE'S LEAD THAN MAKE THE DECISIONS HERSELF: AT LEAST THEN SHE'D HAVE SOMEONE ELSE TO BLAME FOR HOW MUCH SHE'S SWEATING RIGHT NOW.

Who ever thought hiking was a good idea?

Elsie knows—she knows it was her! She chose this. Ginny said they could do anything Elsie wanted, and for some reason Elsie wanted to huff and puff and sweat through her clothes. She thought it'd be good to move their legs after their long travel day yesterday, thought they'd come away with an appreciation of the island's natural beauty. Sure, it's lovely or whatever, but the real thing she's appreciating right now is winter in Minneapolis, when all the bugs are in hell where they belong.

"Fuck!" She coughs. That's the third bug she's swallowed so far.

"You good?" Ginny says.

Ginny has been walking behind her, carrying more weight on

shorter legs and not issuing a single complaint. Probably because Elsie has been inhaling all the bugs before they get to Ginny.

"I'm sorry I made us do this." The whine in her voice just makes her pout more.

"Nothing to be sorry about."

"Don't act like you're not breathing just as hard as me."

"Didn't say I wasn't," Ginny says. "Still doesn't mean you have to be sorry."

Elsie huffs. Sometimes Ginny is so easygoing it's annoying. She doesn't want Ginny to be nice; she wants camaraderie in her grumpiness.

Like always, Ginny seems to read her mind.

"Okay, yes, it sucks," they admit. "I haven't sweated this much outside of woodworking in, like—maybe ever? But you still don't have to be sorry. And I know we're doing whatever you want, so we *can* turn back if you want, but at this point I wanna see that waterfall, and it better be serene as shit."

A laugh bubbles out of Elsie. "Shit being known to be so serene."

She looks over her shoulder to watch Ginny roll their eyes at her. Exasperating her best friend is one of her favorite activities. Maybe she should've put it on the list.

The last mile is a lot easier knowing she's not alone in her discomfort.

She can hear the waterfall before she sees it. *Well* before she sees it. She keeps thinking it must be only a few steps away, surely they've made it by now, it's going to appear any second, if she eats another bug before they get there she's going to scream. Then, finally, the trees they've been plodding past for the last hour open up, and—

Oh.

Oh.

It was worth it, swallowing all the bugs.

Large boulders give way to a still turquoise pool. The waterfall must be thirty feet tall and about half as wide, a white cascade down rocks covered with plants so green they look like they've had the saturation turned up. To one side of the pool there's a flat boulder that looks perfect for sunbathing and—that's a penis.

That's *two* penises.

Elsie can't contain a snort of laughter, which sends the couple who had been taking advantage of the perfect sunbathing rock scrambling. They fumble their way to sitting up, hands over their crotches.

"Um," one of them says.

"Hi," the other one says. "Sorry. We, uh, had the place to ourselves for a bit."

Elsie bites her lip to keep from laughing any more.

Ginny, somehow, is unfazed. "Totally understandable, dude," they say. "Tell you what, you don't watch while we change into our bathing suits, and we won't watch while you change into yours."

"Deal."

Ginny turns their back to the pool, takes off the daypack they refused to let Elsie carry even for a moment.

Elsie giggles as Ginny hands over her suit. "Nothing like naked strangers in the morning."

"Can you blame them?" Ginny says, moving to a little alcove on the side that provides at least a semblance of privacy. "This place is unreal."

"Serene as shit?" Elsie asks.

"You're goddamn right."

Putting a bathing suit on when you're sweaty is disgusting. Luckily Elsie brought the same one she wore yesterday—it's mostly string ties rather than anything she has to shove her damp skin into. Ginny, on the other hand, brought their two-piece with the compression top. They're still trying to get into it when Elsie's done.

"I got you," Elsie says.

"No, I'm gross. I—"

Elsie has already helped before Ginny can finish the complaint. The top had been bunched around Ginny's ribs; Elsie got her fingers under the edge from behind and straightened it out. The skin of Ginny's back is slick with sweat. Elsie wants to lick it, or at least lick her fingers, but she's aware that's *stalker* behavior, not best-friend behavior.

This is how it goes, most of the time. She can be fine, normal, buddies with her favorite person since before she hit double digits—and then, in a split second, she sees Ginny differently. Suddenly she's wanton. She feels bad, usually—kinda skeevy—but it's not like it's her fault Ginny looks delicious in this bathing suit.

The high-necked black top flattens their chest, and the royal-purple bottoms come up just over their belly button, leaving a tantalizing strip of pale pillowy skin between. Ginny never seems to notice how amazing they look, how, every summer, Elsie has to keep her panting appreciation in check. Or maybe they do notice and just have never said anything so as not to humiliate Elsie.

"Thanks," Ginny says quietly. Then louder, over their shoulder, "You decent?"

Bathing-suit-clad Ginny momentarily distracted Elsie from the other couple, from the entire waterfall and swimming hole itself.

"We're good!"

When Elsie turns around, the couple is clambering off the rock, both in shorts and tank tops now. Not a penis in sight.

"We should get going, anyway. Sorry about that!"

"No worries," Ginny says. "Have a good one."

It's so Minnesota nice, Elsie's surprised they don't tack an *eh* on the end.

The couple disappears down the trail, and Elsie and Ginny have the place to themselves. Ginny was right: it's unreal.

"I have to get pictures," Elsie says.

She digs through the daypack to find her cell phone. The oasis is not big enough for a panoramic shot, but she takes three photos at different angles to capture the whole thing.

"Can I take one of you?"

Ginny normally refuses. They've never particularly liked being the center of attention. Elsie, the fourth of five kids, can't relate.

This time, though, instead of an immediate no, Ginny sighs. "Do you want to?"

Elsie beams. "Yeah."

"Fine."

She makes Ginny pose—*Hands on your hips* then *Arms up over your head like you're celebrating* and eventually *Blow me a kiss!* She didn't think they'd do the last one, but Ginny manages it with only the slightest roll of their eyes. Elsie giggles. She could definitely get used to this.

"Okay, selfie."

She smushes herself against Ginny's side at first, then slips behind them instead, almost tall enough to rest her chin on the top of their head. The waterfall doesn't even end up in the picture, it's just Elsie planting a kiss on one of Ginny's cheeks, which is the cutest pink from their hike.

"You're ridiculous," Ginny says.

"You love me," Elsie says.

"Whatever."

Elsie grins as she puts the phone away and sets the daypack out of the way so they can swim. Turning back to Ginny, she says, "Tell me."

"What?"

"I want you to tell me you love me."

"I'm regretting telling you that you could have whatever you want."

"Ginnifer." It's not even their full name—Ginny is just Ginny—but every once in a while, Elsie pulls out *Ginnifer* or *Virginia*, just so her best friend knows she's fake serious.

"I love you, stupid," Ginny says.

"I know," Elsie says, and marches into the pool.

There are plenty of waterfalls in Minnesota—*Land of 10,000*

Lakes and also a bunch of waterfalls; there are six in the Twin Cities alone—but none of them look like this, even in the height of summer. The tropics are just *different*. Which makes sense, obviously—it's not like the climates are anything alike. But this place still blows Elsie's mind.

The water is the perfect level of cool. Enough of a chill to be refreshing after the hike without making Elsie gasp. Her hair sticks to her damp shoulders when she takes her ponytail down. She ignores how gross that is, and dives under.

Heaven might have to be a swimming hole at the bottom of a waterfall. It's perfect. She surfaces from the dive to float on her back. A few fluffy clouds dot the bright blue sky above her. With her ears under the surface, the waterfall sounds like constant, rolling thunder. She feels weightless. This is exactly what she needed.

Suddenly she's flailing, yanked underwater by her ankle. She comes up sputtering, blinking water out of her eyes while Ginny laughs nearby. Elsie has to bite down on a smile at the sound.

"You're dead, Holtz."

She hurls herself at Ginny.

Elsie maybe should've thought this through. Ginny spends every evening, every weekend, moving lumber. Lifting and sawing and holding in place. Elsie's skinny enough you could see her abs, except she doesn't have any; meanwhile, Ginny's fat covers layers of muscle underneath. When Elsie tries to dunk them, fingers laced on top of their head and whole body trying to pull them down, Ginny laughs and leans forward until Elsie's the one going under.

The only way Elsie has a chance is to get them into the deeper water, where Ginny's legs aren't long enough to touch. Getting there, though, is practically impossible, given how damn *sturdy* Ginny is. Plus, they won't stop laughing at her, and their laughter makes Elsie giggle and lose focus as she tries to climb Ginny like a tree, or a jungle gym, or maybe just a big soft comfy couch— she's doing anything she can to get the upper hand, and it does not seem to be working one bit.

Eventually they stop, both breathing hard, Ginny clutching tight to Elsie's shoulders. She succeeded, she realizes—Ginny can't touch the bottom. Her hands find their hips to help keep them afloat.

Elsie grew up with no personal space. Her parents had five kids in the span of eight years, raised them in a three-bedroom house. They'd had to pile together, in the car or on the couch, too many limbs and not enough space.

Elsie complained about it, but it must have affected the wiring in her brain, because when she goes too long without physical touch, her skin feels itchy. So, she and Ginny touch. They touch a lot. She doesn't know what it is that flips something in her sometimes, that makes friendly touch suddenly heavy, meaningful. They were just all over each other, and it was fine. But the handfuls of Ginny's hips switch something on in Elsie. It's not friendly anymore.

Ginny's lips are pink and full and parted, slightly. They look so soft. They're wet—all of Ginny is wet, hair a mess, water droplets sneaking down their neck—and it makes them look glossed, shiny, begging to be kissed.

Except Ginny's not begging at all. They're just looking at Elsie, eyes dark. Fuck, how long was she looking at Ginny's mouth? Elsie wishes she could read their thoughts.

This trip is supposed to be about what she wants.

She wants to kiss Ginny.

"Oh my *god*—Mom! Dad! It's so cool!"

Elsie lets go of Ginny's hips, and they go underwater up to their eyes.

"Fuck, sorry." She grabs at them again.

"I'm good," Ginny says.

They tread water, kicking themselves out of Elsie's reach.

The child who broke their reverie is still shouting. "Look at this place!"

Elsie looks at the kid so she doesn't have to analyze Ginny's face. They're small, and adorable, wearing a sun hat with their socks pulled up to their knees. Their parents appear, both obnoxiously not even breathing hard.

"So what's next?" Ginny asks.

Elsie cuts her eyes to Ginny, whose face is unreadable. She swallows hard. "What do you mean?"

"You wanted to go on a hike, we've been on the hike. What's next?"

Right. What's next on the trip, not in this moment of almost kissing.

Because *this trip* is about what Elsie wants, but real life isn't.

It doesn't matter that when the hotel worker assumed Ginny was her partner, Elsie liked the idea. It doesn't matter that she wanted to say yes when Ginny asked her to the dance sophomore year. It doesn't matter that sometimes, watching Ginny work in their garage-turned-woodshop, when Ginny is wearing a Twins hat backward and sweating through their tank top if it's summertime, pushing up the sleeves of their hoodie if it's winter, Elsie wants to kiss them.

Elsie's occasional indecent feelings for Ginny get filed away next to her ideas for the store. Interesting. Fun to think about sometimes, when she's alone. Never gonna happen.

She lifts her feet and lets herself float once more. "Jesus, Gin, can't we enjoy this before we're on to the next thing?"

It's good, she decides. It's good they were interrupted. Elsie can't ruin what she and Ginny have always had just because they're in a romantic place, far from reality, and she wants to kiss them. It's good.

She's gonna float until she stops seeing Ginny's lips every time she closes her eyes, and they're gonna be fine.

12

About how long she and Elsie weren't quite the same after the dance, how awkward everything was. It doesn't really matter. It was forever ago—more than eight years by now. Basically, a third of their lives has passed since then. They've both moved on.

That Ginny hasn't actually moved on doesn't matter.

Sure, if sophomore year had never happened, Ginny might say something. They might even ask Elsie how she feels. They're a lesbian—they love talking through feelings. But Elsie already rejected Ginny once, and their friendship barely survived. It's not worth risking again.

Plus, Ginny is never sure if they're reading things wrong. Did Elsie really look at their lips? Did her fingers linger on Ginny's skin? Maybe the moment at the waterfall was just a fluke of Ginny's senses, the way time moves slower when Elsie touches them. No reason to make it into anything it's not.

When Ginny gets out of the shower back at their bungalow, Elsie is already in her other bathing suit. She tosses Ginny theirs.

"A swim is gonna feel better than a shower," Elsie says.

Ginny was hoping to get some distance from all that skin. Elsie didn't put on a top for the return hike, and Ginny spent a full hour and a half trying not to get distracted by the muscles in her back.

Still, Elsie isn't wrong: the water is heaven.

Shallowness is relative—when the surface hits Ginny at their chest, it's barely over Elsie's belly button—but they're both able to wade in all directions. Elsie had spent their first swim yesterday exploring; she circled the bungalow, ducked under the dock it's connected to, chased glittering schools of fish.

Ginny found the floats in a storage trunk on the deck.

That's what they both use today. Elsie sits on a pool noodle and Ginny lounges in an armchair float with a mesh bottom that keeps them half in, half out of the water. Everything is so blue it doesn't seem real. Ginny spares a moment to wonder how this all works—why is Caribbean water more turquoise than the Great Lakes, why is this area so shallow and free of waves, how do tides work—but, god, she really doesn't care.

"Don't let me float away," they say, and Elsie catches their hand. She's floating, too, but at least wherever the ocean takes them it'll be together. "What else you wanna do today?"

"This," Elsie says.

Nothing is indeed on the list.

The afternoon feels like summer vacation in middle school. No responsibilities. The world is warm and golden and still. Time passes neither quickly nor slowly, because the clock doesn't matter. They spend hours alternating between the hammocks and the deck chairs and the ocean. Ginny's never changed swimsuits as much as she has today: a constant rotation to keep things dry, each bathing suit getting hung over the deck railing as soon as it comes off, the other being grabbed from its place in the sun.

GINNY HAS SHARED A BED WITH ELSIE MORE TIMES THAN THEY CAN COUNT. Summers in their preteens they would bounce back and forth between each other's houses, a night here, three there, then back again. Tonight is the same as every night they've fallen asleep beside each other; Elsie tosses and turns until her ankle presses against Ginny's.

"Good night," Elsie says with a sleepy murmur of content.

Ginny's heart skips a beat.

None of that is unusual, but normal aspects of their friendship can suddenly feel heavier if Ginny thinks about them for too long.

She lies still and listens to Elsie drift off.

Ginny knew they were a lesbian before they knew they were nonbinary. It was before they met Elsie. They don't have a specific ring-of-keys moment so much as there was never a time in their life they weren't awed by women. The way they acted out enough to get sent to the hall in first grade on their student teacher's last day. Their alarming devotion to Sally from *Cars*. The stern math teacher everyone else said was mean who Ginny would have done anything for.

The only time Ginny and Elsie have ever kissed, they were eleven years old. They both knew they were queer, but it wasn't that kind of kiss. They just wanted to see what the big deal was. They'd kept their eyes open and broken the kiss with giggles.

"That was weird," Elsie had said. "Let's watch *The Johnson Dynasty.*"

That was a fluke. Just like their moment at the waterfall. They've had a lot of flukes over the course of their friendship, but not enough for them to mean anything. Elsie's pansexual, but she's never seriously dated anyone who wasn't a cis man. There was Sahar in eighth grade, but that was a middle school thing. Elsie's bound to be curious, just like when they were kids kissing in Ginny's bedroom. Ginny had felt like their whole body was on fire afterward, hyperaware of how close Elsie sat on the couch. Elsie, meanwhile, had been fully engrossed by the television.

A few years later, when Ginny got up the nerve to ask her to the dance, Elsie said no.

Ginny is happy with their friendship. She almost lost it once, and she refuses to risk it again. So no matter how many moments they have like the one at the waterfall, Ginny will never ask Elsie if she feels the same way they do.

Elsie is the most important thing in Ginny's life. She's not willing to fuck that up.

∼

SLEEP ALWAYS HELPS GINNY GET THEIR HEAD ON STRAIGHT. Or, as straight as anything about them can be, so. Not very.

Whatever—in the morning, they wake up alone.

Elsie, ever the morning person, has left a note on the pillow saying she already ordered breakfast. The shower is running on the other side of the wall, Elsie's voice loud enough for Ginny to know it's off-key, but not enough for them to know what she's singing.

They sneak their hand under the mosquito netting and grab their phone from the nightstand. Yes, they're in paradise, they should unplug and all that, but they do actually have some real-life stuff they should pay attention to.

Ginny logs in to their banking app. They've been doing that a lot the last week, checking and double-checking their savings account. They hated their job—and it didn't pay much regardless—but still, quitting without a backup plan maybe wasn't the smartest idea.

They've got options, at least. Beyond their emergency fund, they'll have some income. Woodworking always brings in decent money, and now Ginny will have more time to devote to that. As long as they can get enough work. Maybe Sue has a connection who could help.

Ginny met Sue in a woodworking class at Lowe's when they were in college, not even twenty yet. Sue was older, midthirties or something, an Ojibwa woman who introduced herself with a strong handshake and an unforgettable line.

"Take the workbench next to me. Us queers gotta stick together. I know I have a perfect bisexual bob, but I'm a dyke."

"Me too," Ginny said.

Sue snorted. "Uh, yeah."

Everyone else in the class was a man. Ginny and Sue got so much extra attention from the instructor, so many "tips" from the other attendees, they went for lunch together afterward and agreed to never go back. They started working on projects in Sue's garage instead, and when Ginny bought a house in bad need of a remodel, they did all the new cabinets and flooring together, with Elsie's so-called supervision, which was mostly her standing around talking about stain colors and how her parents' store really should do classes of its own, where they could kick out any condescending men. They're a perfect pair: Ginny tending toward Adirondack chairs and dining room sets and thousand-pound entertainment centers, and Sue using all their scrap wood to make smaller stuff—cutting boards and cooking utensils and the like.

Sue has brought in some work for Ginny from her day job as an interior designer. Every so often, someone wants new built-ins, or a dining room table they can pass down to their children and grandchildren, or even something small like a bedside table. Usually Sue and Ginny split the project, their day jobs keeping them both too busy to complete it on their own. Now that Ginny quit, they'll have plenty of time.

Their life in Minnesota is going to be so different when they get back. And even though they're in paradise, they're actually excited to go home. They don't have an exact plan yet, but figuring it out is going to be a lot more fun than their old job.

There's a knock on the door. That must be breakfast. By the time Ginny gets out of bed to get it, the delivery person has disappeared. At least that saves them the guilt of not being allowed to tip.

"Yay! It's already here," Elsie says, emerging from the bathroom squeezing her hair in a towel.

She's in a spaghetti-strap tank top and black underwear.

Ginny's head is very much not on straight. They drain half their iced coffee and set everything up on the deck table under the umbrella.

"I ordered lots of protein." Elsie has put on shorts to eat, thank god. "Eat up. We're going snorkeling."

"That so?" Ginny spears a piece of fried sausage with their fork.

"Snorkeling this morning and dinner at that fancy restaurant tonight," Elsie says. "Gonna check 'em both off the list."

~~~

PROTEIN CONSUMED, BATHING SUITS ON UNDER THEIR CLOTHES, AND DAYPACK STRUNG OVER ONE SHOULDER, GINNY FOLLOWS ELSIE TO THE OFFICE ON THE BEACH WHERE MOST OF THE HOTEL'S ACTIVITIES BEGIN.

A worker with a name tag reading NICHOLAS, HE/HIM—Ginny loves that pronouns are included—issues them both masks and flippers and life jackets, all for free. He almost has Ginny convinced they should rent wet suits—one of the few add-ons available that's not already covered—when they finally think to ask the water temp.

"Oh," Nicholas says, like he's talking about a horror movie. "It's *only* seventy-four degrees."

Elsie snorts, and Ginny bites down on a grin. Their preferred Great Lake is Superior, a balmy 62 degrees at the height of summer.

"We're good."

While they wait for the boat to the reef, they sit on the edge of the dock, Elsie's feet dangling in the water, Ginny's legs not long enough for hers to reach.

The beach is crowded with people, on chaises, under umbrellas, kids and adults both playing at the edge of the water. Thank god for the seclusion of their bungalow. Vacations are not for being around people. Though, squinting at other travelers from behind her sunglasses, Ginny realizes that at least there seem to be plenty of queer folks.

A lot of them, actually.

There was a mini rainbow flag on display at the front desk when they checked in. The staff's name tags all have pronouns on them. And now there are more white men in Speedos than Ginny has seen in their whole life.

"Weird question, but, uh . . . is it possible Derrick booked your honeymoon at a gay resort?"

Elsie kicks her feet in the water below the dock. "I was hoping you wouldn't figure that out."

Ginny raises their eyebrows, smirking. "Els."

"Don't laugh," Elsie says, then that's exactly what she herself does, a giggle breaking through. "You know it's important to him to support my identity."

"And obviously the way to do that is taking you to a gay resort for your honeymoon."

Elsie's whole face scrunches up as she laughs. "He actually said—he said—" She wheezes for a moment. "He said, 'It's an LGBTQ resort. *P* might not be in the acronym, but that means pan, too!'"

Ginny presses their fist to their mouth, trying to contain their laughter. "*P* may not be in the acronym."

"He was always kinda offended about that, to be honest."

"He's not the brightest bulb in the box, but at least his heart's in the right place."

"Yeah," Elsie says, all quiet, and Ginny realizes maybe they shouldn't talk about her ex that way.

Before Ginny can decide if they should apologize, Elsie pulls her cover-up over her head. Ginny looks out at the water.

"If we're not doing wet suits, can you sunscreen me?" Elsie asks. "I got burned a little even with how often we sprayed it on yesterday, so will you rub it in, too?"

So much for getting their head on straight. Ginny would rather go back to talking about Derrick. Well—they'd very much not, actually. They'd like to put their hands on Elsie. That's exactly the problem.

Elsie's creamy skin is indeed pink in places, outlines of the straps of her other bathing suit. She's in the one-piece for snorkeling, thank god. Ginny couldn't have handled touching that much skin. They can barely handle the racerback straps and open back of this suit.

Elsie gasps at the first touch of Ginny's hands.

No. At the coolness of the sunscreen. Not at Ginny's hands.

"Go all the way under the straps," Elsie says.

Ginny takes a breath. Lifts the straps to get underneath. She thinks about the Minnesota Twins, about how *Jaws* gave sharks a bad rap, she even thinks about Derrick—anything other than sliding these straps down Elsie's shoulders. The wide expanse of skin. The freckles they connected with a Sharpie one sleepover when they were kids.

The boat arrives before the moment can turn into another fluke.

13

"THERE ARE THREE THINGS THAT CAN HURT YOU, BUT ONLY ONE IF YOU
FOLLOW THE RULES."

The yacht has anchored, and the guide is doing the safety
spiel. Ginny wishes Elsie would listen rather than take pictures of
the island, though they admit Santa Lupita's iconic twin moun-
tains are stunning from this angle. They're not as far offshore as
Ginny expected, in what is apparently a popular snorkeling spot;
three other boats are anchored nearby, and countless people bob
in the water. Ginny would've liked a bit more privacy.

"As long as you wear your life jacket, which you must, you
won't drown," the guide says. "As long as you don't touch anything, which you shouldn't, you won't have a problem with fire
coral. That only leaves the jellies, and they're so small it's more
like a zap of static electricity than anything else."

Ginny loosens the straps of the provided life vest as much
as possible, but still has to suck their stomach in to buckle it.

Great. They have to spend the whole morning squished into this thing.

The tightness of the life vest is forgotten the moment Ginny puts their face in the water. The boat is anchored off the reef, of course, but even here there are schools of fish flitting in and out of the occasional coral. They forget about their desire for more privacy, too; when they follow Elsie over to the reef, there could be a thousand people around and Ginny wouldn't notice.

It's like an episode of *Planet Earth*. Coral and anemones and sea urchins and *fish,* so many fish. Ginny can't count how many different kinds, sun flashing over colorful scales as they dart through the water. She wants to ask Elsie if she saw the one that looks like Dory, wants to never stop looking at the reef. There's too much to see.

At first, Ginny swims all over, trying to see everything, though they'll never have enough time. Eventually, they manage to stop being so desperate to take it all in and instead let themself enjoy the experience.

Ginny is floating, as still as possible, hands motionless in front of themself, trying to see how close the schools of striped fish will get, when something thrashes in their peripheral vision. It's not a sea turtle or an octopus, but their best friend.

"Fuck!"

Ginny is at Elsie's side in half a second. "Are you okay?"

She is, Ginny can tell upon closer inspection. She's floating just fine, mask pulled off her face and one hand to her mouth.

"Something stung me! On my lip!"

She pulls her hand away and sticks her chin out at Ginny, but there's not even a mark.

"It looks okay," Ginny says, reaching out to touch Elsie's lip before thinking better of it. "It was probably one of the tiny jellies they told us about."

"On my *lip*," Elsie huffs like it's a personal affront. She flips around in the water and holds a leg out toward Ginny. "I jerked away when it happened and accidentally kicked a coral and now my shin feels like it's on fire."

That did leave a mark, an angry stripe of red across Elsie's leg.

"You must've kicked fire coral," Ginny says. "Let's go ask the guide what to do."

They shepherd Elsie back toward the yacht. Once there, the guide flushes the area with salt water, then vinegar. Elsie pouts, but she's not in pain anymore.

"They could've warned us about fire coral," she grumbles.

Ginny tries not to chuckle. "They definitely did, Els. You were a little focused on taking pictures."

"Oh," Elsie says. "Well. Whatever. I got great pictures. Even if I got stung on the lip and attacked by fire coral."

"*You* attacked the fire coral."

"Oh my gosh, I can't believe you're blaming the victim like this."

Ginny laughs and bumps their shoulders together. "I love you."

Elsie beams. "Love you. Thanks for taking care of me. You can go back in if you want."

"Nah," Ginny says. "I'm good here."

They are. Snorkeling was amazing, and they could've done it forever, but they could do this forever, too, sitting in the sun on a boat beside their best friend. Life is good.

———~~~———

SUNRISE IN SANTA LUPITA IS AT 6:30 A.M., SUNSET AT 6 P.M. It means they get a full two hours' more daylight than Minneapolis this time of year, but it also means that if they want dinner at sunset, they have to eat like they're AARP members.

The restaurant is a la carte, separate from the buffet they ate at before, and it's the first building they've been in that isn't fully open-air. Still, they eat outside, the host leading them through candlelit tables and out a wide door to the restaurant's deck.

All the servers wear ties, and Ginny would, too, for a restaurant this fancy, if they were back in Minneapolis. On vacation, though? They're in a chambray button-down French-tucked into chino shorts—joggers, because in addition to no ties, Ginny refused to bring any pants with a zipper on this trip.

Elsie looks like a dream in a kelly-green linen jumpsuit with wide legs and a square neckline. Ginny keeps getting distracted by her collarbones.

"I can't believe I got stung by a jellyfish on my fucking lip," Elsie says for the fifth time once they're seated.

"You know," Ginny says, trying for nonchalant but unable to stop a grin, "*P* may not be in the acronym, but I could pee on it if you want me to."

A beat of silence. Ginny can only pretend to look at the menu for so long before glancing across the table. Elsie's glare makes it impossible not to laugh.

"I hate you," she says.

Ginny tries to swallow their laughter, focusing on the menu

again. "The boat captain did say they have lots of water sports here, but I don't think that's what they meant."

"Water sports is distinctly *not* on our list of things to do this week."

"I didn't realize it was that kind of list."

"You're so stupid," Elsie says, but she's giggling, too.

The server arrives then, in a long-sleeve white button-down and a black tie matched to black pants. "How are we doing tonight, ladies?"

Ginny bites their lip to keep from smirking. The gendered term is annoying, but the lecture Elsie is about to launch into is endearing enough to outweigh it.

"Excuse me," Elsie checks the server's name tag, "Juliana, is it? This resort specifically caters to queer people, right?"

The server's eyes are wide. She nods.

"And I see your name tag has your pronouns on it," Elsie continues. "So you must know that you can't assume someone's pronouns or gender by looking at them. Why would you greet anyone with *ladies*?"

"I'm so sorry. I shouldn't have."

"No, you shouldn't have. There's plenty of nongendered ways you can greet a table."

"Anyway," Ginny says before Elsie can start listing them. They appreciate that Elsie uses her privilege to address the rampant gendering that people do for truly no reason, but— "We're good. How are you doing, Juliana?"

The server looks at her. Glances nervously back at Elsie. "I'm good. Thank you. Are you enjoying your stay?"

Ginny is more interested in looking at the menu than making small talk, but they chat, all smiles and gentle voice, before giving Juliana their drink order and sending her on her way, hopefully a little less anxious about serving them all night.

"You know I'm okay with getting *she*'d," Ginny says to Elsie once the server is out of earshot.

"*I* know that," Elsie says, "but she doesn't. And what about when there's a customer who isn't okay with that? Plus, she didn't *she* you, she *ladies*'d you. It's different."

"I know, Els."

Ginny's chest feels warm. Elsie just . . . she cares, and she gets them, and Ginny fucking loves her for it.

"Should I not have said anything?"

"No, no, that's not what I mean." Ginny reaches for her hand on top of the table, squeezes it. "I love that you stand up for me, and for nonbinary folks in general."

"But?"

If they're pushing Elsie on what she wants on this trip, why not push her on this, too?

"Where does that boldness come from?" Ginny says. "Why are you so good at speaking up for me but not for you?"

Elsie pulls her hand away. She looks at her water glass. Picks it up and takes a sip. Puts it back down. It takes her a moment to respond, and when she finally does, Ginny can barely hear her. "You deserve it."

"So do you," Ginny says.

"I know, I just—" Elsie huffs. "I don't always know what I want, so how am I supposed to speak up about it? I *know* it's not right to greet strangers with gendered terms."

Of course that's when the server returns with their drinks. Ginny puts on her nicest smile. It'd be really helpful if they could tip to make up for how terrified this kid looks. She delivers the drinks and takes their food order and scurries away.

Ginny's mojito comes in a crystal highball glass with a lime twist, muddled mint swimming among the ice cubes. It's positively boring compared to Elsie's Bahama Mama, which looks like a sunset in a hurricane glass. Pink and yellow and orange melding together, a maraschino cherry and a huge slice of pineapple as garnish.

Ginny waits while Elsie takes pictures: of their drinks with the actual sunset as a background, then a selfie with hers, and lastly one of Ginny holding their drink. They're going to continue the conversation once she's done, but Elsie picks it back up herself.

"Even with Derrick, I didn't *know* I didn't want to marry him until it was right in front of me. Until it was really happening. Fuck, I'm lucky I didn't make it all the way to the altar before I figured it out."

You and him both. Ginny doesn't say it; Elsie feels guilty enough already.

"I don't even know who I am separate from Derrick. I've never been an adult without him."

"Okay, but you know *some* stuff you want," Ginny says.

"Oh my gosh, this drink is so good. Try it."

Elsie holds the glass across the table, straw angled so Ginny can lean in for a taste. It tastes like it looks: sunny and beachy and tropical. Too sweet by half, but Ginny knows that's how Elsie likes it.

"Delicious." But they refuse to let the topic drop. "What if, in addition to *doing* whatever you want on this trip, we use the time to *think about* what you want? In real life, I mean, not just here."

"*We* think about what *I* want?"

Ginny needs to think about what they want, too, what they're going to make of their life now that they're not chained to a desk forty hours a week. But Elsie still doesn't know about that, and this is about her.

"Well, yeah," Ginny says. "I can help. Talk through it and stuff. Help you figure out who you are, even though I'm pretty sure you know more than you think."

Elsie considers it. "So, like, not just a fun game where I get whatever I want. But a real thing."

"A real thing," Ginny agrees. "What you want matters. Both when it's fun and when it's real."

Elsie looks at her. There's a weight to the look, something heavy between them all of a sudden. Ginny would give anything to be able to read her mind.

"What if what I want . . ." she starts, looking toward the sunset. She pauses. It's probably only for a moment, but it feels like hours to Ginny, their breath caught in their throat. When Elsie speaks again, her voice is stronger. "What if what I want is to enjoy dinner and not think about real life until tomorrow?"

There's no way that was what she first planned to ask. There's no way she had to break eye contact to talk about enjoying dinner. Ginny would give absolutely *anything* to be able to read her mind. But as always, they refuse to push it.

"I don't know," they say instead of asking what Elsie was

originally going to say. "Enjoying dinner with this view seems tough."

The sun has fully dipped below the horizon, the sky all pale orange with bright pink clouds, the water opalescent.

"I think we can manage it," Elsie says.

She smiles and Ginny gets her pulse under control, and they manage just fine.

Elsie gets a different cocktail with each course. The Bahama Mama goes with a shared appetizer of scallops and pork belly so tender their forks go straight through it. The next drink, a rum punch, is overshadowed by her entree; it's the first time in her life she's had lobster. Ginny, meanwhile, orders lemon pepper shrimp and linguine that's so good they practically lick their plate. For dessert, Elsie gets an espresso martini, and together they order chocolate cobbler with banana ice cream. It's possibly the best meal of Ginny's life.

All the *bests* in Ginny's life have Elsie in them. Best meal. Best vacation: this one, probably, but also spring break their senior year of high school, when they spent a week driving around the Great Lakes with no itinerary, just going wherever they felt like that day. Their best concert: seeing girl in red at First Avenue.

This would be the best date, if that were something it could be. Stars are beginning to blink into existence above them. Lights from the island glitter reflections across the water. Their table is small enough they could easily hold hands across it or play footsie beneath. While parts of the resort cater to traveling families, everywhere they've been has emphasized privacy. Intimacy. You mostly can't see the other bungalows from theirs; only if you lounge in the hammock on the side are you aware that anything exists besides the endless ocean.

Even if this whole place weren't built for romance, any date with Elsie would be the best. She's Ginny's favorite person. It's taken Ginny a long time to figure out how to be themself in life, but it's always been easy with Elsie.

This dinner does feel different, somehow. Like maybe it *could* be a date. There's just something in the way Elsie looks at them, and Ginny can't stop wondering what it was she was going to admit to wanting earlier.

Regardless of all that, this cobbler is definitely the best dessert Ginny has ever had. They scrape their spoon against the plate, refusing to let any go to waste.

"Okay, I'm not gonna lick the plate in public, but I will do this." Elsie swipes her index finger through the leftover dessert, then sucks it into her mouth.

Ginny chokes. "*Elsie.*"

"What?" Elsie giggles. "You sound like my mother. *Elsbeth, that's not very ladylike.*"

She drags her finger across the plate again. This time, her tongue comes out, licking up one side of her finger before sucking it into her mouth.

She is not looking at Ginny the way she looks at her mother.

"Anything else I can get you two?"

It takes a second for Ginny to break eye contact with Elsie to look at the server. They wish she'd misgendered them again, anything to interrupt whatever is happening here. This fluke.

"I'm all set," Ginny says. "What about you, Els?"

Elsie hasn't stopped looking at them. "I'm good."

As the server reaches for the empty dessert plate, Ginny stacks their silverware on it, tosses her napkin on top just for something else to do with their hands. They watch the server walk away for as long as possible before finally looking at Elsie again. Elsie's index finger idly traces the edge of her martini glass. Her head is tilted down, so when she looks across the table at Ginny, it's through her lashes. Candlelight dances across her face.

"What if I want something that could ruin our friendship?"

Ruin it, Ginny thinks, no hesitation.

But no, they can't say that. They want to be a good friend. Besides, maybe Elsie doesn't even mean it like that. They can't let their libido and this romantic place mess up a decade and a half of friendship.

"Nothing could ever ruin our friendship," Ginny says. "You're stuck with me for life, Hoffman."

Elsie blinks and looks away. "A real hardship, being stuck with you."

14

Ginny wanted to go to the dance with *her*. Elsie had let herself imagine it: Ginny in a suit—navy, maybe, or charcoal, their tie matching Elsie's dress. They'd get her a corsage with an orchid, even though they were expensive, because it was Elsie's favorite flower. Elsie's mom would be obnoxious about pictures before dinner somewhere fancy where Ginny would open doors for Elsie and pull out her chair and pay after—with their parent's credit card, but still. Ginny would go to the dance even though they didn't really care, and Elsie would only make them stay through one slow song, maybe two, just so she could feel their arms around her. Then they'd ditch and go to Steak 'n Shake in their fancy clothes. They wouldn't share a milkshake, even though that'd be cute, because Ginny would want Butterfinger and Elsie would want cookies and cream. If they were gonna kiss, it would have to be before they got home, where Elsie's parents would probably be watching through the window.

But what would happen after that? People broke up, all the time. Just because Elsie's parents were high school sweethearts didn't mean she knew how to be in a relationship forever.

She'd dated people before—Sahar Nelson in eighth grade, though only for two weeks and they didn't do anything but talk on the phone, and a couple of boys here and there—and it never ended well. Sahar broke up with her via text before they'd ever even kissed. One boy told everyone he got to third base with her when she didn't even know what counted as third base, but unless it was French-kissing, he hadn't.

The thing about her romantic relationships was they always ended.

All Elsie was sure of at fifteen was that she wanted to be best friends with Ginny forever.

It's all she's been sure of most of her life.

Everything else has fluctuated. As a kid she played with dolls and wanted a big family, five children, just like her parents. As a teenager, fighting with her siblings what felt like every time they interacted, she swore she'd never have kids. She's gone from wanting to work at the store to being forced to work at the store when she'd rather do anything else to wanting to do more at the store but no one in her family will listen to her. Even this past week, Elsie's gone from engaged to single. Things *change,* a lot. The only thing that has never changed is that Elsie wants to be best friends with Ginny forever.

So she said no and refused to let Ginny pull away, no matter how awkward it got after.

Staring up at the mosquito net draped around the bed the morning after their fancy dinner, Elsie realizes there's one other thing that has never changed. She has wanted to kiss Ginny since before they did it for the first time, eleven years old—at Ginny's house because they didn't want to risk Claire or Danielle walking in on them in Elsie's shared bedroom. She wanted to kiss Ginny when they asked her to the dance. She wanted to kiss Ginny in college, tipsy at house parties where they didn't know the host, Ginny always close but never hovering. She wanted to kiss Ginny at the waterfall, and when their eyes lit up talking about snorkeling—even though Elsie's lip hurt from the jellyfish sting—and last night, when Ginny told her that what she wanted mattered.

Ginny told her to think about what she wants. Sure, they meant it more like in an overall *life* sort of sense, but what if what Elsie wants is to act on every moment of longing, every time she looked at their lips too long, every time she watched Ginny build furniture and wanted to test its sturdiness by letting them fuck her on it?

What she wants matters.

Before she can talk herself out of it, Elsie climbs on top of Ginny.

Ginny's hands find Elsie's thighs before they're fully awake, at which point they promptly let go. Elsie grabs each of Ginny's wrists and moves their hands back where they were.

"This is what I want," she says. "I want you to fuck me."

Her voice doesn't shake, though she's got butterflies swooping through every vein in her body. Ginny's fingers flex against her thighs.

Elsie thinks about being eleven. Kissing Ginny, then giggling instead of admitting she liked it. Not looking at Ginny for three whole episodes of whatever show she suggested as a distraction. Her heart hammers against her sternum just as hard now as it had then, waiting for Ginny to reject her.

But Ginny doesn't reject her. They take a few moments, blink the sleep from their eyes. Then they say *okay,* and lean up to capture Elsie's mouth with their own.

The first thing Elsie feels is *relief.* Thank fuck. *Thank fuck.* This is what she's been waiting for. This is what she's wanted for over a decade. She knows now: *this* is what she ended her engagement for. Ginny's lips are as soft as the rest of them. When their tongue connects with hers, Elsie gasps. Desire overpowers relief. Ginny's mouth is warm and wet and perfect, and Elsie wants it all over her. Wants her mouth all over Ginny, wants to kiss every warm, wet, perfect part of them.

Elsie never let Derrick kiss her in the morning until he'd brushed his teeth. Ginny's mouth is stale, and still Elsie licks into it. Ginny doesn't kiss like Derrick.

Kissing Derrick had become routine, almost thoughtless. Even when they were intimate, it never felt particularly special. It never lit her up inside. Before Derrick, she can barely remember; it's been years since she kissed anyone else. Still, she's pretty sure it's never been like this. The sun is barely up, the world around them all soft light, but Elsie feels fluorescent, feels on fire. Not a candle but a firecracker. All heat and sparkling explosions.

Elsie wants to take her time, but she doesn't want to go slow.

She didn't ask Ginny to kiss her—she wants Ginny to *fuck* her. She wants to fuck Ginny.

Ginny, though, never moves anything along. They kiss Elsie like they could do it forever, which—yeah, Elsie, too, sure—but she also wants *more*.

"Can I—" she starts, plucking at the tank top Ginny slept in. They kiss her again, and it takes her a minute to finish the question. "—take this off?"

Ginny nods.

Elsie has seen Ginny's boobs before. They've been best friends forever, they've changed together plenty of times. She's even inspected them once, when Ginny was afraid they had a lump on the underside of one, where they couldn't see. Elsie had claimed it was a third nipple, but it was just an ingrown hair.

So yes, she's seen Ginny's boobs. But not like this. Those times were obviously not sexy. This time is sexy. This time Elsie *notices* things, like how Ginny's nipples are more brown than pink, the left more at attention than the right. Their boobs are uneven, too, the right a bit smaller. Elsie doesn't blink as she takes one in each hand. The right one fits perfectly into her palm, like it was made for it, but the left might be even better, the give when Elsie squeezes, the flesh overflowing what she can hold.

Elsie has never slept with anyone but Derrick. She's never gotten under someone's bra before. She felt up Camryn Miller in the dressing room after opening night of *A Midsummer Night's Dream* senior year of high school, still remembers the way her nipples hardened through two layers of fabric. Ginny's nipples do the same, but Elsie actually gets to see it happen. She rolls them between her thumb and index finger, both at the same time. Ginny groans. Elsie needs them to make that noise again. She ducks her head, gets her mouth on one.

The noise Ginny makes at that is even better.

And Jesus, the feeling against Elsie's tongue. Soft skin and pebbled nipple and somehow, even when they've been in Santa Lupita for three days, Ginny still smells like sawdust. Why has it taken them so long to do this?

Elsie licks her way to Ginny's other nipple. Their boobs really are perfect. Elsie bites without even meaning to, and Ginny gasps. They're so reactive. It makes Elsie feel powerful, makes her feel good at this, even though she's not actually sure she's doing anything right. Is this too long to be spending on Ginny's boobs? They're just so nice, shiny with Elsie's spit by this point. Elsie doesn't want to move on, but she also *does*. She wants to get to the main event. She's never had foreplay take this long. But Ginny hasn't even made a move to take off Elsie's shirt.

"You gonna be a pillow princeling," she uses Ginny's preferred royal title, "or you gonna take my shirt off?"

Ginny's face slides into a smirk. "I'll do anything you want, but not until you ask."

Elsie rolls her eyes, even while the thought of Ginny doing *anything* she wants sends a thrill through her. So does Ginny's voice, low and husky. Elsie has a knee on either side of their hips, her legs spread about as wide as they can go. She adjusts, gets one of Ginny's thighs between hers, and takes off her own shirt.

"Fuck."

They both say it at the same time—Ginny at the sight of Elsie's boobs and Elsie at the feel of her center against Ginny's thigh. She closes her eyes, and when she opens them, Ginny is still staring. Elsie wonders what they notice that they've never noticed before. She rolls her shoulders back, pushing her chest out. Ginny's hand comes up, reaches, before dropping back to their side, the look on their face almost embarrassed.

Elsie beams. "Do you like my boobs so much you almost touched them without me telling you to?"

"I don't know what you're talking about," Ginny says. But they lick their lips and don't make eye contact—still too busy looking at Elsie's chest.

"Touch them."

Ginny doesn't need to be told twice. Their touch is gentle, but their calloused fingers are rough against Elsie's nipples. Elsie gasps, rolls her hips and gasps again. Her underwear is just a wet scrap of fabric. Everything feels so good she can barely think.

Maybe it should be weird. Or Elsie should be nervous. But Ginny has always made her feel safe. And this—it feels impossible and inevitable all at once. Elsie can't believe they're doing it. She can't believe they waited so long to.

Elsie wants Ginny to keep playing with her nipples. She wants Ginny's mouth on them, or on her neck, or *anywhere*. Ginny brushes their thumb back and forth, and Elsie can't stay upright anymore. She collapses down, and for the first time, their upper bodies are skin to skin.

Fuck.

Ginny is warm, and soft, and *perfect*. They turn their head to bite gently at Elsie's jaw. Elsie could get lost in this. She could give herself over to Ginny. And she will—she will, she wants to—but she can't yet. If they keep going like this, it won't be long until Elsie can't think at all—her whole body feels like molasses, slow and sticky and sweet, and there's something she needs to do while she can still focus.

She slides down the bed to settle between their legs. Ginny's blue plaid boxers are soft and paper-thin under Elsie's fingers. She leaves them on, for now.

"I've never done this before," she says, like Ginny doesn't know that. They know everything about her.

"You don't have to."

If Ginny thinks that, maybe they *don't* know everything about her.

"I thought I got to do whatever I want." She smirks, then bites Ginny's thigh.

Ginny's response is half laugh, half gasp.

"Thank god," they say. "I was just trying to be gentlemanly."

"How about you come all over my face like a gentleman?"

"Jesus."

Jesus, indeed. Elsie doesn't even know where that came from. She's never been much of a dirty talker, never been much of a noisemaker during sex at all, but it's fun to surprise Ginny.

Elsie pulls their boxers off. She takes great care in sliding them all the way down, over one ankle, then the other, before looking back up. There's Ginny's cunt.

"Oh," Elsie says. A jungle of dark curls covers Ginny's mound, spreading down to their inner thighs.

"I, uh, haven't done any landscaping recently," Ginny says like that's somehow bad.

"You're perfect." Elsie says. "I've never seen a prettier pu— wait, can I call it a pussy?"

Ginny breathes out a laugh. "What else would you call it?"

"Well, I didn't know if that felt gendered or something."

"You're very sweet but I could not care less."

There's this undertone in Ginny's voice, not quite a whine but close, and Elsie would very much like to stop talking about terminology. Whatever you want to call it, Elsie puts her mouth on it. The gasp Ginny lets out is heaven.

Elsie has tasted herself before. Derrick liked her to lick his fingers after—okay no, not thinking about Derrick right now. Elsie has tasted herself before. Elsie likes the way she tastes. Ginny tastes better.

Elsie always knew she'd like eating pussy—she never knew she'd like it this much. She gets why they call it *eating* now. It's so much more than just mouth to cunt, tongue to clit. Elsie bites and sucks and nibbles and licks.

It's ludicrous, but she thinks of the Minnesota State Fair. At the end of every summer, Ginny and Elsie go to the fair together. When they were kids, their parents would give them twenty dollars to spend on games and they'd go on a wristband day for unlimited rides. The fair before they started college, Ginny signed them up for the pie-eating contest.

Eating Ginny out reminds Elsie of that pie-eating contest. It seems absurd, but the similarities are obvious—the different textures between the plump flesh of Ginny's lips and the sweet slickness inside and their clit, round like a blueberry. The way Elsie wants to be thorough, licking every crevice. The way her face gets messy and she doesn't care one bit. It has its differences, of course. Ginny hadn't writhed during the pie-eating contest. They hadn't cursed, hadn't reached for Elsie's head but stopped themself before holding on.

"You can," Elsie pulls away to say. Then she remembers— "I want you to."

Elsie gets what she wants.

Elsie has always liked the power of blow jobs. Derrick was never more at her mercy than when his dick was in her mouth. But here, she doesn't feel in control. Ginny isn't, either, though. They're both free-falling, Elsie's mouth on Ginny and Ginny basically humping her face. Elsie doesn't even know what she's doing with her mouth anymore, what her tongue is licking, what her teeth are scraping against. Her brain isn't translating anything beyond how much she wants Ginny to come. She's feral with it.

Ginny's fingers clench in Elsie's hair. It hurts, but in a way Elsie can't actually process. Like rationally she can tell her brain registers pain, but everything feels so perfect, it's not really there. Elsie squeezes her legs together, desperate for some kind of friction. The underwear she slept in is soaked.

"You want me to come?"

Elsie *mmhmm*s against Ginny's clit and again, she gets what she wants.

Ginny tastes even *better* then, not exactly a gush of wetness, but more, certainly, the taste stronger. Elsie keeps going until Ginny pushes her away.

"*Fuck.*"

Elsie wipes her mouth discreetly on the sheet before scooching back up the bed to be face-to-face. "That means I did good, right?"

Ginny's laugh is breathless. "Yeah, Els. You did great."

They butt their head at her, capture her lips with their own. It's soft, for a moment, before Ginny's tongue comes out, insistent, like they want to lick their taste from Elsie's mouth. Elsie loves it—both Ginny's voracity and the way they taste. She would've stayed down there longer, but she needs something else.

"I want you to go down on me," she whispers, looking Ginny right in the eye.

Whenever Ginny encourages Elsie to break the rules—to take an extra-long lunch break or ignore a NO TRESPASSING sign on a private beach or sneak candy from the dollar store into a movie theater—they have a specific smile. That's what's on their face now, a grin that's equal parts mischievous and thrilled.

"As you wish," they say, and slide down the bed.

Elsie clenches her fists. She almost rescinds her request; this is scarier than going down on Ginny. No one but Derrick has ever seen her like this, has ever touched her. Ginny has touched other people. Elsie knows the first girl they went down on— Annie Walker senior year of high school.

What if her vagina is weird?

Ginny's hands stroke Elsie's bare thighs and Elsie tries to focus on the feeling.

"I don't know if I could've held out if you didn't ask soon," Ginny says. "Really wanted my mouth on your cunt."

As though the words didn't elicit goosebumps all on their own, Ginny presses their tongue against Elsie's center through her underwear. Elsie makes a noise somewhere between a whimper and a squeak.

"God." Ginny's voice is all gravel. "You taste so good."

They keep licking at her like that, Elsie's underwear so wet it's like there's nothing there, but there *is*, there's a *barrier* and it's not long before Elsie can't take it anymore.

"Please," she gasps. "Please, Gin. Take it off."

"Take what off?"

Elsie's too desperate to mind being made to voice it. "My underwear. Take off my underwear. I want your mouth on me. Directly. Nothing in between."

"Of course, Els," Ginny says, already tugging the ruined panties down Elsie's legs. "Wanna give you everything you want."

Elsie is so turned on she forgets to be nervous about Ginny seeing her bare, but even if she'd remembered, Ginny is so obviously into her it doesn't matter.

"Speaking of pretty pussies . . ." Ginny presses their face into Elsie and takes a deep breath in. "God, you smell as good as you taste."

Their nose bumps Elsie's clit and their tongue snakes out again and Elsie's hips come straight off the bed.

A thing about that pie-eating contest: Ginny won.

Elsie can't—she doesn't know what Ginny's doing. She can't keep track. She can't form a coherent thought. Everything is *yes* and *fuck* and *Ginny.*

Ginny Ginny Ginny

Afterward, Ginny brings Elsie a glass of water for her dry throat.

"I fucking love the way you say my name," they murmur, and it's only then that Elsie realizes she was screaming.

She downs half the glass and sets it on the nightstand, holds her arms out and wiggles her fingers at Ginny to make them climb back into bed and give her a kiss.

"You're really good at that," Elsie says.

Ginny smirks. "I know."

They kiss Elsie again. Deep enough Elsie can't help but whimper.

"You wanna come again?"

"Oh, it's okay, I—"

"I didn't ask if it was okay," Ginny says. "I asked if you wanted to come again."

Honestly, Elsie didn't know that was an option. They've had sex. They both came. She might've already come more than once, actually—she couldn't tell if it was a new orgasm or just a second wave as Ginny kept sucking her clit. But that was it, right? That was sex. Of course, she'd love to come again. Saying it, though— she had no problem in the moment, in the middle of it, telling Ginny what she wanted, but now that she's not desperate, it's harder to admit.

"Elsie."

"I wanna make you come again, too."

Ginny gives a nod. "I'm amenable to that."

"Will you just kiss me for a while first?"

"I'll do anything you want."

They don't have to keep saying that. They're being sassy, committing to the bit, but it also makes Elsie's blood run hot to hear it.

Everything Ginny does makes Elsie's blood run hot. The way they kiss, not aggressive but not soft, just *present*. Like they are fully here; there's nothing they'd rather be doing. Like there's nothing better than this. And maybe there's not. Ginny's soft lips and warm tongue and occasionally even their teeth, digging into Elsie's bottom lip. Elsie whimpers, every time, but even that doesn't make Ginny do it more. She's sure they would if she asked, but she doesn't. She wants this—Ginny on top of her, taking their time. It's different than when Elsie was on top. Elsie likes Ginny's weight, likes the way their body is big enough to cover hers, even though they're shorter.

They kiss like they're teenagers. Deep and wet and desperate. With so much tongue it feels obscene. Every time Ginny dips their head to suck at Elsie's neck, Elsie gasps, shudders, asks for more. A necklace of hickeys is worth it for how good Ginny's mouth is.

Ginny keeps grinding down against Elsie's thigh. Their cunt is slick, sliding against her skin. Elsie wants them to rub it all over her body. They shove their hips down again, gasping.

"Can you come like this?" Elsie asks.

Ginny's eyes are closed. They nod.

"I want you to," Elsie says immediately. "Come on me."

It doesn't take long.

Ginny rolls off after they've come, collapses into Elsie's side. Elsie presses a kiss to their forehead. One to the bridge of their nose. And a last one to their lips, softly this time. She wants to tell them she loves them. She does—not like *that,* but she loves them. She's always loved them. They've said it to each other countless times over the years. But Elsie doesn't say it this time. She doesn't want Ginny to think it's weird.

Ginny props themself up on an elbow and looks down at Elsie.

"Your turn," they say, then drop another kiss on her mouth. "How do you want me to make you come?"

Elsie clenches around nothing. She looks at Ginny's chin instead of holding eye contact, but they don't let her get away with that.

"Hey." Ginny ducks their head to catch her eye. "Whatever you want is okay. If you don't want to come again, that's—"

"No, I do," Elsie interrupts. "I do! I just . . . I want you inside me."

Ginny's face breaks open with a cheeky grin. "Yes, please."

Speaking up for what she wants, it turns out, is pretty fucking great.

Five seconds after admitting she wants Ginny inside her, Elsie is coming. It's the moment Ginny slides two fingers in, not fast or hard or even moving them at all—just that first penetration and Elsie's gone.

Ginny kisses Elsie hard as she recovers. "You're so fucking sexy."

Then they start pumping their fingers.

Elsie always thought Derrick was good at sex. He made sure she came, every time, even if he came first. That's not something that all guys do, but he did. One morning with Ginny and Elsie's realizing that maybe giving your partner an orgasm is actually the bare minimum. Or maybe Ginny's really fucking good in bed. Either way, Elsie comes again, then *again*.

"You want another?" Ginny asks while Elsie's still too lost to know how to open her eyes.

"Do you want me to *die*?"

Elsie can imagine exactly how Ginny's face looks when they chuckle in response. Seriously, she should've fucked her best friend years ago.

There's not even any awkward silence after. It's silent, sure— except for how hard Elsie is breathing, still—but it's not awkward. It's just them. They've lain next to each other in bed hundreds of times before. It doesn't feel that different even though they're naked and satisfied.

"So what else do you wanna do today?" Ginny asks after a while.

"Virginia Marie Holtz." Again, *Ginny* is their full name. "If you think I want anything that involves either of us leaving this bed, you're dumber than you look."

"Oh geez, thanks."

"I'm kidding, I'm kidding." Elsie rolls over so she can pepper their face with kisses. "Though you did look pretty dumbstruck while you were riding my thigh earlier."

Elsie really could stay in bed all day. There's so much she wants to do to Ginny, so much she wants Ginny to do to her. She may have only ever had sex with Derrick until now, but she's seen porn—she knows there are options. Positions and toys and probably things she's never thought of before. She wants to get her fingers inside Ginny, wants Ginny to grind on her face the way they grinded on her thigh. She wants to do *everything*.

"You just said you would die if I made you come again," Ginny says.

"Well, who says I can't make *you* come again?"

"We've gotta eat something at some point."

Elsie smirks. "I don't know, I think we've been doing a lot of eating this morning."

15

THEY DO GET BREAKFAST, EVENTUALLY, BUT IT'S LATE. Elsie wanted her fingers inside Ginny, and they weren't about to say no. Thankfully, the resort serves all-day breakfast. They order with their naked limbs still twined together in bed. They pick the "leave at the door" option, and Ginny just hopes Elsie wasn't actively screaming while it was delivered. Because there was a moment there, between ordering and breakfast, that Ginny made her. Just in case she hadn't already come enough that morning.

Once they're finally out of bed—but not out of reach, even as they sit on the deck, breakfast spread out on the table in front of them, their legs tangle under the table. Now that Ginny is allowed to touch Elsie like this, they can't seem to stop—but once they're finally out of bed, worry begins to niggle at the back of Ginny's mind.

What are they doing? What have they done?

When it was actively happening, there was too much skin

for Ginny to think about ramifications. They've wanted this for longer than they can remember. Their desire for Elsie feels like a part of their body by this point; missing it would be like missing a limb. That desire is something they know how to deal with, how to handle. They know how to move through their day-to-day life with it.

This? The consummation of that desire? They have no idea what to do.

What does this mean? feels like dark clouds in the distance.

Then Elsie reaches for the syrup at the same time Ginny does, and their hands touch. Elsie giggles, and the coming storm seems so far away.

"I can't believe you insisted on putting on clothes for breakfast." Elsie fakes a pout.

"Oh yes, I'm sorry I won't sit bare-assed on our deck and spill syrup all over my tits."

"I'd lick it off."

Jesus, this girl.

"Calm down," Ginny says, but they can't help the grin that takes over their face. "We need *sustenance* or we're gonna pass out."

They're only in a ribbed tank top and a pair of boxers—a different pair than the one they slept in, since those were damp after how long Elsie kept her mouth on their tits. Elsie's wearing an oversized T-shirt over nothing. Her nipples are hard through the cotton, and it's almost enough for Ginny to abandon breakfast even though she *just* said they needed sustenance.

"You know, I do kind of want to swim," Elsie says.

"Gotta wait thirty minutes after eating."

She half rolls her eyes. "I'm gonna stand in waist-high water, not swim laps. Somehow I think it'll be fine. The bigger issue is those perfect tits would still have to be covered up."

Ginny almost chokes on their bite of French toast. They did not expect Elsie to have such a mouth on her. The smirk on Elsie's face says she likes surprising them.

"Can't we just skinny-dip?" Elsie asks.

This conversation is moving a few steps faster than Ginny's brain is. "I know it feels like we're alone, but the other bungalows are not that far away."

"What about after sunset?"

Ginny considers it. "Maybe."

Elsie plucks Ginny's phone from the table between them. She inputs the passcode, which Ginny has kept the same since Elsie programmed it into their very first phone—0712. Elsie's birthday. Ginny would feel a little pathetic about it, except Elsie's passcode is their birthday.

"Skinny-dipping," she says aloud as she types. She holds up the phone to show Ginny. "Now it's on the list, so we have to do it."

"You know I shared that note with you and you could've just done that on your own phone?"

"My phone's far away." She looks around. "Actually, where is my phone?"

She puts both hands on her tits like she's going to find her phone in a bra she isn't even wearing. Before Ginny can get too sidetracked by *boobs*, Elsie heads into the bungalow to search. Ginny tries to focus on the French toast in front of them. The last time Ginny saw Elsie's phone, Elsie had been taking pictures of last night's chocolate cobbler. Before she said she wanted something that might ruin their friendship. Before she straddled Ginny's thighs, came on their fingers. How was that barely twelve hours ago?

"Oh shit." Elsie returns to the deck, brow furrowed and phone in her hands.

"What?"

"There's a storm at home. I missed so many messages. Fuck."

Ginny has lived through more snowstorms than they can remember, which means they know how to get through them, but also respect their power. "Everybody good?"

"So far. It's supposed to be worse today." Elsie climbs back into her chair, hugs both knees as she scrolls her messages. "Alec and Brandon are already talking about closing, but you know Dad likes to keep the store open during a storm because that's—"

"When people need the most help," Ginny says the end of the sentence with Elsie. It's Mr. Hoffman's motto for every big winter storm.

"I wish he would shift to focusing on storm preparedness and just close the damn store when it's not safe for customers to get there anyway."

Her thumbs fly across her phone screen, likely typing a similar message to the family group chat.

Ginny takes another bite of French toast. Elsie scowls across the table, the furrow accentuating that scar on her forehead from when she and Ginny set up a zip line from Ginny's bedroom to the tree at the far end of their backyard.

"He's so *stubborn*." Elsie scoffs and types another message.

Ginny reaches to put a hand on her wrist. For the first time since she found her phone, Elsie looks at them.

"There's literally nothing you can do about a storm in the Midwest right now, Els," they say. "Turn off notifications for your group chat. Or, you know, maybe you were right—just use my phone to look at anything. You're supposed to be relaxing. You don't need to worry about the store or whatever other family drama is happening right now."

"It's not *family drama*. It's my dad making everyone else unsafe. It's how he's so stuck in his ways about the store, he won't change anything, even if it would be good for business."

"You're not going to change his mind from however many miles away we are."

Ginny watches Elsie's face as she works through the decision. They're not going to *make* her put her phone down—she's a grown woman—but they release their breath when she does.

But she immediately picks it back up. "Do you think I should text Derrick to remind him to put the cover over his truck bed so it doesn't fill with snow?"

"No," Ginny says, almost before she finishes the question.

"But you know he always forgets—"

"If this was about the apartment you're still on the lease for even if you're not sure what's happening when you get back, yes. For his truck that you have no financial stake in? No."

"But—"

"You're not responsible for him anymore, Els. I mean, you shouldn't have had to be responsible for him then, either—he's an adult. But it's definitely not on you now."

Elsie doesn't respond. They haven't actually talked about the end of her engagement since it happened. Ginny checks in sometimes, but just a *how you doing?*, nothing beyond that. She seems okay, right? She's certainly been happy this whole vacation. She was happy this morning, that's for sure.

Ginny swallows a sudden rock in her throat. What if this morning was a rebound? Elsie's engagement is over and she doesn't know what comes next, and she rebounded with the first person available. The last piece of French toast on Ginny's plate suddenly looks unappetizing. She moves it around with her fork.

They're supposed to be pushing Elsie to think about what she wants. Last night, Elsie said she wanted to enjoy dinner and wait until today to think about real life. Ginny doesn't want to know what she thinks about real life today. Not after this morning. If she's going to break Ginny's heart, Ginny would rather she put it off a little longer.

Ginny knows what they want. Ginny could tell Elsie everything. They've been in love with her since before they knew what love was. The girl with white-blonde hair who moved in next door. Elsie has so many siblings, but Ginny didn't notice a single one that day. Once the moving truck had gone, Ginny's parents sent them over with brownies. Elsie answered the door. That was it for Ginny, even if she didn't know it at the time. She was a goner.

They don't need to tell Elsie any of that. Don't need to embarrass themself. This can be whatever this is, and that's fine. That's enough.

"Okay." Elsie's voice pulls Ginny from their spiral. "Swim time?"

"Swim time," Ginny says.

They go into the bathroom to change. Not to *hide*, obviously. Elsie has seen plenty, even before this morning. They just have to pee, so it makes sense to bring their bathing suit in with them.

They leave the water running after they wash their hands and look at themself in the mirror. Everything is fine. It's good, even. They're in paradise with their favorite person. If this is just a vacation fling, it's worth it. Ginny is never going to regret any of this. Elsie will always be their best friend. That friendship can change without ending. If they made it through sophomore year, they can make it through anything.

16

GINNY IS TOO QUIET.

Elsie's heart thumps hard in her chest. Do they regret this morning? Did she ruin their friendship after all?

If Ginny weren't acting strange, Elsie wouldn't want to talk about what they're doing. Whatever it is—it's great. They have two more days here, and if they could just keep fucking and having fun and not talking about it, Elsie would. That sounds *ideal,* actually.

Because Elsie doesn't even know what she wants. What if Ginny wants to date? How shitty of Elsie would that be—to return from what was supposed to be her *honeymoon* with Derrick with a new partner? How would they even date? They already see more of each other than anyone else.

And what if Ginny *doesn't* want to date? Elsie wants to fuck Ginny over and over and over. What if Ginny wants this to be a vacation fling? What if when they get back to Minnesota, this will just be a fun memory? That seems worse.

Maybe she's reading Ginny wrong, though. Ginny is quiet, their eyes hidden behind their sunglasses, but maybe they're just enjoying the water. It does feel incredible. Elsie wants to enjoy it. She wants to kiss Ginny again. But what she wants more than anything is for her and her best friend to be okay.

"So, like"—she takes a fortifying breath—"do you wanna talk about this morning?"

Ginny wasn't moving, but Elsie swears that, somehow, they freeze.

"Do you wanna talk about it?" they say, tone neutral.

"I mean—we don't have to make it a big deal. Like, friends can fuck," Elsie says with more bravado than she feels.

"Of course."

"It was fun, right? You had fun?"

Ginny laughs, and all of Elsie's body relaxes. "Yeah, Els, I had fun."

"Me too! So, that can be enough."

"For sure."

Friends can fuck, Elsie says, as though she hasn't avoided even considering the possibility for years now. Every time she was speechless with want, she told herself not to think of Ginny that way. She told herself satisfying her horny itch wasn't worth risking their friendship. Now she's out here trying to claim it's no big deal.

That's the only explanation that allows her to keep doing it, though, and she *definitely* wants to keep doing it.

She looks at Ginny—actually *looks* at them—in a way she's never allowed herself to before. She doesn't worry there's too much desire in her eyes. She can barely see Ginny's eyes through their sunglasses, but she isn't imagining the desire in them. It's there. She knows it's there, as Ginny stares at her in her yellow string bikini. Ginny keeps staring as Elsie reaches out and traces a water droplet down their neck.

"Why did we go swimming again?" Elsie asks.

"We're doing what *you* wanted to," Ginny says.

"I'm stupid."

"Hey." They step closer, sending little ripples against Elsie's skin. "Don't talk about my favorite person like that."

"Kiss me," Elsie says, and Ginny does. Because Ginny does everything Elsie wants. And even though Ginny said they weren't allowed to skinny-dip, when Elsie whines that she wants Ginny's hands on her, it turns out fucking in the ocean is acceptable. It's hard, though, the water washing away too much of Elsie's wetness to be fully comfortable. Her legs are wrapped around Ginny's waist, ankles locked behind their back. Barely enough room for Ginny's hand between them, but Elsie can't stand being anything but this close.

She clutches Ginny's shoulders. "Take me to bed."

They barely make it all the way back inside. Ginny carries her—*carries her*—and it's so hot Elsie rolls her hips, which makes Ginny lurch at the top of the steps.

"Fuck." Their voice is the bottom of the ocean. Deep and dark and all-encompassing.

Elsie unlocks her ankles to stand on her own two feet—she doesn't want Ginny to drop her and also she *needs* to be naked. *Now.* She strips her top off, then tugs at Ginny's when they take too long with their own. Once Ginny's tits come out, though, Elsie abandons the undressing task to Ginny so she can put her mouth on their nipples.

They're still on the deck. Ginny stumbles backward and Elsie follows, mouth anywhere it can reach. They're both dripping in more ways than one. Ginny takes her to the shower first, turns the water on hot and strips their soaked bathing suit bottoms off. Elsie pushes Ginny under the spray, then just stares. She can't believe she gets to look. She can't believe she gets to do any of this—stepping closer, not caring about water getting in her eyes if it means she can meld her body against the softness of Ginny's. She can't believe she hasn't done it before. Why haven't they been doing this all along?

Kissing Ginny is heaven. Their tongue is like the rest of them, thick and strong and certain. It brushes Elsie's bottom lip, curls into her mouth, a wet slide against her own tongue.

"I said take me to *bed*," Elsie murmurs while Ginny kisses her neck.

"Just a little detour."

They squirt body wash onto a washcloth and take Elsie's hand. Oh.

This is an acceptable detour. Ginny's touch is full of tenderness and promise. They drag the washcloth up Elsie's arms, over her chest much more thoroughly than necessary for cleanliness, across her stomach, down one leg and back up the other.

Ginny has always been Elsie's safe space. Nothing could ruin this. Ginny wants her, too. That's enough. That's all Elsie needs to know to know they'll be okay. Ginny makes her feel like she could do anything, like she could take over the world.

Ginny washes between Elsie's legs, first the front, then behind. They wring out the washcloth before reaching for her center again, nothing but their fingers this time.

They make Elsie come until she can barely stand up anymore.

"Gin, fuck—wait," Elsie says when they start moving again after she's come down from her third orgasm. "Take me to *bed*. I want you to sit on my face."

Saying it out loud is terrifying but the ragged breath Ginny takes makes it worth it. Ginny saying *yes, please* makes it worth it. Ginny turning off the water and reaching for towels makes it absolutely worth it.

Neither of them takes the time to dry off fully. Elsie's wet hair soaks the pillow beneath her head as Ginny puts one knee on the mattress beside it. Their other foot is on the other side of Elsie's head, holding themself up and open. Elsie breathes in. Ginny smells so fucking good.

"Okay?" they ask.

Elsie responds by licking a stripe up their center.

"Fuck."

It's different, to have Ginny's cunt above her face like this. She could drown in them, could suffocate, and she'd die happy. Their lips are soft and thick. If Elsie thought too hard, she'd still worry she wasn't good at this, but with Ginny's hips rolling above her, she can't think. All she can do is lick and suck and let her hands wander, squeezing Ginny's ass, digging fingers into their thighs, pulling them closer and harder onto her mouth.

As soon as Ginny comes, shaking and moaning and making Elsie so wet she can feel it on her thighs, they move off of her and fall hard to the mattress.

"Fuck," they gasp. "My legs were about to give out."

Elsie giggles and kisses them, face messy. Ginny groans.

"Thank you, Gin," Elsie whispers. "That was amazing."

"You're amazing," Ginny says. After some more kissing and heavy breathing, they nudge to suck under Elsie's jaw. "What do you want?"

"*You.*" It's as much as Elsie can come up with.

"You got me." Ginny breathes the words into Elsie's ear, sending a full-body tremor through her. "Now how do you want to come?"

It's always easier to tell Ginny what she wants to do to them rather than what she wants them to do to her. "Your mouth?"

"Is that a question?"

"You're so annoying." Elsie doesn't mean it for one second.

"So you don't want my mouth?"

"Did I say that?"

Oh fuck. Ginny's teeth are on Elsie's neck, only for a moment, but long enough to make Elsie's body shake.

"Do that again."

Ginny does.

"Work your way down my body like that."

"Yes, ma'am."

Ginny stays at her neck, at first. They bite hard enough Elsie's going to have to wear coverup for a week. It's worth it. Their mouth on her nipples almost makes her come right there. They lick down her stomach, dig their teeth into her hips. Elsie's so fucking ready. But then Ginny keeps going down, almost all the way to Elsie's knee.

"Ginnifer," Elsie admonishes.

"What?" Ginny is a picture of wide-eyed faux innocence, except for how their mouth is swollen from its work on Elsie's skin. "You said to work my way down."

"To my cunt," Elsie says. It might be the first time she's ever said that word. It feels fucking amazing. As does Ginny's tongue, when they stop being dense and drag it between Elsie's lips. "Fuck."

Ginny's tongue dips inside of her, then laps upward, ends with a swirl around her clit. They do it again. And again. And again. Elsie rolls her hips and it makes Ginny's tongue touch her lower, for a split second. Not *low* low, but.

Derrick liked Elsie on top of him, but more often than not, it was him on top, or occasionally behind her. That was about as adventurous as they got. She's never even considered having a tongue on her . . . her . . .

It feels dirty to think about, even though she knows that's society's fault. Jesus, she can't think this through right now. Not with Ginny's head between her legs. She can't think of *shame* or societal constructs or anything other than how good this feels. She rolls her hips again, gets Ginny's tongue a little lower still. The next time she tries, Ginny's ready for it, and holds back, doesn't give Elsie what she wants.

Elsie is going to have to ask.

"Ginny." She drags out the end of their name.

Ginny keeps their lips on Elsie, so when they respond, Elsie feels it more than she hears it. "Something you wanted?"

She has to ask. Ginny won't do anything unless she asks.

"Please," she says anyway.

"Please what, Els?"

Finally, Ginny takes their mouth fully off her, and Elsie can think again.

What if it's too much? What if they don't want to? Is it, like, *coercion* to ask for a sexual act they haven't talked about before while Ginny says she can have whatever she wants?

Ginny's always been able to read her mind. "Els. There's nothing I don't want to do to you."

Elsie swallows. "Nothing?"

Ginny shakes their head.

"Promise?"

"Promise."

Elsie looks at the mosquito net draped over the bedposts above them, but that's not enough—she closes her eyes completely.

It comes out all one word instead of as a sentence. "Willyoulickmyasshole?"

"What was that? You're not looking at me and you said it so fast I'm not sure I understood."

"No," Elsie snaps, but she does look down at them. "That's not fair. There wasn't a rule that I had to say it slowly or look at you while I say it. I'm supposed to get what I want as long as I ask, and I want your tongue on my asshole and— Oh, *fuck*."

Elsie slams her eyes closed again.

Ginny's tongue is *low* low now. Ginny's tongue is *perfect*. Elsie pounds her fist against the mattress beside her.

"Jesus *Christ*."

Any thought of this being dirty or wrong or something Ginny might not want to do—it's all out the window. Everything is out the window, nothing in Elsie's brain except *yes*. Elsie doesn't know what Ginny's doing, because she has exactly zero experience with rimming, but holy shit, whatever it is, it's working. Elsie feels like a million nerve endings, like fireworks, like a whole house of winter lights all lit up, everything glowing and sparkly and beautiful.

"Oh fuck."

Elsie's hips come full off the bed. Ginny's thumb has found her clit. It's almost too much, overstimulation even while it's also the best Elsie has ever felt in her entire fucking life.

"I don't—I don't know—"

"Don't know what, Els?"

"*Put your mouth back on me.*"

Okay so maybe it's not too much.

Elsie doesn't even want to come. She wants to keep doing this forever, wants to never ever let go of this feeling. Everything in her body coiling tight.

Her orgasm is a tidal wave. It's the entire ocean. She floats in it, gets rocked back and forth and back again. Her mind feels too small to comprehend its vast endlessness.

When Elsie finally comes down, she is boneless. Limbs like wet noodles. She wants to do that to Ginny. She's never really even considered butt stuff before, but Jesus, she wants to do that to Ginny. As soon as her bones resolidify.

Before she can express that, though, Ginny clears their throat. Elsie looks at them.

"So, uh." They scratch the back of their head. "We maybe should talk safe words? Probably already should've, but especially if we're doing, like, uncharted territory?"

Right. Safe words are a thing. Elsie's never needed them—as established, she and Derrick weren't exactly adventurous.

"Right, yeah, they're supposed to be something we wouldn't normally say, right?" She sounds so stupid, Jesus Christ. She barrels on. "So, like, mom or dad, or one of my siblings' names?"

Any of those would work as a safe word, because Elsie absolutely does not want to be thinking of her family while she's having sex.

"Uh." Ginny doesn't make eye contact. "Mommy and daddy are not always uncommon words during sex."

Elsie's face flushes.

"But yeah, I've found traffic-light safe words are the easiest," Ginny says so Elsie doesn't have to die from embarrassment. "Green means go, yellow means slow, red means no."

Imagine if Elsie had kept her mouth shut and let Ginny talk. That makes so much more sense than *mom*.

Whatever. It's fine. She is powering through this.

"So, if I said I wanted to do to you what you just did to me, what color would you give me?"

Ginny weighs it for a moment. "Yellow-green?" Another pause. "I've never done that before."

It feels special, somehow, to be the first person to do this to Ginny, the only person who has ever done it. At the same time, Elsie knows that's not what makes this special. It's not the exclusivity; it's that it's *Ginny*.

She shutters that thought. This is whatever it is, and it's enough. Ginny is important, obviously. They're special, but that's as far as Elsie lets her mind go.

"Yellow-green," Elsie repeats. "So, go slow?"

"Well . . ." Ginny looks at her. "With anyone else it'd be yellow-green, but just green with you. I trust you."

Elsie preens, but only for a moment. "Okay then. Face down, ass up."

Ginny bursts out laughing, but they do what they're told.

Ginny has a really great butt. It's wide and round and dimpled. Elsie slaps it, gently, just to see it jiggle.

"You have no idea how long I've wanted to do that."

"We played on a softball team together," Ginny says. "You've definitely smacked my ass before."

"Not while it was naked."

They look over their shoulder, arching an eyebrow. "You been thinking about my naked ass a lot?"

"Like, all the time." Elsie hits it again. "I've also wanted to do this."

She digs her teeth into Ginny's cheek. The softness, the way it gives—Elsie hasn't actually been thinking of their ass *all* the time, but it's even better than she'd ever imagined. She sucks the flesh into her mouth.

"Is this okay?"

Ginny *mmhmm*s, and Elsie pulls back.

"Not just because I want to," she says. "Do *you* want me to?"

"God, Elsie, yes."

Elsie never in her life would've thought she'd love putting her tongue on someone's asshole, but holy shit. The way Ginny gasps. Like it's the best thing they've ever felt.

Ginny groans. "Jesus, your tongue is perfect."

Elsie's brain goes haywire at the praise. She licks harder. Faster. The noises Ginny makes hit Elsie right in the clit. Is it possible to come from making someone else come?

Elsie takes a breath. This isn't about her. She slows down, focuses on Ginny's reactions rather than the slick between her own legs. Ginny had touched Elsie's clit while they did this, but this position makes that difficult.

"Rub your clit," Elsie says.

Ginny snakes a hand under their body and Elsie gets her tongue back on them. Ginny's next moan is even sweeter than the last. Elsie refuses to take her tongue off Ginny again, not until they come. It doesn't take long—Elsie licks at that tight hole, and Ginny rubs their clit, and before long, they're burying their face in a pillow to scream.

"I am a puddle of blissed-out goo," Ginny says when Elsie returns from brushing her teeth.

Elsie knows the feeling. She teases Ginny anyway. "I was unaware goo could be blissed out."

"This is perhaps the first evidence of such," Ginny says, their eyes still closed. "You should probably write a scientific paper about it. Though I don't know that I want you to publish your methods for people to replicate."

Elsie doesn't even know if that's a thing—she never was very good in science class. She wants to replicate it, though—giving and receiving, both. She climbs back in bed and lies beside her best friend.

There's no sound but the ocean lapping gently at the deck and Ginny's still slightly labored breathing. Elsie swallows. It's awkward now, suddenly. The bungalow is mostly open-air, but somehow it feels like the walls are closing in. When they're actively fucking, it's easy not to think about the repercussions. It feels so *normal* with Ginny. It's amazing and mind-blowing and so hot Elsie can barely breathe, and somehow it's also just . . . normal. Ginny is still her best friend, like always.

It's not until they're out of the moment that Elsie starts to worry. She's the one who said friends could fuck. She's the one who said it didn't have to be a big deal. But how could this possibly not be a big deal?

They should talk about it.

"I need a nap!" Elsie announces.

They sleep instead.

17

YESTERDAY GINNY WOKE UP TO ELSIE STRADDLING THEM. Today, they wake up as Elsie rolls over within the cocoon of their arms.

The two of them barely made it out of bed the day before. Only ate two meals—late breakfast and early dinner—went swimming at sunset, cleaned up and got dirty again in the giant bathtub. They'd fucked until they were exhausted before falling asleep, then fucked some more in the middle of the night. Ginny's not sure the last time Elsie was out of arm's reach.

Elsie yawns and stretches, and Ginny wants to climb inside of her. Wants to make a home out of her. They settle for leaning in for a kiss, but Elsie puts one hand on their chest and the other over her own mouth.

"Oh my gosh, no. Morning breath. Let me brush my teeth."

"I don't care," Ginny says, but Elsie is already out of bed.

Then—"Oh, shit!"—she's on the floor.

What? Ginny props themself up with one arm to see her better. "What's happening right now?"

"There's a *boat*."

Sure enough, a dinghy like the one that delivered Ginny and Elsie to their bungalow is puttering past. It could be the exact same one; it's too far away for Ginny to be certain, but still close enough that the passengers *might* be able to tell they're naked. It's probably people going to or coming from one of the other bungalows.

Elsie has started army-crawling across the transparent glass floor to the bathroom.

"God, I wish I was a fish under this bungalow right now," Ginny says.

"Because you haven't seen enough of my naked body?"

"Uh, *never*."

Elsie giggles.

"Brush your teeth," Ginny says. "Then we're gonna give those folks an enthusiastic welcome."

"*Ginny*," Elsie admonishes, but she doesn't say no.

In fact, she says *yes,* a lot. Screams it, really.

～～～

AFTER THEY GIVE THEIR NEIGHBORS A WARM WELCOME AND SHARE BREAKFAST IN BED WITHOUT GETTING DRESSED, GINNY TRACES HER FINGERTIPS OVER ELSIE'S SKIN. "So what's on the docket for today?"

"Can't it just be this?"

"Elsie, my tongue is *tired*."

"Okay, so no oral for the rest of the day."

Ginny pokes her in the side, and Elsie squeals.

"No tickling!" She keeps giggling even after Ginny has stopped. "I don't know what I want to do today."

"What about when we go home?"

Elsie goes stiff in their arms. "Like . . . can we do oral when we go home?"

No. No, Ginny is not asking about that.

"No, like, we said we were going to talk about what you wanted to do in real life." That was two nights ago by this point. They'd forgotten all about it yesterday, lost in too few clothes and too much sex. "What do you want when we go home? Like, with the store, I mean."

Elsie doesn't want to talk about what's happening between them, and Ginny is doing whatever Elsie wants. So they pretend nothing is awkward, go back to tracing their fingers over her body.

"Or—it doesn't have to be with the store," they say. "Are you just at the store because it's your parents'? You could do *anything*, you know?"

"You're saying I should just quit my job when we go back?"

Maybe now would be a good time to mention Ginny already quit her own. But no, this is about Elsie.

"If that's what you want." Ginny shrugs. "I just mean—if you're figuring out who you are separate from Derrick, what about separate from your family?"

"No, I like working at the store," Elsie says. "I don't want to be separate from my family. I just want them to actually listen to my ideas. You know we've had the same signage for more than two decades?"

Of course Ginny knows. The store has looked exactly the same for as long as they can remember.

"Not just we haven't changed the design, but we haven't even repainted the signs. They're old. Even if we went with the exact same design, they could be upgraded. My dad acts like it'd be a waste of money." Now that Elsie's started, she's on a roll. "I'm not saying we need a whole new brand or anything, just some upgrades to make the place look nice. Dad acts like we'll always have enough customers, like we don't need to even try."

"The store's doing okay, though, right?"

"I don't want it to just do *okay*," Elsie says. "You know I got my dad to start putting aside money for upgrades when I graduated? Kind of begged him—a graduation and an engagement present both." She rolls her eyes. "He's never let me actually *use* it, but it's there. There's a budget."

"So you just gotta convince him when we get back."

"I don't wanna think about going back," Elsie whines.

Ginny's with her. "Well, we *have* to get up at some point. It's our last full day here and we haven't finished the list."

"Why didn't we put sex on the list?"

They didn't put sex on the list because when they made it, they'd never had anything but one childhood kiss.

Well, one childhood kiss and one rejection.

Ginny doesn't want to think about that, either.

They get their phone off the nightstand to look at the list.

"Okay, the only for-sure things we have left are horseback riding and a massage." They look over at Elsie, her blonde hair spread out on the pillow. They really should've put sex on the list. "Which do you want to do?"

Elsie sticks her bottom lip out. "I want to stay in bed all day."

"We did that yesterday."

"Yes, and? This vacation is supposed to be about what *I* want, and I want you."

Ginny could've made a hundred guesses as to how this trip would go, and they never would've guessed this.

"Pick an activity," they say, "and I'll make you come again."

"Horseback riding!" Elsie chooses with no hesitation, and climbs into Ginny's lap.

~~~~~

THEY BARELY MAKE IT TO THE FRONT DESK ON TIME, ELSIE'S FINGERS STILL COMBING THROUGH HER SEX-MUSSED HAIR. As they load into a golf cart to be driven to the stables, a hotel staff member quietly informs Ginny they missed a button. They fix it with more grin than blush.

It's hard not to touch Elsie, sitting together on the back of the golf cart. Not hold her hand—which they're already doing—but *touch her* touch her—slide a hand between her legs, up her thigh to the warmest part of her. She's probably still wet from this morning, from their escapades that made them late.

But they're supposed to be focusing on an activity other than sex, so Ginny behaves themself. Anyway, they're excited about horseback riding. Both they and Elsie went through a horse-girl phase as kids, passed the Misty of Chincoteague books back and forth between them until the paperback covers fell off.

The driveway to the stables is long, pasture lining both sides. At the edge of the fence stand two horses, one black and the other pinto, big blocks of brown and white hair. Elsie's soft gasp reminds Ginny of her noises from earlier.

"It's Black Beauty," Elsie whispers, clutching Ginny's arm.

It's so goddamn cute Ginny feels sheepish about being such a horndog. Though swooning over Elsie's adorableness isn't much better.

Elsie only lets go of Ginny's hand once she's assigned a horse—an Appaloosa, mostly tan, with a white patch spotted with brown over its rear. She murmurs, "Hi, beautiful," as she rubs the horse's muzzle, and butterflies flutter through Ginny's stomach.

"Wives, am I right?" the person beside them says.

Ginny blinks. They had barely noticed the other people in the stable for the ride: two couples—queer of course—one of whom has a kid, plus the guide.

"You're looking at yours like I look at mine," the person says, rubbing a hand over their shaved head. "I don't even like horses, but I can't say no to her."

"Right," Ginny says. *Wives.* "I can't, either."

That much is true.

Ginny focuses on their assigned horse instead of Elsie or the swooping in their stomach at the word *wives.* The horse is a deep-chestnut gelding with a blaze of white down his forehead. As far as distractions go, he's a pretty good one, soft coat and softer muzzle, the tallest horse in the barn.

Ginny hasn't been on a horse since five-dollar pony rides at the state fair when they were a kid. Mounting is a little terrifying—their momentum almost takes them all the way over the other side—but once they're up and going, it's not so bad. The pace is slow, and the scenery is gorgeous.

Elsie rides in front of Ginny, glancing over her shoulder almost constantly to beam at them. It's so easy to ignore real life, to ignore that they have no idea what they're going to do when they have to go home. Most of the time it doesn't even feel like they're ignoring anything. It all feels so *normal*. Sex seems to be the only thing that's changed about their relationship. If they'd never slept together, Elsie would still smile at Ginny as they rode, checking in to make sure they were having fun. Yesterday, after their tongues were on each other's assholes, there'd been teasing and giggling and Elsie's ankle against Ginny's while they took a nap. It was the same as always. They're just *them,* now with sex.

And god, the sex. Ginny honestly isn't thinking about Minnesota or their job situation or the future because they're sex-addled. Can't think of anything but Elsie—her skin, her mouth, her cunt. If what Elsie wants is to fuck and not talk about life back home, Ginny is happy to oblige.

After a slow trail ride through the tropical forest, they end up on a white sand beach where they can spread out instead of walking single file.

"Does everyone feel comfortable going into a trot?" the guide asks.

The group agrees. As the guide offers safety tips, Elsie pulls her horse up beside Ginny's.

"What do you say, Gin? Wanna race?"

"We're going to trot, not gallop."

"Sounds like someone's scared of losing."

When they dig their heels in to speed the horses up, Ginny doesn't even try to beat Elsie. Bragging rights mean nothing when losing means they can watch Elsie bounce in the saddle. They've behaved themself the whole ride, but now all they can think about is how their horse doesn't feel as good as Elsie between their thighs. They focus on the spots across the back of Elsie's horse.

They manage to keep behaving themself right up until the end, when they're putting their helmets away, Ginny and Elsie the only two in the barn. Then they push her against the wooden railing of an empty stall. Elsie's giggling, so Ginny's kiss lands on her teeth.

"You gonna take me for a roll in the hay, Mx. Holtz?"

"Gonna take you home." Ginny's hands have somehow found their way to Elsie's chest. "To the bungalow," they amend. "Want you to be loud again."

"Let's go."

The golf cart ride back is excruciating.

When Ginny thinks about it, they can't believe they're allowed to do this. To hold Elsie's hand. Look at her with so much unhidden desire.

But still, it also feels normal. Elsie's always been their favorite person. She's always made them laugh. Ginny would always rather spend time with her than anyone else. They're just allowed to spend that time naked now.

Back at the bungalow, though, they don't actually get naked immediately. They don't even make it to the bed—Elsie's back is up against the door as soon as they're inside.

Ginny has never had this much sex. Dating queer women can often mean moving fast—a first date that was only supposed to be drinks but turns into dinner and a sleepover and breakfast the next morning. Queer sex is different, too—not that Ginny has experience with cishet sex, but it seems really focused on penetration. There's so much more than that.

Of course, there's also penetration, and after making out against the door until Elsie is squirming, when Ginny finally slides two fingers inside, Elsie comes immediately, clutching at their shoulders. Ginny loves how easily she comes for them, loves how easy they are for her, too—they're still fully clothed, pants aren't even unzipped, when they come against Elsie's thigh.

That could be it, maybe it would be it if they were cishet, but Elsie bites at Ginny's earlobe.

"Now take me to bed where you can fuck me properly," she murmurs.

Maybe the next orgasms should be enough: Elsie on top, licking Ginny's cunt while Ginny licks hers, both needing breaks because they can't focus when they feel so good. But it's not enough. Ginny gets Elsie on her back next, needs their fingers inside her again.

How did they ever live without this? How will they ever again, now that they know how good it is?

"Please," Elsie gasps. "Please please please."

For someone who gets whatever she wants, she's still incredibly polite. *Please* might be the most used word in her vocabulary the past twenty-four hours.

"More, Gin, *please*."

"I can't give you more, Els. I've got four fingers in you already."

"Your thumb. Put your thumb in, too."

"Jesus."

Ginny truly can't, is the thing. Elsie's cunt is clamped down on the four fingers inside her. Ginny can barely move them, much less fit the rest of her hand inside.

"You're too tight, sweetheart," Ginny says. "And we don't have any lube. But you're taking my fingers so good."

Elsie whines. Ginny can't tell if it's a happy or frustrated sound.

"When we get—" They cut themself off. *When we get back to Minneapolis*—that's what they were going to say. They were going to say they'd fist her when they get home, next week, next month, whenever she wants. And they would, if she'd let them, but they're not talking about that. Nothing exists but right now. This is all that matters.

"You're so tight," Ginny says. "Can you unclench for me?"

The vise around Ginny's fingers loosens and retightens in stops and starts.

"That's a good girl." Ginny shifts their hand, sliding out slightly and then back in.

"Shit."

"That's right," Ginny says. "That's a good girl."

Elsie whines again, and it's definitely pleased this time.

Ginny doesn't always talk much during sex. If the girl she's fucking is into it, sure, but sometimes it can be awkward. Sometimes it feels more performative than authentic.

It does not feel performative with Elsie.

"You know how much I love your cunt, Els?"

"Yeah?"

"Love all of you," Ginny says, and it's not performative at all. They fist a hand in Elsie's hair. "All this hair." They let go and trail their fingers down her face. "Those eyes. This mouth." Elsie bites at the pad of Ginny's thumb, then sucks it into her mouth. Thank god they're not still against the door—Ginny's knees might've gone weak at that. Instead, she curls the four fingers in Elsie's cunt just to make her gasp, to make it feel like they're on a level playing field. "I love your boobs. These perfect nipples." Ginny pinches one, then the other. They look too good—she leans down to take one in her mouth. Elsie arches off the bed.

Ginny gets distracted there for a bit, forgets that they were in the process of complimenting every part of Elsie's body. Her boobs are small, pert. Ginny wants to put an entire one in their mouth. Elsie's skin is easily marked, is something Ginny has learned in the last twenty-four hours. She has love bites all over: her collar-bone, behind her ear, the inside of her thighs. There's even one on her ankle. Elsie clenches tight around Ginny's fingers as they add another star to the constellation of hickeys across her chest.

"Love your skin," Ginny says, admiring their purpling hand-iwork. "And I love your cunt. Tight and wet and delicious. You feel so good around me. Never wanna do anything else but this."

They pump their fingers and Elsie moans.

"Well . . . maybe there's one thing I wanna do."

They pull out suddenly, which is mean, but they can't help but revel in the way Elsie cries out.

"Roll over," they say.

Elsie pants. "Gin."

"Get on your knees."

The top in them forgot they're supposed to be catering to Elsie's whims. Elsie doesn't seem to mind. She scrambles to roll over. Just like Ginny yesterday: face down, ass up. God, she's got a nice ass.

"Love this, too," Ginny says, then spits directly onto Elsie's asshole before licking it.

The noise Elsie makes.

The way she sounds *shocked* at how good it feels. Ginny could come just from that.

Elsie's hips pulse backward into Ginny's tongue, which Ginny flicks back and forth and back again, against that tight little hole.

"Love this," Ginny says again, mostly to themself, honestly. Then, unthinkingly, "Love you."

Elsie comes before Ginny even gets their tongue back on her.

18

ELSIE HAS NEVER HAD THIS MUCH SEX IN HER LIFE.

Maybe if she'd ever had sex this good, it would be the same—the way she's insatiable. The way Ginny can make her come until she almost blacks out, and two minutes later, she's ready to go again. Her cunt is *sore* by this point, after only a day and a half, and still, she can't help but keep going.

That's clearly not a problem for Ginny, who returns from brushing their teeth to press their entire naked body against Elsie's, capturing her mouth in a kiss.

"You're so fucking sexy," Ginny says, like Elsie had been doing anything more than lying there. "I really want to lick your cunt right now, but I just brushed my teeth so I'll give it a minute."

"Oh, is minty fresh not good for a vagina?"

"Trust me, it is *not*."

There's a niggling moment of jealousy. Not jealousy exactly—it's fine that Ginny has experience, obviously. Elsie is incredibly grateful for any experience that has led to Ginny being so fucking hot in bed. Plus, she'd bet Ginny hasn't told that many girls they love them while they fuck. So. It's not jealousy, it's more that Elsie wants that experience with Ginny. Elsie wants memories, sex gaffes, everything. Ginny says Elsie gets everything she wants on this trip, but what about when they get home?

Elsie doesn't engage with that thought.

"Just because you can't put your mouth on me doesn't mean you can't make me come again."

Ginny grins. "You're goddamn right. How do you want it?"

"Fingers."

Giving voice to her desires has somehow gotten a lot easier over the past few days. At least when it comes to sex.

"As you wish."

Ginny rubs the pad of their thumb between Elsie's legs, next to her clit but not right on it, not too much.

"You know, resorts like this really should have lube," Elsie says.

Ginny practically guffaws. "What?"

"Like how they have shaving kits or toothpaste if you forget them. There's an iron under the sink in the bathroom. I bet most of the people who book here need lube more than they need an iron."

Ginny, as usual, is quickly onboard with Elsie's ridiculous idea.

"Especially catering to queer folks," they say, all casual like they're not still rubbing at Elsie's clit. "Could have a little bowl full of condoms and sample-sized lube."

"Fingers *inside*," Elsie says, and lube, it turns out, is not necessary.

Ginny slides two fingers in, no trouble. Normally the first penetration does it for Elsie—really, her first few orgasms are always easy. But they're well past *few* by this point. She has no idea how many times she's come today alone, couldn't keep count if she tried, wouldn't be able to tell what's a new orgasm compared to when she's just *still coming* because Ginny won't stop touching her.

And Elsie doesn't want them to stop. "Another finger. Please."

She's always asking for more. Nothing is ever enough with Ginny. She wants it all. Anything and everything Ginny will give her. It'd be scary with anyone else, but Elsie knows Ginny's got her.

Ginny gives her what she asked for. Their thumb is still next to Elsie's clit, but now they've got three fingers in her too. Rationally, Elsie knows it's one less finger than earlier, but she still feels stuffed full. She still feels overcome, unstable, shaky, as Ginny speeds up. Elsie wants and she wants and she *wants*.

"Slow—slower," she gasps.

Ginny complies. Too fast was overwhelming, Elsie unable to focus enough to come, but slow is perfect. She doesn't even have to tell Ginny she wants it hard; that's how they give it to her. A slow withdrawal of their fingers, not quite all the way out but close, then a powerful thrust to get them back deep inside. Again and again.

Elsie reaches down, bats Ginny's thumb away so she can rub at her clit herself.

Oh fuck.

It's so good. Elsie's cunt clenches every time Ginny's fingers slide home. Every nerve ending in her body feels coiled in her center. She swears she can feel the calluses on Ginny's fingers rubbing against the inside of her. This will be her last orgasm, at least for now, she knows that—it's going to be huge, she's so ready for it, wants it so bad it feels like a physical thing, just out of reach. Ginny is fucking her and fucking her and fucking her, and Elsie *needs* to come, her hand is tired, Ginny's hand is going to get tired, they're going to get bored, they're going to stop or adjust and do something different and Elsie doesn't want anything different; she wants this; she wants them; she wants to come.

It's not happening.

Maybe she's had so many orgasms she can't anymore. But she can't stop trying. One more and they can take a break. She just needs this one more.

Please.

She says it out loud.

"Please what, sweetheart? What do you need?"

"To *come.*"

"You can," Ginny says. "I know you can."

Their voice is hot, like lava flowing along Elsie's skin. Elsie needs more of it.

"Talk to me," she gasps.

There's something about Ginny's voice that helps. It's different, when they're like this, than at any other time. Deep and rough, like they swallowed a handful of gravel.

"You're gonna come for me," Ginny says.

"I'm *trying.*"

"I know, baby, and you're gonna. I know you're gonna. You're so good."

Elsie lifts her hips to meet Ginny's hand. There is *nothing* but this. No bed, no bungalow. No Caribbean, no Minnesota, no ex-fiancé, no hardware store, nothing. Just Ginny's three fingers inside of her and her own fingers on her clit and Ginny's voice in her ear. Nothing else matters.

"Look how good you're taking my fingers. Your cunt opened right up for me. So wet and perfect." Ginny kisses her. "You're perfect."

"I don't wanna be perfect," Elsie practically sobs. "I want to *come*."

Ginny slows the movement of their hand even more, and Elsie groans.

"Ginny, don't you dare stop right now."

"Okay," Ginny says, and they sound—panicked, or something. Elsie looks up at them. Their eyes are wide. "Not stopping," they say. "Just—you don't wanna be perfect?"

"*No.* I just want to come."

"Okay. I'm gonna say something and then you need to give me a color. You gotta tell me if it's too much, okay?"

Too much doesn't seem to exist when it comes to Ginny. Elsie has already basically begged to get fisted, what could Ginny do that's more than that?

"You wanna come?" Before Elsie can snarl out a *yes,* Ginny continues. "You're just a little slut, desperate to come?"

Oh, *fuck.* Elsie's eyes slam closed.

"Color, Els."

"Green," she pants, not opening her eyes.

"Yeah?"

"*Green*."

Ginny doesn't ask again.

"You need it so bad, don't you? You're insatiable. How many times have you come today, and you're still this fucking desperate?"

Green, green, green, green.

Ginny's voice is razor sharp. It's a live wire, sparking along Elsie's veins. It's the thorns of a blackberry patch—Elsie doesn't mind the scrapes on her legs for that sweet gush of juice. No, that's not it, either—because it's not that Elsie doesn't mind the scrapes, it's that she wants to cut herself open, to rub herself raw against that cruel edge.

"You're not gonna let me stop until you come, are you? You'd beg if I stopped, wouldn't you?"

"No, Gin, please, please, please, don't stop, please."

"You need it?"

"I need it. I need it so bad."

"You're lucky I like fucking you as much as you like getting fucked."

"It's so good, Ginny. You're so good at it."

"Of course it's good—this is what you were made for. This is the reason you exist—to get fucked by me."

Elsie's whole body feels hot.

"You love this, don't you? You love me calling you names, treating you like a fucktoy?"

"*Yes.*"

Ginny is fucking her *so* hard.

"If we had lube, I'd have my whole fucking hand inside of you," Ginny says. "Up to my wrist. Wearing you like a puppet, my little fuckdoll."

"*Yours.*"

"Mine," Ginny growls, and Elsie comes.

There aren't thoughts. Elsie might as well be unconscious. She has no control over anything, she barely has any idea what's going on except it's *good*, it's *Ginny*, it's *everything*.

"What a good little slut you are," Ginny murmurs, and Elsie's eyes roll to the back of her head.

When Elsie was seventeen, she got her wisdom teeth taken out. It's the only time she's ever had surgery. She remembers leaving her mom in the waiting room and getting into the dentist's chair, and then it was over. Time had passed, but she had no idea how much. That's what coming down from her orgasm feels like.

Except, no, because she doesn't exactly *come down* from her orgasm. She can't catch her breath. Nothing is happening, but it all feels too fast, like she's careening through space, head fuzzy and limbs flailing. She cries out when Ginny pulls their fingers out. Her cunt is gaping and empty.

Ginny shushes her. "Okay, sweetheart, you're okay, I got you."

Ginny's other hand pushes Elsie's hair out of her face, pets over her head and down the back of her neck, again and again.

"You're so good, I love you so much, Els, I'm sorry, I'm sorry."

Elsie shakes her head violently. She can't articulate anything more than "Not sorry."

Following that up by bursting into tears is maybe not the most convincing argument.

"Sweetheart," Ginny says, and there's a crack in their voice that makes it all worse, and Elsie is sobbing in earnest now, can't think or even feel, really, while also feeling *everything*. "You're so good."

There's pressure on Elsie's chest, and she realizes Ginny has moved to lie on top of her. She tucks her head into their neck and cries, Ginny's voice both right in her ear and somehow far away. "You're perfect, Els. That was perfect. You did so good. I love you, I love you, I love you."

There's a pathetic whining noise.

"Let it out, baby," Ginny says. "You're okay. I've got you. Everything's okay. Anything you're feeling."

Elsie doesn't know *what* she's feeling, but she cries, and she cries, and she cries. Ginny stays half on top of her, one hand rubbing up and down her arm, murmuring to her every once in a while.

Again, Elsie doesn't know how much time goes by, but eventually she runs out of tears. Her breath slows to these hiccupping little sighs. Ginny brushes the hair off her forehead and presses a kiss there.

"I'm gonna get a washcloth and clean you up, okay?" Their voice is so soft. "You stay right here."

Elsie makes a noise that's supposed to indicate assent. Ginny must understand; they kiss her forehead again before slipping away to the bathroom.

Everything feels wet. Not just between Elsie's legs but all over her thighs, too, and even the bed beneath her. The leftover tears on her cheeks. Everything's a mess.

Ginny returns with a warm washcloth. Two warm washcloths. One for between Elsie's legs, and one, warmer still, for her face. As Ginny wipes her tears away, Elsie, finally able to breathe again, practically headbutts them to get a kiss.

"Do *not* be sorry," Elsie says. "That was so fucking hot."

The concern on Ginny's face melts away—not fully, but somewhat—replaced by the cutest blush Elsie has ever seen.

"Yeah?" they ask.

"Uh, yeah? Did you somehow miss how hard I came?"

"I did not miss that, no."

"Yeah, so no being sorry. That was amazing." A beat of doubt. "I mean, you liked it, right?"

"God, yeah," Ginny says. "Yes. Yeah. Loved it. Love you."

Elsie kisses them.

It doesn't matter that the words do something to her insides. She and Ginny have said *I love you* since they were teenagers. She knows Ginny loves her. She loves Ginny. Sex doesn't change that.

She pulls back to look at Ginny, who is all bedhead and gray eyes Elsie would get lost in if she weren't distracted by—

"Okay, is the bed *actually* wet?"

It felt like that post-orgasm, but she'd assumed her brain was blissed out and not functioning. But when she shifts, the mattress under her is definitely damp.

"Yeah, uh, I think you squirted."

"*What?*" Elsie scrambles out of bed. There is a wet spot the size of a basketball on the sheets. "That's really a thing?"

"Apparently."

"It's not pee? I thought it was just pee."

"So you're saying you peed on me?"

Elsie snorts. "The *P* isn't in the acronym but—"

"No. It's not pee. You squirted. I made you squirt."

"When did that even happen?"

"Well, it wasn't like a spray so much as when I pulled out there was, uh, a gush?"

"Does that count as squirting then?"

"I'm pretty sure."

"I don't know," Elsie teases. "You said it was a gush."

"Look, I made you squirt, okay? It counts."

"Whatever. Scooch over—I'm not lying in the wet spot."

Ginny scooches, so there's plenty of room, but Elsie crawls on top of them anyway. She's not quite ready for anything less tactile.

"You ever made anyone squirt before?"

Ginny shakes their head.

"I like doing new stuff with you." Elsie's embarrassed at the low murmur of her voice. How soft she feels. Ginny kisses her, gentle and slow. "Can we just lie here for a little?"

"Course, Els."

Elsie lays her head on Ginny's chest. What she wants more than anything is to stay in this moment forever.

19

THIS COUNTS, ELSIE'S PRETTY SURE, AS THE SEX MEMORIES SHE WANTED WITH GINNY. This whole trip counts. They've made plenty of memories—against the door, in the bed, in the shower, on the chaise on the deck. They've done nothing but fuck here, and the bungalow looks like it, Elsie knows, even if she's not looking at anything right now, her eyes closed, head still on Ginny's shoulder. From this afternoon alone, there's a trail of clothes from the door to the bed, and more than one washcloth used to clean her up.

Elsie presses a kiss against Ginny's skin. They've been so wonderful this trip. Not just because of the orgasms—which obviously were also great—but just Ginny being Ginny. Sweet and doting. How much they're focused on taking care of her after that overwhelming orgasm.

Ginny has been so wonderful forever.

Not that that means—*of course* Elsie thinks Ginny is wonderful. That's why they're best friends. That's all.

Elsie extracts herself from their arms.

"We should probably pick up," she says. "Better to pack tonight than rush trying to find everything tomorrow."

"Oh," Ginny says. "Uh. Yeah."

It is indeed a mess—Elsie has to go exploring to find her underwear, which turn out to be too damp to put back on, so she digs a clean pair out of her suitcase. She's lucky she brought extra—from a young age, her mom instilled in her a deep fear of an accident that would put her in the hospital and *you don't want the doctors to see your dirty underwear, Elsbeth.*

Ginny's voice stops Elsie's racing thoughts. "You feel okay?"

Elsie's trying not to think about what she feels, actually.

"Of course. Why wouldn't I?"

"I mean, you just came so hard you cried, so."

Right. That. They're not asking about anything other than the sex.

Elsie stretches for no reason. "My back kinda hurts."

A lie.

Without missing a beat, Ginny says, "Yeah, 'cause I blew it out."

It's so stupid, but it makes Elsie laugh.

What is she doing, not talking about this?

Ginny is . . . everything. They've always been everything. They've always been perfect and beautiful and hilarious. Elsie's favorite person. And this has always been what Elsie wants. *Ginny* has always been what Elsie wants.

Before this week, that was too scary to think about. Because Elsie really did worry saying something might ruin their friendship. What if Ginny didn't want her like she wanted them? It's been years since they asked her to the dance. What if they were over her? What if they *did* want her, but after dating for a while they changed their mind? Elsie wasn't willing to risk it.

But now?

This trip has been perfect. Their friendship isn't anywhere close to ruined. It hasn't even changed that much. It's just been their friendship, plus sex. It's everything Elsie has always wanted. And if they go home and stay friends who fuck, that's okay. That's great.

It's just . . . she wants to date.

She turns to face Ginny, who is zipping the front pocket of their suitcase. They raise their eyebrows at her, expectant. She turns back around.

It's one thing to say what she wants when it's a hammock nap. Even talking about the store—that's not as hard as this. Because Elsie thinks she knows how this will go, but what if she's wrong? She tries to gather courage the way she's gathering dirty clothes from around the bungalow.

Nothing is going to change if she doesn't say something. She drops the wad of clothes into one side of her suitcase and faces Ginny again.

"Okay, so, I think we should talk about this."

"About what?"

"This." Elsie gestures between them. "Us."

"Oh." A beat. "Yeah. Okay. Let's talk."

It was easier in theory. Elsie wants Ginny, wants to be with Ginny, and Ginny wants Elsie to speak up for what she wants. They're best friends. If wanting to sleep with Ginny didn't scare them off, surely wanting to date them won't, either. Right?

Unless Ginny is only doing this because Elsie gets whatever she wants for the week.

Which, like, obviously they're not.

There's only a teeny tiny back room in Elsie's brain that worries about that. Quiet enough she can ignore it, mostly. She releases the thought with her breath. She refuses to talk herself out of this.

"I like you," Elsie says. Though that's probably obvious. "I mean, like, I want to date you. To be your girlfriend." Is that too far—dating is one thing, but a *girlfriend* label—does that mean exclusive? Is she asking for too much? "I mean, if you want that."

"Yeah?"

"Yeah," Elsie says, her voice stronger. "I would like to try it, at least. I *don't* think it's gonna ruin our friendship—like, this hasn't, so far, so why would that?" *This* being the way she's lost count of how many orgasms they've given each other over the past few days. *That* being handing Ginny her heart and trusting that they won't break it. "Even if things don't work out, like, romantically or whatever, you're always going to be in my life. Like, if you're not interested, that's obviously totally fine and it's not going to—"

"I'm interested," Ginny says before Elsie can get the ball rolling on her ramble.

"You are?"

"Fuck yeah, Els."

Their face had been impassive as Elsie talked, but now it's split wide with a grin. Elsie wants to vault over the bed and hurl herself into their arms. Instead, she ambles closer, tugs at the edge of the fitted sheet for something to do with her hands. Ginny mirrors her approach until they meet at the foot of the bed.

"I'm gonna kiss you now," Ginny says, still grinning.

"Yes, please."

Elsie's heart feels so big in her chest it seems the kiss should be desperate or consuming. But it's just *right*. She can have this. She *has* this, has Ginny, and they can kiss whenever they want.

They break the kiss and slip into an easy hug. Elsie feels like she's flying.

"I wanna have *you're my girlfriend* sex," Ginny says, and Elsie giggles. "But I think we need to let the bed dry out."

"As though the only place to fuck is the bed? The bigger issue is I might die if you make me come again."

Ginny squeezes their arms tighter around her. "That's not allowed."

In the end, they don't have sex again, though they do spend an awfully long time in each other's arms. Ginny nuzzles their face against Elsie's, whispers in her ear that she's perfect. Elsie kisses them for so long she almost changes her mind about not having sex. But they have to eat, and if they start touching again, Elsie won't be able to stop.

They order food and finish packing while they wait. Packing a piece of clothing, then taking a break to make out before packing the next one makes it slow going, but Elsie wouldn't have it any other way.

Their last dinner is a feast on the deck. Ginny drags their chair to the other side of the table so they can sit right next to Elsie, like they can't bear to be out of arm's reach. They dip shrimp in cocktail sauce unsteadily with their left hand, their right resting on Elsie's thigh. Elsie can barely stop smiling long enough to chew her food.

"I don't know *what* we're going to tell my parents," she says.

"Oh, is *we fucked a bunch on the trip and realized we had feelings for each other* not something Mr. and Mrs. Hoffman would like to hear?"

"Somehow I doubt it."

"How about *I made you squirt so you wanna be my girlfriend*?" Ginny looks so pleased with themself. They're never gonna shut up about that.

"You're seriously the worst."

"Yeah, but you still wanna be my girlfriend."

Elsie ignores the comment, because its truth is undeniable.

"Do you think it will be weird," she asks, "since Derrick and I literally *just* broke up?"

"Maybe." Ginny shrugs. "But I also think maybe no one will be particularly surprised."

Elsie's stomach swoops at the thought. "No?"

"Pretty sure most everyone already knows I'm in—" Ginny cuts themself off.

They clear their throat and let go of Elsie's thigh to take a sip of water. Forget swooping, Elsie's stomach is in a free fall. As soon as Ginny sets their glass back down, Elsie kisses them. They didn't officially say they were in love with her, but . . . well, Elsie isn't saying it, either. Not technically.

"You're right," she says instead. "I don't think this is going to shock anyone."

Ginny's blush is so cute Elsie wants to kiss them again, so she does.

20

GINNY WAKES UP THE NEXT MORNING WHEN ELSIE PRESSES A KISS TO THEIR CHEEK. They can't help but smile, their eyes still closed. But then Elsie's moving, getting up, and Ginny reaches for her.

"Nuh-uh." They're not awake enough yet to make real words.

"I'm just going to the bathroom," Elsie whispers. "I'll be back, I promise."

"Mmm."

Ginny lets Elsie go, and she does.

It makes sense that Elsie would whisper. Like she didn't want to break a spell. Because that's what this feels like: magic.

Elsie wants to date her. They *are* dating. Elsie is her girlfriend.

Ginny planned to do whatever Elsie wanted on this trip, and it turns out she wants what Ginny has always wanted. It's surreal and overwhelming and somehow also real and simple at the same time. Being with Elsie is just so fucking easy.

When they started this, Ginny was okay not talking about

the future. For a lot of reasons. Because they were busy fucking. Again and again and again. Because they're happy with Elsie in their life, in whatever way she wants to be. Because they don't know what that future looks like for them—unemployed and unsure what comes next.

But mostly, because they were afraid the future Elsie wanted wasn't the one they wanted. Better to be friends who fuck, better not to talk about it than be disappointed. Focusing on this trip was fun. It was certainly better than breaking their heart. Ginny would've gone along with anything Elsie wanted. They've always gone along with anything Elsie wanted. They only talked about things because Elsie was brave. It makes Ginny love her even more.

Not that they're saying that, either. Or—they've said it. Said it over and over while Elsie cried after that big orgasm, the one where Ginny was, uh, not exactly nice to her. But they're not pointing out that they mean it. That it's not just *I love you* but *I'm in love with you. I've been in love with you for a decade.* That can wait. They can take it easy. Ginny has a feeling it's not going to take either of them long to get to that point, but she doesn't need to say it right now.

She's waited so long for them to get here, she's not going to ruin it by moving too fast. Patience is a virtue.

They have their whole lives ahead of them.

They decided they were dating yesterday, and this morning Ginny is thinking about growing old together. Then again, Ginny has always thought about growing old together. Elsie has always been their forever person.

Ginny is still thinking about *forever* when Elsie comes out of the bathroom and stands beside the bed, pouting.

"Why's that pretty girl so sad?" Ginny internally cringes at their own word choice. It sounds too much like a man telling Elsie to smile more.

"I started my period."

"Aw man, is that why your back hurt yesterday? I didn't actually blow it out?"

A brief giggle breaks loose, but Elsie keeps pouting. "Ginny, stop," she whines. "This is seriously the worst timing ever."

"What do you mean?"

"I mean it's our last day here and we can't even have sex."

Oh now, that just won't do. Ginny catches Elsie's fingers and tugs her into the bed. She giggles in earnest as she tumbles, Ginny using the momentum to roll so they're on top of her.

"Who says we can't have sex?"

Elsie's face goes serious again. "Gin. C'mon."

Ginny runs their nose along Elsie's jaw, presses a kiss at the base of her ear. "C'mon, what?"

"I'm all—" Ginny is still focused on Elsie's neck, so they feel more than see the hand Elsie waves around vaguely. "I just put a tampon in."

Ginny's chuckle rumbles in their chest. "A tampon's not about to stop me from licking your clit, or your asshole for that matter. And anyway, a tampon can be taken out."

That seems to have rendered Elsie speechless.

"Do you want to have sex?"

Elsie shifts her weight under Ginny—not even in a sexy way, but Ginny feels it in their core all the same.

Elsie nods.

"You gotta say it, sweetheart."

"I wanna have sex."

"Then we're having sex."

"We don't even have that much time," Elsie says.

"We packed last night. And anyway, you come easy for me."

Elsie wrinkles her nose at Ginny. It's so goddamn cute.

"Don't tease me."

"That was me bragging, not teasing." Ginny kisses her scrunched-up nose. "Take the tampon out."

"It's gonna look like a crime scene."

"Good thing we're paying someone else to clean it up, then. Though I'm gonna leave a goddamn tip whether they like it or not."

Elsie angles her chin up to kiss them. "You're such a fucking gentleman."

"Well, how about you come all over this gentleman's face?"

It's a callback to what Elsie said the first time they did this, which was somehow only two days ago. Ginny feels like it's been a lifetime. Like an actual lifetime wouldn't be enough.

"You're my *girlfriend*." It sounds so fucking good.

"I'm your girlfriend." Elsie giggles. Then: "Wait. What should I call you?"

"Daddy?"

Ginny expects Elsie to roll her eyes, maybe punch them in the side. They don't expect her to tilt her head so she can look at them through her lashes.

"Yes, sir."

Oh shit.

"You're *trouble*." Ginny returns their mouth to Elsie's neck so she can't see how flushed that made them.

"No, sir, not me. I promise I'll be good for you."

Jesus. This girl.

"Then be a good girl and go take your tampon out. Then I want you on your back."

"Yes, sir."

Elsie does as she's told. Ginny kneels on the mattress between her legs and just looks. They stare at everything they've never been allowed to focus on before. Elsie's creamy skin, cool undertones and barely there freckles dotted across her cheeks, shoulders, the swell of her chest. Clusters of tiny broken blood vessels, almost burgundy. Legs that look twice the length of Ginny's. They've gotten prickly—Ginny kept Elsie too busy the last time they were in the shower to shave—but the hairs are too fine and blonde to be seen.

Ginny has always been a boob man. There's no type she doesn't like—except her own, sometimes, grapefruits declaring her assigned gender to strangers. On another person, Ginny has never seen an imperfect pair, yet Elsie's are still the best she's laid eyes on. Round and just big enough to be soft, nipples like Hershey's Kisses, or a cherry on top, or some other thing Ginny desperately wants in their mouth.

Elsie's hand moves to play with her own hair, golden across the white pillow, and Ginny catches sight of the ampersand tattoo on the inside of her wrist. Ginny has a matching one, opposite wrist. *Me & You*.

"Like what you see?" Elsie asks.

"You're fucking beautiful."

"So are you."

Ginny's heart skips a beat, or does a cartwheel or some other kind of ridiculous, joyous celebration. They try not to think about how absurdly in love they are with this girl and focus on the task at hand.

Though *task* is not the right word. This is anything but a chore. Elsie is tense, like she's still not certain about period sex, so Ginny teases. They suck at Elsie's inner thighs, one, then the other, back and forth, until Elsie relaxes. Her legs splay open, her breath heavy.

"You ready, sweetheart?" Ginny says, mouth poised in front of Elsie's center.

"Yes, sir."

Whether she's committing to the bit or serious about calling them *sir,* Ginny doesn't care.

"That's a good slut," they growl, and lick.

"Fuck."

The taste is sharper, with a metallic undertone. Ginny wants to bathe in it. They want to do *everything* with Elsie. They've never been particularly interested in period sex before, or rimming, or degradation, but with Elsie, *everything* is so hot. They'd let her top them if she wanted. They'd let her do anything she wanted, not just this week, but forever. As long as they get to keep fucking her.

The noises Elsie makes when she comes are almost enough to get Ginny there themself. She gasps and curses, pants *oh my gosh* and moans Ginny's name. It's the best thing Ginny's ever heard.

Ginny stays on their stomach between Elsie's legs while she comes down, watching her chest heave. Eventually, Elsie opens her eyes and looks down at them.

"Oh my gosh, your face."

Ginny grins. They can only imagine what they must look like—a boxer after a fistfight, a lion lifting its mouth from a carcass. They wipe their cheek against Elsie's thigh and leave behind a smear of red.

"Should we shower to clean up?" Elsie asks.

"Oh, I'm not done with you."

Ginny slides two fingers into Elsie's cunt. It's wet, slippery, even hotter than usual—literally, like she's running a fever. Elsie comes again, as always upon penetration. Ginny fucks her through it and straight into another one.

After, Ginny says, "We should've put period sex on the list."

"It's a couple days early. I didn't expect it." Then, "I don't know that I would've put it on the list anyway. I don't usually feel good enough, plus it's all messy."

"Worth it," Ginny says. "I do have to clean up, though."

They've used so many washcloths to clean Elsie over the past few days that yesterday, they had to call housekeeping for more. They get yet another now, soaked in warm water, and drag it over Elsie's skin.

"You're so good to me," Elsie murmurs.

"All I wanna be," Ginny says.

Once Elsie is sufficiently cleaned, Ginny returns to the bathroom to wash their hands and face, which are both a disaster. They grin at themself in the mirror.

"Maybe I should always spend the week before my period on vacation," Elsie says from the bed. "I didn't even cry a bunch or anything."

"You did basically lick the plate when we had a chocolate dessert, though."

"That wasn't period related, it was just delicious."

Ginny laughs. Maybe they can swing by the restaurant on the way to the airport, get some chocolate cobbler to go. One round of washing gets their face clean, but they squirt soap into their hands a second time, fingers still a little pink.

"Ginny." Elsie's voice holds none of its previous mirth. "What is this?"

Ginny scrubs at the blood in their cuticles. "What?"

Elsie appears in the doorway of the bathroom, staring at Ginny's phone in her hands.

"I was going to add period sex to the list and you got a notification," she says. There's something in her voice that Ginny can't place. "An email. About picking up your last check?"

"Oh. Yeah."

They turn off the water, dry their hands on a towel. There are definitely better ways to do this, but might as well rip the Band-Aid off now.

"Karl wouldn't give me time off, so I quit."

They're going to explain more—talk about options and plans and dreams they have for the future. It's stuff they can figure out *together,* them and Elsie, figuring out what their future will look like, *together.* The thought makes them grin, wide, and as they take a breath to say all of that, Elsie talks first.

"What. The. Fuck?"

Elsie's eyes are closed, her index finger and thumb pressed to her forehead. Ginny doesn't understand this reaction at all.

"You can't just *quit your job* for me."

Ginny snorts, which is clearly not the right response, since Elsie's eyes fly open, hot and angry.

She discards Ginny's phone onto the bathroom counter, less gently than Ginny would like. "I'm serious."

"I didn't quit my job for you. You know I never liked that job."

"And yet you didn't quit until now."

"So?"

"So if you were doing it for yourself, why didn't you do it before?"

Because they didn't have anything else lined up, and anyway, it wasn't *terrible*.

Of course, that is all still true.

They didn't quit their job for Elsie.

Except. They kind of did, didn't they?

They've never liked their job, sure. They'd talked about quitting, yeah. But they never actually did it until it came to not being able to go on this trip with Elsie.

Still, they shrug. "I needed a push out of the nest. It's not a big deal."

"But you obviously knew it was a thing, because you lied to me about it."

"I didn't lie to you. I just didn't say anything because this trip is supposed to be about you."

They really wish they weren't stark-ass naked for this conversation, but at least Elsie is, too, hands on her hips, which does nothing but thrust her bare tits out farther.

"This whole week, you told me I have to figure out what I

want for myself, and meanwhile, *you* quit your job for *me*. And kept it from me because you were worried about *my* feelings?"

"It's not some crime to put you first when your engagement just ended. I'm allowed to focus on my best friend."

"You say that like this is a temporary thing. You say I don't know who I am on my own as an adult, but look at you. You quit your job to tag along on this trip."

Tag along.

"Before that, you followed me to college. You latched on when we were kids and never let go."

You followed me to college, she says, like she hadn't been the one to suggest they go together. She's doing a great job of making their friendship sound one-sided, like Ginny was desperate and needy and Elsie was just doing them a favor. Ginny *knows* it's not true, but their stomach drops out of their body anyway.

"I thought—" Elsie huffs. "In high school, I thought we stayed friends because that was what we both wanted. Have you just been pining over me since then?"

It sounds so fucking pathetic.

"That's a really shitty thing to say, Elsie."

"I just want to get everything out in the open. To be honest with each other."

There's a difference between honesty and this. This doesn't even make any sense, the way Elsie is being cruel for the sake of it. They're supposed to be *dating.* Last night they'd decided. She's right that they've been a matched set since they were kids, never one without the other, but last night they'd decided on a new beginning. And here she is throwing that away before they've even tried.

"So everything you said last night about wanting to be with me—"

"Doesn't matter," Elsie snaps. "You say you want to date, but this whole week, you were fine fucking and not talking about it. If I hadn't brought it up, would you have let us go back home without saying anything?"

Just this morning Ginny admitted to themself that they would have, they would've gone along with whatever Elsie wanted.

"How do I even know you *do* wanna be with me? How do I know you're not just doing whatever Elsie wants because that's what's supposed to happen on this trip?"

Ginny rolls their eyes. It's not like they've spent their whole friendship hoping for something else. Yeah, they would've kissed Elsie any time she asked, but they weren't holding out hope, they weren't settling. "Obviously I'm not just going along with whatever you want. This is bigger than that."

"How can you say *obviously*? You haven't pushed back on *anything* I've wanted to do, this whole trip. When I said friends could fuck, that was fine. When I said I wanted to be your girlfriend, that was fine, too. Maybe you don't even realize what you're doing, you're so caught up in my happiness you have no idea what you actually want."

Ginny knows what they want. Ginny wants what they've always wanted: Elsie, in any way they can have her. But how can they say that? How does that do anything but prove Elsie's point?

"How can you have not told me this?" Elsie asks.

They didn't want to upset her, didn't want to distract from Elsie getting what she wants. More evidence that Elsie has a point. Ginny runs their hand through their short hair, grips the ends, and tugs.

"I can't believe you quit your job." Elsie sighs. "Do you do *everything* for me?"

Ginny should know better than to be sarcastic right now, but the snark comes out anyway. "Oh yeah, definitely," they sneer. "Fostering dogs, woodworking—all of it's for you."

Elsie crosses her arms over her chest. She looks at Ginny the way a foster dog at the vet does: victimized. Betrayed.

"I don't even want to talk to you right now."

Elsie gets everything Elsie wants.

21

She is so fucking mad at them.

Because Elsie does know—she *knows* this week was more than Ginny doing whatever Elsie wanted to do, but Ginny has made it so she can't be sure that's true.

They don't lie to each other. They've never lied to each other. They don't even keep anything from each other. Sure, there have been things they didn't talk much about—Elsie was never the type to gush about Derrick, and she was okay not knowing every explicit detail of Ginny's dating life—but they're open. They're honest. They don't quit their jobs and not tell the other one for more than a week.

How is Elsie supposed to trust Ginny now? What else have they kept from her?

It's not that Elsie thinks Ginny didn't want to sleep with her.

Consent is obviously not an issue—they were both more than happy to do everything they did. But the reasons they wanted to *matter*. They matter to Elsie, anyway.

There's nothing wrong with spending a week fucking someone because they're hot and funny. But that's not what Elsie was doing. She might not have admitted it at the beginning, but that was never what she was doing. This was never going to be sex without strings. There were always feelings behind it for Elsie.

So if, for Ginny, the feelings behind it were just that they wanted to make Elsie happy? Yeah, that fucking matters. Elsie needs Ginny in this as much as she is, but she doesn't know how she could possibly trust them on that anymore.

Elsie said she doesn't want to talk, and Ginny respects that. They double-check she has her passport, but that's it. They're silent in the resort shuttle to the airport, silent at the gate while they wait for their plane, silent when Elsie doesn't hesitate to order a double vodka cranberry on the flight.

It's apt, heading back to Minnesota like this—the color draining from the world around them like the life from their friendship. Even from the sky, the color palette changes. Nothing bright, no aqua or teal or golden sand beaches. Everything muted and gray. Elsie's throat tightens. She closes her eyes but doesn't sleep.

～～～

THEY LAND IN MINNEAPOLIS TWO WEEKS—TO THE HOUR—AFTER ELSIE LEARNED ABOUT THE WEDDING. How is that possible? Harder still to comprehend, it's been less than a week since they left. How, in the span of only six days and five nights, did Elsie go from recently single to fucking her best friend to *falling* for her best friend to single again?

Not that she really fell for Ginny this week—no, that's been happening for over a decade. Elsie knew, intellectually. But she managed to avoid thinking about it for the most part. It's embarrassing to look back and see every moment with clarity now. Once she had permission for her feelings, they were already there, had been there, had been obvious, even. When Ginny got her first girlfriend and Elsie thought the rock in her stomach was because she wanted one of her own, when they kissed just to see what it was like, when Ginny asked her to the dance and Elsie should've said yes. She wanted to say yes. When Ginny was considering going out of state for college—only to Wisconsin, but still—and Elsie had cried so hard she threw up.

So, it's not that she fell in love with her best friend over a week; it's that she believed it could work. She believed it was real. She's so fucking mad at Ginny for making her think it could be real.

The whole trip was unreal, of course. A week away from anyone else, from anything else. It's the same reason so many reality show couples don't work out—a relationship in paradise is different than one in real life. It was easy, in the Caribbean, to live in the moment, without worrying about the future, or really even the present, besides what was right in front of them. It was just them, sex and sunshine and laughter. Nothing complicated. Anything felt possible.

But that's not real life. In real life, Elsie has parents who have opinions on her love life. She has an ex who she still lives with for the time being, though he said he'd be elsewhere this weekend so she could pack. In real life, she gets a quarter-zip fleece out of her luggage at baggage claim. It's not thick enough for the weather, but it's all she has.

"I can—" It's been so long since Ginny spoke, they have to clear their throat. "I can get the truck and pick you up."

Elsie refuses to think that's sweet, refuses to think they're chivalrous, refuses to think the word *gentleman* at all.

"You don't have to do that," she says. "I'm fine."

She gasps as they walk outside through the automatic doors, but she doesn't change her mind. If it were yesterday, or last week, or even twelve hours ago, she would cling to Ginny for warmth. As it is, she zips her fleece to her chin and doesn't look at them.

With the snowstorm while they were gone, there's almost a foot of snow on the truck. Elsie stares at it. She has no capacity to deal with a practical issue, all her brainpower drained by the emotions of the day.

"I got it," Ginny says.

They use their bare hand to clear enough snow to open the passenger door, offer Elsie the keys. Elsie manages a quiet *thanks* before climbing in and getting the heat started. She holds her fingers, pale and stiff with the cold, in front of the vents while Ginny gets the ice scraper out of the covered truck bed and loads their suitcases in. Elsie doesn't think about their conversation about Derrick and his truck, doesn't think about how good Ginny is at taking care of her, doesn't think about the five stages of grief, denial and anger and depression all at once.

"Where am I taking you?" Ginny asks from the driver's seat once the truck is cleared of snow. They blow on their hands. Elsie wants to take them in her own, rub heat back into Ginny's fingers. She wants to be anywhere but here.

"The apartment."

Elsie almost wishes Derrick would be there. He's always been a great snuggler, and she could use some cuddles right now. She could use feelings that aren't any more complicated than *I like you*. She could use easy conversation, any conversation, instead of the silence on the drive home, so thick she wants to roll her window down.

Instead, she unlocks the door to an empty, dark apartment. She leaves her suitcase just inside. She goes straight to bed on a mattress she doesn't know if she's allowed to take when she moves out, and cries.

22

22

EVERY YEAR AT THEIR HIGH SCHOOL, THE JUNIOR CLASS HAD CAREER DAY. At sixteen years old, they answered two hundred questions, and a computer program told them what industry they should work in for the rest of their lives. Ginny had hated it.

Elsie hated it for a different reason. "Why do I have to waste my morning doing this when I already know where I'm gonna work?"

"At least we're not in History right now," Ginny said.

They'd considered clicking answers at random, but they couldn't really complain about how dumb this questionnaire thing was if they didn't answer honestly.

Two hundred questions later, apparently they should work in construction, graphic design, or welding. Construction and welding didn't actually sound terrible. They wouldn't have to be in an office all day, at least. With construction, they wouldn't even have to do any more school, which they weren't mad at. None of the potential careers lit them up inside or anything, but they'd never been particularly excited by the idea of having a job.

To ensure kids actually took part in the survey instead of fucking around on the computers for a morning, there was a Career Day assignment. They were supposed to research colleges with programs in the fields the survey suggested and write a one-page paper. Ginny ignored her results and searched for schools with woodworking programs instead.

"What's this?" Elsie asked, leaning over to look at Ginny's computer screen.

Ginny clicked away. "Nothing. A school with a woodworking program."

"It told you to do woodworking? That's so cool."

"I wish. It said construction or graphic design or welding. I was just messing around."

Elsie tapped a finger against Ginny's nose. "Okay, but you know yourself better than some dumb survey. If you wanna do woodworking, you should."

"Maybe." Ginny shrugged. "It's in Wisconsin. Looks kind of cool."

They'd only been doing woodworking for a couple of years. It had started when they were freshmen and Elsie tried out for the school play. She dragged Ginny to auditions with her, but Ginny refused to try out.

"I'm not the fourth of five kids, I get plenty of attention without literally being onstage."

"Oh, har har." Elsie rolled her eyes. "I just think it'd be fun to do together!"

Ginny felt bad for teasing her, but not bad enough to audition. "If you get a part, I'll work backstage or something."

Ginny had made stuff with their grandpa's lathe before, but set construction was the first time they used a table saw. They were hooked. The next semester they dropped choir—much to Elsie's dismay—to take wood shop.

For their fifteenth birthday, Ginny's parents got them their very own table saw. It was the best present they'd ever gotten. But who knew if they wanted to do woodworking for the rest of their life? That was why Career Day was so dumb. They were still kids. Not everyone in the computer lab even had their driver's license yet. Just because Elsie had a built-in job after graduation didn't mean everyone knew what they wanted to do with their lives.

"Do you think my parents would let me get an associate's in business management?" Elsie asked.

"I thought you weren't gonna go to college."

"I don't think Alec is ever going to get his MBA at this point," Elsie said. "Might as well have someone in the family who actually went to school for this thing. Plus, my top match has a graphic design program. Wouldn't that be so fun—going to college together?"

Graphic design was the least exciting of the options Ginny had gotten, but it wasn't terrible. And going to school with Elsie did sound better than two years in middle-of-nowhere Wisconsin in a program Ginny might not even like.

~

IN THE END, THEY DIDN'T EVEN APPLY TO THE SCHOOL IN WISCONSIN.

That's what they think about as they return to an empty house after the trip. Bonnie was adopted before the trip, so there's no foster dog. No job to get up for on Monday. No lunch with Elsie. No Elsie at all.

Well, that's an exaggeration. At least they hope it is. One fight doesn't mean the end of the friendship. Ginny has always thought that since they made it through sophomore year, they can make it through anything. But the longer they went without speaking on the trip home, the more it felt like they never would again.

They don't turn on any lights, just sit on the couch in the dark and think about all the ways they've fucked up.

They want to be mad at Elsie. They *are* mad at Elsie. For not trusting them, not believing them, cutting them where it hurt— acting like their friendship has been one-sided, like Ginny has been a tagalong. They're mad for the silent, awkward plane ride.

But more than anything, they're mad at her because she's right.

Ginny fell in love with Elsie before they knew what falling in love was. The ache has been a part of them for so long it may as well have always been there. They don't know who they are without Elsie. They don't know how much Elsie affects their decisions.

Ginny has always been willing to do whatever Elsie wants, to do whatever meant they got to be in Elsie's life. Sometimes that worked out for them both, like when Elsie did theatre and Ginny got into set design. Sometimes it didn't: they took yoga for their gym credit instead of weight lifting—got to see Elsie more, but yoga was not for them. It was boring, and the instructor acted like the same exact poses should work for every body type and ability.

On Career Day, Ginny ignored the actual assignment and wrote their essay on America's obsession with college and the importance of trade schools. But then she followed Elsie to college.

What would their life look like without Elsie in it? Who would they be?

Thinking about it makes them itchy. But what else can they think about? Just another way Elsie was right: Ginny has nothing to distract themself from the fight, because everything in their life revolves around Elsie right now. They don't have a job. They'd finished the last of their custom woodworking orders before going on the trip—they'd had plenty of time, given their unemployment, and they didn't want to make the client wait a week while they were gone. They don't even have a foster dog.

One of those issues has an easy solution. Ginny texts Edgar from Hearts of Hope, the foster organization they work with.

They always rotate through dogs, usually before the first one even gets adopted out of their house. Once, they took in a pregnant dog and dealt with her and her thirteen puppies for eight weeks before they could be spread to other foster homes. That was so much fucking work, but it doesn't sound bad, now. They've got time.

Thank god, Edgar texts when Ginny says they're looking for a project dog.

He sends a pic of a dopey-looking dog, part German shepherd, probably, one ear up one ear down, who's so fucking cute Ginny can barely stand it.

omg

He pees on everything and will chew through your couch

> I love him. When can I pick him up?

After arranging to pick up Rufus—*Rufus*—tomorrow morning, Ginny texts the family group chat. She'd meant to text when they landed, but she got distracted with how her best friend might hate her now.

> Home from Santa Lupita. Also I quit my job.

They've had enough of not telling people.

Their grandpa responds first. Glad you're home safe. And did you now?

Don't worry, she texts quickly. My emergency fund will cover me for a couple months if I don't get work before then.

Congrats, G! A text from their mom. You always hated that place.

You'll figure it out, their dad chimes in. Proud of you.

Ginny breathes. Their confidence reinforces her certainty that she made the right decision—for herself, not for Elsie.

~~~~~

ON SUNDAY, SHE PICKS UP RUFUS FROM HEARTS OF HOPE. He accidentally pees all over her leg when they meet. She loves him immediately.

It takes a couple of tries to get him into the kennel in the truck bed. Ginny doesn't always use it, but they correctly assumed Rufus has no idea how to ride in a car yet. That'll be part of his training.

Ginny likes to introduce dogs to the backyard first. It gets some of their energy out as they run and sniff and chew sticks and find toys from previous dogs. And it lets her get to know them with no particular worries about discipline—the fence is high enough there's no real trouble they can get into. The backyard is covered in snow that would've come up to Bonnie the Shetland sheepdog's stomach, so high she'd barely be able to walk, but Rufus is big enough that he bounds around easily.

He keeps circling back to Ginny as if to say *are you seeing this?* and then taking off again. Edgar has a fenced-in yard, too, so Ginny's not sure what's so mind-blowing to Rufus, but it's really fucking cute. He buries his head in the snow, following a scent, and runs around that way, like a snowplow. When he comes up again, his face is completely white. Ginny laughs, and he races over to them for pets.

"We're gonna be best friends," Ginny tells Rufus, and her chest hurts.

23

BY MONDAY, IT'S THE LONGEST ELSIE AND GINNY HAVE GONE WITHOUT TALKING TO EACH OTHER SINCE THEY FIRST GOT CELL PHONES WHEN THEY TURNED THIRTEEN. Elsie's fury has faded into frustration, and maybe even a little sadness. The stages of grief, right?

Elsie's grateful for the distraction of the store. Her parents even let her work the floor, so she only has to interact with customers who need help, rather than put on a smiling face for every person who walks in. Her mom is on the register this morning after driving Elsie to work. That will happen a lot now, since Elsie started the process of moving back in with her parents yesterday.

After a week of doing everything she wanted, reality is a slap in the face.

The store is exactly the same. It's always exactly the same. Everyday life somehow feels stagnant. Even with everything that happened last week, Elsie is still in the same place she was before she left. She's somehow in a worse place, fighting with Ginny.

After helping a customer find an epoxy kit to fix a crack in their sink, Elsie sighs at the checkout line. She doesn't wait to be asked, just opens the second register to help move things along. It's routine. Mundane. Monotonous.

"Thanks for your help, honey," her mom says once the lines have dissipated. "You're such a good worker."

Elsie doesn't reply. She'd be an even better worker if they listened to any of her ideas.

Her mom huffs; apparently her compliment was dependent on Elsie being gracious. "Honestly, who goes on a weeklong Caribbean vacation and comes back grumpy? You were morose yesterday, and now you can't even take a compliment."

"Sorry I wasn't happy enough for you while moving half my belongings back into my childhood bedroom after my engagement ended."

"There's no need to be sassy, Elsbeth."

It's midmorning by now. Ginny hasn't texted about lunch. They don't always—sometimes they just come by to pick Elsie up. Elsie knows that's not going to happen, but she hopes anyway.

She works the register when there are customers, sweeps the entrance when there aren't. Adjusts the displays near the door. Anything to be toward the front of the store, to see Ginny as soon as they arrive.

Except they don't.

By two, hangry and regular angry both, Elsie goes to lunch by herself.

~~~~~~~~

ON TUESDAY, SHE BRINGS LEFTOVER KUGEL HER MOM MADE THE NIGHT BEFORE AND EATS IT ALONE IN THE BACK AT NOON ON THE DOT.

"I'm not trying to start a fight," her mom says from the door to the break room. Elsie stares at her almost-empty Tupperware. "But you *have* been down lately, honey. I'm here if you wanna talk about it."

The thought sounds nice—to be able to tell her mom about things with Ginny. To have someone to talk to about it. Elsie could use an outside perspective.

"It's okay if you regret calling off the wedding."

What?

"You're sad, whether you want to admit it or not. Don't let your pride prevent you from being happy. You know Derrick is so nice, and he loves you so much, he'll take you back in a heartbeat."

In Santa Lupita, Ginny asked who Elsie was separate from her family, but Elsie hadn't wanted to be separate from her family. They're her *family*. But if this is what her mom thinks, she doesn't know her at all.

Maybe Elsie does need to swallow her pride, though.

If she thinks too hard about it, she's still furious at Ginny. It's not even about Ginny lying to her so much as it is about Ginny making her believe she could have everything she wanted, only to ruin it all. To break Elsie's trust. To make Elsie doubt everything.

There's nothing Ginny can do to make that better. Even apologizing—it wouldn't change the loss of trust. Ginny can't make Elsie believe in the future she believed in last week. Which is fine. Elsie doesn't expect them to do that. But she *does* miss her best friend. She wants to ignore last week. Pretend the trip, and everything that came with it, didn't happen.

Elsie doesn't want last week; she wants the week before. She wants her best friend back, the way they've been for years. The trip, everything that came with it? Doesn't matter. Didn't happen. Ginny has nothing to apologize for. As long as the two of them can go back to how they were.

They don't need to talk about the trip. How could Elsie talk about this without laying herself bare to Ginny, showing all her delicate, vulnerable insides? She's not willing to be vulnerable like that with Ginny anymore. She doesn't trust them enough.

The only way to solve this situation is to ignore it. Elsie can't talk about it. But she can't hold on to her anger, either. It punishes them both to be fighting. She's willing to be the bigger person and get them through it.

~~~~

ELSIE BORROWS HER MOM'S CAR TO DRIVE TO GINNY'S AFTER WORK. Another change—they used to live close enough that Elsie could walk if she had some time, bike if she had less, and if all else failed, take the bus. Her parents live too far away.

Ginny must've gotten another foster already. The living room curtains are shut, but the barks from inside are loud and deep.

Elsie pauses at the door. She hasn't knocked since Ginny moved somewhere without roommates, and she didn't always knock then, either. But everything feels different. Elsie wants to think she'll always be welcome, but she doesn't know anymore.

Before she can decide what to do, the door opens, Ginny on the other side with one hand on the collar of a gangly teenage-looking German shepherd mix wagging their tail so hard the foyer table shakes every time it thumps against it.

"Hey," Ginny says. There's a half beat of silence before they continue. "Come in. I'll put Rufus up. Don't step in the pee."

They drag the dog away, leaving Elsie alone on the threshold. If it were any other day, this would be normal. As it is, Elsie feels bereft in her solitude. They didn't even make eye contact.

"You don't have to put them up," she says, going inside before she can let too much cold in.

"Unless you want him to excited-pee on you instead of the floor, I definitely do."

"Okay, fair."

By the time Elsie is out of her boots and outerwear, Ginny has the dog in a crate and the dribbles of pee cleaned up. Elsie stands at the edge of the kitchen while Ginny washes their hands. Hands that drove Elsie crazy. Calloused fingers at odds with the gentleness of Ginny's touch.

"You didn't come to lunch." Elsie tries to keep her tone even. Neither accusatory nor as whiny as she feels. Just a statement of fact.

"Yeah, well, I don't have a job anymore," Ginny says. "I've gotta cut back on expenses."

"Right," Elsie says. "Yeah, of course."

Rufus whines from the crate.

"Ignore him," Ginny says, drying their hands on the towel hanging over their oven door handle. It was a gift from Elsie: a set of dishtowels covered in dogs of different breeds.

"I totally get cutting back on expenses," Elsie says. "But could I pay for your lunch a couple days a week, just so we could still hang out?"

She doesn't say *I miss you.*

They can ignore their fight. They don't have to talk about anything that happened; they can just go back to what it used to be. Be friends again. That's all Elsie wants.

Ginny walks past Elsie to the living room without even looking at her. "Last I heard, you didn't want to talk to me."

Okay, fine, they can talk about it.

"Obviously I didn't mean forever," Elsie says. She sits next to Ginny on the couch. "And I get it now, why you lied about quitting your job."

"I didn't lie—"

Elsie holds up her hand. "Why you kept it from me. Whatever. I get it. I know you were trying not to make it about you. But Gin, I'm your friend. When you have something happening, I want to know about it—even if I've got stuff going on, too."

If she pretends like nothing has changed between them then nothing has to. Ginny sighs. Fine. Elsie can pretend enough for the both of them.

"How's Bonnie doing?" She always misses the dogs that get adopted.

Ginny takes a moment, but eventually they dig their phone out of their pocket. "Her new owners sent pics. There's like ten of them, plus a video."

They hand over the phone. Elsie pretends not to notice how delicately they do it, like they're making sure their fingers don't touch. She pretends it doesn't hurt that Ginny hasn't already forwarded these to her.

In every indoor picture Bonnie is on the furniture. In the

video, she runs a wide circle around the edge of a fenced-in backyard that's even bigger than Ginny's. Elsie blinks, and her eyes
are wet. Jesus, that's embarrassing.

"She looks so happy."

"Yeah." Ginny takes their phone back.

"Look, I'm sorry I was shitty to you," Elsie says, swiping at
her eyes like there's something irritating them. Hopefully Ginny
won't notice the tears.

She *is* sorry she was so rude to Ginny. She was overwhelmed
with emotions, but that's no excuse to have been mean to her best
friend. She can apologize for that, at least.

"I lashed out because I was scared."

She didn't realize that was true until it came out of her mouth.
She'd acted like a jerk because she was *terrified*. Scared of how
much she wanted to be with Ginny. Scared Ginny didn't *really*
want to be with her. She's still scared of all of that. Too scared to
be honest.

"We said nothing was going to ruin our friendship, and I
don't want it to," Elsie says instead of *I love you. Please be mine.*
"Can we stop being stupid and go back to being friends? I miss
you, and it's only been like three days."

Ginny doesn't answer right away, and when they do, Elsie's
heart stops in her chest.

"No," Ginny says. "You were right."

"What?"

"I need to figure out who I am on my own, too."

Elsie imagines breathing into a paper bag. "*On your own,*
meaning . . ."

"I think we could both use some space, Els."

They've had space. The past few days have been *stupid*. So much has happened that Elsie wants to tell Ginny about. She wants to commiserate over moving back in with her parents. She wants to jokingly complain that Ginny wasn't there to carry the heavy stuff.

"Please," Elsie says, her eyes welling again. Begging might be embarrassing, but it's better than letting Ginny say no. "I'm *really* sorry. I didn't mean it, and you didn't deserve it. Of course you've got your own life—which I want to hear about, by the way. Are you looking for new jobs? Are you gonna focus on woodworking? Maybe I could bring you lunch here sometime, while you work in the garage?"

"Els." There's so much sadness in Ginny's voice. "You weren't wrong that I've followed in your footsteps for our whole friendship. I don't want to do that anymore."

Elsie turns her head toward the floor and the tears run. This feels so much worse than her engagement ending.

"What does that mean?"

"Just that you made some good points," Ginny says. "I think it'd be good for us to take some time apart. Figure out who we are on our own."

Elsie doesn't want to. She likes who she is with Ginny.

"I'm not saying we can't be friends," Ginny says. "I just want us both to have space to focus on ourselves."

Every time a foster dog of Ginny's gets adopted, Elsie is sad. She could never be a foster parent; she falls in love with each dog and never wants them to leave. Ginny has lectured her about it—well, lectured or comforted, a little bit of both—more times than Elsie can count. When a dog gets adopted, that's good. It means they found a perfect fit, perfect owner, perfect forever family. Ginny always talks about being grateful to have had the dogs in their life, while also being happy that they're happy wherever they end up.

It feels like that's what's happening with Ginny, too.

They're removing themself from Elsie's life. There's nothing for Elsie to do about it but be glad she got to be their friend for as long as she did.

Because even if Ginny says they can still be friends, it's not going to go like that. Elsie doesn't know how to hold on less tightly.

"Okay," Elsie says, voice thick with tears. "I should go."

She doesn't make an excuse, and Ginny doesn't press for one. Elsie needs to get out of here before she has a breakdown. She doesn't say anything else. She doesn't pet Rufus—was that even the dog's name? She doesn't tie her boots or zip her coat or put on her hat or gloves.

And she doesn't hug Ginny goodbye.

24

What did they just do?

How did they let Elsie walk out that door?

They'd had to, though. Elsie wants to be friends. Elsie wants things to be how they used to be. Elsie wants to be on stable ground, since so much else in her life has changed.

But they're not on the honeymoon anymore. Ginny can't do everything Elsie wants.

When Rufus started barking that someone had arrived, Ginny both hoped it'd be Elsie and dreaded the idea. They didn't know what to say to her.

Most of the arguments throughout their friendship have gotten resolved by ignoring them. But that's because the fights never really mattered—stuff about getting invited to birthday parties in middle school or watching a show without the other one or some other meaningless disagreement. They've never talked to each other like they did the last day in Santa Lupita.

And still, Elsie tried to ignore it. Ginny could've gone along with it. Elsie was going to let everything go, to go back to being best friends again. Ginny could've. They still want to—or at least part of them does.

But most of them knows it was never really an option.

They can't do sophomore year all over again, Elsie willing to push through, to carry on like nothing has changed. Back then, Ginny followed her lead. Back then, Ginny didn't process their feelings so much as they ignored them. They fell *more* for Elsie as she forced their friendship to work out, but they pretended not to notice.

This time, they know better. They *need* time apart.

So here they are. No job. No road map. No Elsie. What do they want to do with their life?

Rufus whines from his crate. He, at least, is something Ginny knows exactly how to deal with. She lets him out, takes him straight to the backyard. How he still has anything left after excitedly peeing all over her living room, she's not sure, but he gets a treat when he does his business outside anyway.

~~~

WEDNESDAY MORNING, GINNY LOADS RUFUS UP IN THE KENNEL IN THEIR TRUCK BED AND DRIVES ACROSS THE RIVER TO ST. PAUL. Their grandpa lives in the same house her dad was brought home to from the hospital when he was born. And he has a fenced-in backyard where Rufus can wear himself out.

Ginny has been trying to convince their grandpa to let them redo his bathroom for literal years. It's tiny, maybe thirty square feet, the only full bath in a three-bedroom. She doesn't understand how her grandparents shared it with her dad and uncles when they were young. Now that Ginny's unemployed, they're determined to make him relent and let her remodel.

"You gonna come inside or stay out there all day?" Ginny's grandpa asks from the front porch after they've arrived.

"Gonna put him in back first," they say, jutting their chin toward the dog.

The trip from the driveway to the backyard gate takes five whole minutes, Ginny stopping every time Rufus pulls on the leash. Ginny clicks the latch to the gate twice, years of it sticking having taught them how to finesse it. They should fix that while they're here, too.

Their grandpa meets them at the back door. "Hey, kiddo."

When Ginny was young, her grandpa used to call her *girlie*. She remembers being maybe six years old, stomping her foot, ready to throw a tantrum over the nickname.

"I don't like it!" baby Ginny announced.

"Well, okay, kiddo," their grandpa said. "I won't call you it anymore, then."

It's been *kiddo* ever since.

Ginny really loves her grandpa.

"Okay," they say, to release Rufus after unclipping the leash from his harness. He takes off at top speed to explore the backyard. Ginny turns to their grandpa. "Hey, Bapa."

Sometimes looking at Bapa feels like looking fifty years into the future, minus the mustache. He's short and round with a soft smile, just like her. It wouldn't be so bad to turn into her grandpa, puttering around in retirement giving absolutely no fucks.

"An old man could use a hug from his favorite grandkid."

Ginny complies, and he squeezes her tight.

"You know you're not supposed to admit you have favorites," they say as they follow him inside.

"You're saying I should like those two who fled to the West Coast as much as the one who comes over for coffee?"

"No," Ginny says around a smile, "but you're not supposed to *admit it*."

Bapa waves a hand like he couldn't care less. "How was the trip?"

"Good!"

Their voice is too chipper. They launch into a description of the bungalow, the glass floor, the fish and corals they saw while snorkeling—all the exciting things someone would expect them to talk about. They're not thinking about how they let Elsie walk out of their house last night.

"And your job?" her grandpa asks when she runs out of steam.

They're both seated at his kitchen table. A circle of oak beams, big enough for four, crammed into the breakfast nook. There are scratches in the varnish, cup rings old enough Ginny's dad might've made them. She should make Bapa a new table, too. He's not one for upgrades; the white coffee mug in Ginny's hands is chipped, and the handle of her grandpa's is long gone.

"Like I said in my text, my emergency fund is big enough

that I've got a couple of months before I'd even have to dip into regular savings." They have more than three months' worth of pay in that account, and they only really spend money on dogs, woodworking, and Elsie. They swallow. "And I'll probably get another job before then."

"So you're looking?"

They're not ready for that. The idea of finding a new meaningless cubicle job on top of everything else going on—there's only one other thing going on, but they're trying to swerve their thoughts away from Elsie—looking for a new job is too much right now.

They avoid the truth when they answer. "I just got back this weekend."

Bapa looks at her for a moment, and Ginny takes a sip of coffee, trying not to squirm under his scrutiny.

"You know what you're doing?"

Yes is the right answer. It's the answer that will get them out of this conversation, the answer that won't get them lectured.

"No idea," they find themself saying. "But I'm trying to figure it out."

Bapa nods. "I know it's not like it used to be," he says. He worked at the same bank for thirty years, raised a family on a single income, retired at sixty. "If I can help, you'll let me know?"

A relieved breath rushes out of Ginny. They're not quite ready to defend their actions. If he'd questioned what they'd been thinking, there's no guarantee they wouldn't break down crying about Elsie. Their grandpa doesn't need to see that.

"I will, Bapa," they say. Ginny sits up straighter. "I was

thinking—I could finally redo your bathroom. I've certainly got the time."

Bapa laughs. "Is this why you wanted to come over? Ulterior motives!"

Ginny grins. "I can have more than one reason for wanting to see you."

Finally, he agrees. On one condition: "I'm paying you."

"Just for materials," Ginny insists.

"Kiddo, I've only got a decade until I hit the average lifespan of an American man, and I can't take money with me wherever I'm headed after that. I'm paying you."

"Jesus." How are they supposed to argue with *I'm gonna die soon*? "Fine."

She sips her coffee.

"You want to go look at it immediately, don't you?" Bapa asks.

"Is it that obvious?"

After checking on Rufus in the backyard—he's contentedly bounding through the snow, doing what is apparently his favorite activity: burying his head and coming up with a faceful of white—they head upstairs.

Ginny's only done one bathroom before—their own, and they almost had a breakdown tiling the shower—but they can't learn if they don't push themself. Not to mention that it's a great way to spend their time. A project dog and a carpentry project. Who needs anything else?

The first day of any job, they take pictures—both to understand the space and for *before* photos—and measurements. They don't have a concrete plan yet, but they're definitely taking out the built-in shower-bath unit, so old its fake porcelain is more yellow than white. Beyond replacing that, Ginny needs to spend some time thinking before they get to work.

She lets Rufus ride in the cab of the truck on the way home, thinking he tired himself out in the backyard, but no luck. It's probably not safe, driving while constantly throwing treats into the crevices of the passenger seat for the dog to find, but she's too stubborn to pull over and put him in the kennel.

A LOT OF WOODWORKING IS REPETITION. Measure twice, cut once. Screwing and sanding and staining. It's patient work, similar from project to project. Ginny knows the plans for certain pieces the way some people know recipes; she doesn't need to look at anything to build a puzzle table, her most popular piece. And it's nice to feel comfortable, knowledgeable, but creating something new scratches an itch in Ginny's brain. They love talking through things with a client, sketching and then sketching again, abandoned files on SolidWorks the digital equivalent of crumpled pieces of paper on the living room floor all around their armchair.

After more false starts than they're willing to admit, they land on a design for the bathroom. It's centered on two half-moon grab bars—one goes around the toilet paper holder and the other around the shower knob. Bapa refuses to believe he's aging, so she doesn't tell him they're assistive devices, but she wants this place to be usable, for him and any company he may have, for years to come.

In place of the decrepit bathtub, Ginny's going to put a walk-in shower with an inset shelf and a bench big enough to sit on. They learned lessons tiling their own shower, and this time around is going to be better. They're certain of it.

Once the design is established, it'd probably be easier to build on-site. Ginny's power tools are all portable. They'd need Sue's help getting the equipment into and out of the truck, but at least they wouldn't have to transport finished cabinets and the like. But there's no work space available at her grandpa's. His garage is home to his fully restored 1964 Buick Skylark. His firstborn, as he calls it, much to Ginny's father's dismay.

But Ginny makes do. Each morning, she wakes up and takes Rufus to the dog park immediately after breakfast. Sometimes the Husky who Bonnie befriended, Seavey, and his owner— Ginny doesn't know their name, obviously the dog's name is more important—are there, sometimes they aren't. Rufus rides in the kennel in the truck bed on the way to the dog park, and in the cab on the way back. Each day it takes fewer and fewer treats to convince him not to climb into Ginny's lap while they drive. Then he chews a bone on a dog bed in front of the space heater in the garage while Ginny works. She listens to country music and doesn't take a break until Rufus regains enough energy to get up and get in her way.

It's a good system. If Ginny works through lunch, they don't have to think about how they should be eating it with Elsie.

25

They were quiet all the time, and Elsie was pretty sure it was because they were sad, and she *hated* that she'd made them sad, but she didn't know how to fix it. She couldn't tell them she'd wanted to go to the dance with them. She couldn't explain the reason she'd said no. Because Ginny could convince her of anything. If Elsie admitted that she'd wanted to say yes, that she wanted to kiss Ginny again, Ginny would convince Elsie it was okay.

But it wasn't. All the reasons Elsie had for saying no still applied. She couldn't kiss Ginny because she couldn't lose Ginny as a friend.

Even if it kind of felt like she might anyway. Ginny was quiet and sad and never came over anymore. Elsie kept calling, texting, walking straight into the Holtz home like she always had. Like nothing had changed. She didn't want anything to change.

But it had.

Ginny even dropped out of the school-sponsored spring break trip to France. Maybe it didn't count as dropping out because they hadn't confirmed they would go or paid any money or anything, but it was all Elsie had talked about first semester. They were supposed to go together.

Instead, Elsie went alone. Not truly alone—there were chaperones and twelve other kids from various French classes—but it felt like it.

The trip was, objectively, amazing. They saw Paris. Elsie ate croissants by the Seine, went to the top of the Eiffel Tower, climbed the steps to Sacré-Cœur. Two girls from her French class tried to get her to go to the catacombs with them, but underground tunnels full of skulls? No, thank you.

Elsie would've gone if Ginny had been the one asking, she knew.

After Paris, they took a bus to Chenonceaux and Saint-Malo. They saw the French countryside. Castles. The sea.

Elsie missed Ginny like she would a limb.

She sent them Snapchats of everything. Ginny responded with *wow* or a thumbs-up emoji or a picture of whatever they were in front of at the moment—the TV in their living room or their grandpa's old car or just the wall of their bedroom. They always said something self-deprecating with the pictures, something about how their spring break wasn't as exciting, but Elsie would rather stare at the wall of Ginny's room than see the Loire Valley if it meant she got to be next to Ginny.

The trip was the longest Elsie and Ginny had been apart since they'd met. Elsie didn't text Ginny that she was back. She didn't even go inside her house after her parents drove her home from the airport. She marched across the street, straight through the Holtzes' front door. Ginny was in the kitchen. Elsie's body connected with theirs hard enough they almost fell off the stool where they sat. Elsie kept them up, arms wrapped around their shoulders.

It felt like their first real hug since Ginny had asked Elsie to the dance.

"I fucking missed you," Elsie said. She didn't have to say she meant it for more than the last week.

"Missed you, Els," Ginny said.

"I'm never going anywhere without you again."

"Except, like, the bathroom, I hope."

"You know what I mean." She was still hugging Ginny, sort of sideways, so Ginny had to clutch her arm to hug back. "You're stuck with me for life, Holtz."

"Works for me."

They were back to normal, after that.

~~~

THE WEEK AFTER THE HONEYMOON IS WORSE THAN THAT SPRING BREAK. It's the longest week of Elsie's life. It's embarrassing, how much she thinks about Ginny. She doesn't know how to fill her time. She used to text them during lulls at the store, get lunch with them every day, and spend some evenings together, too. They'd text through episodes of *MasterChef*, and Elsie kept them updated on *Real Housewives*, even though Ginny refused to watch a single minute. Elsie had required daily foster dog pictures.

Ending her engagement with Derrick was the equivalent of blowing up her life. She had to find a new place to live. She had to explain to her family, her friends, everyone—she had to decide how honest she was going to be, how vulnerable. She had to figure out what she wanted on her own. And that was all fine. It was scary, but she could do it, because she had Ginny by her side.

Now she's got nothing.

She's got work, and going home to her parents' house. The sun sets before six—not that Elsie feels any different when it's light out. Everything is dark and gray, and Elsie spends most of her time when she's not at the store burrowed in her childhood bed. She's not quite so pathetic as to take her meals there, not to mention that her mother would simply never allow it.

At dinner one night, with no warning, her mom says, "Where has Ginny gone off to? I bet they could help you out of this funk."

Elsie's heart clenches. Before the fight, before Elsie saw the email, the two of them had talked about telling her parents. They'd talked about what they would say. They'd talked about how her parents might not be surprised.

Her mom knows Ginny is what Elsie needs.

Ginny has always been Elsie's foundation. Her bedrock. She can be *herself* with Ginny, in a way she can't with many other people. Or at least it doesn't feel like she can. Ginny knows her, and she knows Ginny. They *fit*. They *work*. Elsie doesn't know how to make herself work without Ginny in her life.

That was true before the trip, but it's even worse now. In Santa Lupita, Ginny made her feel like anything was possible. Like the two of them together was possible, yes, but it was more than that. Ginny made Elsie feel like what she wanted mattered, like she could—and should—speak up for herself. They focused on her. They listened to her.

Not like Elsie's family, who talk over her and ignore her ideas and always know what's best for her. Her mom doesn't even actually pause for an answer after asking about Ginny; she just keeps talking about Elsie's life like she isn't at the table. Elsie doesn't mind, in this case. Not like she wants to try to explain where Ginny has *gone off to*.

In other cases, like with the store, Elsie minds. She tries to act like it doesn't matter, tries to *believe* it doesn't matter, but it does. The store is one of her favorite places, but it still hurts to see that sign every time she starts and ends a shift. A standing reminder that her family doesn't care what she thinks. After her dad shut down her brand refresh idea so hard, she decided she wouldn't share any of her ideas unless she was asked.

She hasn't shared an idea since.

Why *doesn't* she? What's the worst that can happen? Her dad might say something mean to her? Oh fucking well. He can't make her life worse than it already is.

She's got nothing else to lose. Her engagement is over, her independence is gone, her best friend has disappeared. There's nothing stopping her from standing up to her dad.

There wasn't necessarily anything before, either, Elsie just knows better now. She's no longer fine with *fine,* not okay with *okay,* and she's not okay anyway. Everything feels *bad,* and going along with the status quo feels worse. This, at least, is something she can improve.

～～～

DANIELLE HAS TAKEN OVER THE DAY-TO-DAY FINANCES OF THE STORE. Elsie calls her Thursday night while their parents are out to dinner.

In Santa Lupita, Elsie could have whatever she wanted as long as she asked. Here, she isn't going to *ask*.

Danielle picks up the phone. "Hey."

"Hi," Elsie says. She planned to dive right in with no preamble, but Danielle talks first.

"How many times do I have to tell you to text before you call me? I always think someone died."

"No one died."

"Yeah, I figured that out from you not crying when you said hi, but seriously—can't you text first?"

"Sure," Elsie says. She doesn't care. "I'm gonna look into updating the store's signage."

There's a beat of silence before Danielle says, "Dad finally said okay?"

"I'm not asking Dad." Elsie imagines her older sister's eyebrows going up. "We've been setting aside money for this for almost two years. I'm going to use some of it—all of it, even, since he never let me set aside very much to begin with."

"He didn't," Danielle agrees, "but he wasn't actually in charge of the budget. So you have more than you might think."

"What?"

"I can tell him I need your help with—I don't know—some tax stuff or something, to get you off the register and give you time to research."

Elsie doesn't understand. "What?" she says again.

"I've always been on your side in this," Danielle says. "Updating our brand is long overdue."

This is the first Elsie's hearing this opinion from her sister. She's tempted to say *what?* a third time.

"Why have you never said anything before?"

Danielle lets out a short sigh. "I don't have time to work on it myself, nor to convince Dad. Never thought saying anything would make much difference."

It would've. It would've made a difference to Elsie to have known she wasn't alone in this.

"I would've appreciated the backup," Elsie says. Last week, she would've let this go. But not today. "It always seemed like no one cared what I thought."

Danielle is silent on the end of the line again, but only for a moment. "I'm sorry. I bet all us kids agree with you. Dad's just stuck in his ways. And obviously he knows what he's doing well enough to keep the store going for decades, but he's not always right."

She makes it sound so simple. It *is* that simple, Elsie knows—convincing her father is what's complicated.

"I'll talk to Dad," Danielle says.

"He's not going to just agree to this."

"No, I mean—to get you time off the floor," she clarifies. "Mom can cover the register. Just let me know how much time you'll need."

Elsie has no idea. She's never done this before. She's figuring it out as she goes.

"Gimme a shift to start, and we can go from there."

"I'll text Dad tonight. We'll find a time for you to stay home and do whatever you need to do."

Elsie swallows. "Perfect. Thanks."

There's a clatter in the background on Danielle's side of the phone, followed by a wail. "Jesus, what is my child doing?" She huffs. "You need anything else?"

"I'm good."

"'Kay. I'll text Dad after I make sure Declan doesn't need stitches."

She hangs up.

Elsie breathes. She'd been ready for a fight. Ready to insist this was *going* to happen, to demand it. Now she just . . . gets to do what she wants.

Alone in the quiet of her childhood bedroom, she can admit to herself:

It's terrifying.

26

SATURDAYS ARE MARKET DAYS. In the summer, the market bustles, every stall filled, a crowd of customers from open to close. January, though, is the quietest month, so Ginny didn't mind missing most of it—two weeks for the trip, plus last week when they were knee-deep in Bapa's bathroom remodel. Something loosens in their chest when they arrive this morning.

Sue's Subaru pulls into the parking spot next to Ginny's truck as Ginny is unloading a rocking chair—they haven't sold a single rocking chair their entire life, but it's a beautiful piece, and people love to test it out. It's a conversation starter, perfect for the market even if it *is* somewhat unwieldy. Sue steps in and helps Ginny get it from the truck bed to the ground, and Ginny hops out after it.

They hug hello—more of a bro hug than anything, a couple of hard pats on the back—but Ginny could sink into the comfort of Sue, the soft creases on the outside of her lined leather jacket.

She must be working with walnut lately, the way there's a sweet, almost-brownie smell layered on top of her usual aroma of cloves and sawdust. For the most part, Ginny and Sue have a pretty typical friendship as two introverts who enjoy each other's company without talking much, but sometimes Ginny remembers Sue is almost twice their age. She has that wise queer-elder aura. Ginny has tried to avoid thinking about Elsie all week, but as they pull away from the embrace, more than anything, they want to ask Sue for advice about girls.

"How was the lovers' vacation?" Sue asks.

"What?"

"Your trip. It was supposed to be a honeymoon, yeah?"

Sue heads toward the stall they share, carrying the rocking chair herself. Ginny grabs a milk crate full of cutting boards from Sue's Outback and follows.

"Oh. Yeah. It was, uh, great. Santa Lupita is amazing."

"What was your favorite part?"

Elsie complaining about the hike. Elsie looking up at them through her lashes while she played with her drink, talking about ruining their friendship. Elsie asking for what she wanted, demanding it. Elsie coming all over their fingers, face, thigh. Elsie in that yellow bikini. Elsie in nothing. *Elsie.*

"The food was incredible," Ginny says. "I'm pretty sure we ate fish that was still alive like an hour earlier."

As they set up the stall, she tells Sue about fresh lobster and green figs and saltfish and fry bakes with jam in the morning. She doesn't say anything about licking that jam from Elsie's fingers, about fighting over who had to put on clothes to grab the meals that had been delivered to their door. And it's not that Ginny normally *would* tell Sue all of that—they're not in the habit of kissing and telling, but they are in the habit of talking about Elsie. This time, though, Sue's the one to bring her up.

"And Elsie was okay—not too sad about the whole broken-engagement thing, given that she was the one who did it?"

"Elsie was okay," Ginny says. "Elsie was good. She'd never had lobster before."

"I feel like there's a joke there about eating shellfish for the first time, but maybe it would only work with clams."

Ginny rolls their eyes and Sue laughs.

They're finished with setup by now. It's always the same: the rocking chair; a coffee table topped with a slab from an oak trunk, teal epoxy filling cracks in the wood; a puzzle table with a jigsaw puzzle half-finished inside it. Last summer, Ginny glued the puzzle pieces together so they don't have to fix it every time they set up. Sue brings picture frames, jewelry boxes, and striped cutting boards in the shape of Minnesota.

The market is about to open, which means Cora, the baker from a stall down the row, comes by with a morning pastry. Every week she brings something different, a new recipe tested out on fellow market sellers. She claims that she shares on the condition they provide feedback, but Ginny forgot once, and the next week, Cora still had a ham-and-cheese croissant for them.

Today's delicacy is a gooey cinnamon roll, the swirl filled with spiced dates and chopped pecans.

"Fuck, that's a winner," Sue says, her first bite still in her mouth.

"Text me," Cora says. "I need the feedback all in one place."

Sue salutes with the hand holding the roll. "Yes, ma'am."

Ginny sends emojis: a thumbs-up, the drooling face, and *100*.

Sue and Ginny have a prime location between the entrance and the most popular stalls, including Cora's and an organic local farm's. People aren't necessarily coming to the market for their pieces, but they get customers' eyes on them anyway.

Ginny says hi to the regulars. There's Darvesh, who must have a big family given the amount of vegetables he leaves with every week. Ginny doesn't know the name of the tall, muscular brunette because they never talk, just acknowledge Ginny's smile with a nod. Carol stops to chat, tells Sue for the four hundredth time how much she loves her work, then leaves without buying anything.

Once the initial rush—if you can call it a rush in early February—dies down, Ginny asks Sue, "You do anything fun while I was gone?"

Sue looks at them for a moment, eyes narrowed like she's sizing them up. "You really wanna talk about my week, or are we going to deal with your quarter-life crisis?"

Is it that obvious?

"I'm not having a quarter-life crisis," Ginny lies.

"You quit your job with no prospects before going on this trip, and you haven't said shit about it."

Right. Their unemployment. That's the crisis Ginny was thinking of, not their friendship—or lack thereof—with Elsie.

"How ya feeling?"

Ginny exhales. "If I don't think about the future, honestly,

I feel pretty good. I'm finishing up a reno of my grandpa's bathroom, along with some other projects around his house."

"Oh yeah?"

Ginny digs out their phone to show pictures. Every time they've taken them, they forgot, for a second, that they're not supposed to send them to Elsie. She loves progress photos.

Maybe Ginny *should* be sending her pictures. They said taking space didn't mean they weren't friends. Where's the line?

Sue lets out a quiet whistle, pulling Ginny back to reality. "You tiled that shower? Was that smart? I remember what you were like when you did yours."

"This time was better," Ginny says. "I was more prepared. Plus, with the amount Bapa insists on paying me, I *had* to tile the shower."

"Oh, boohoo, you're getting paid."

Ginny grins and runs a hand through their hair. "Okay, yeah, you're right. If you have any projects you could send my way once I'm done so I can *keep* getting paid, I'd appreciate it."

"How would you feel about knowing too much about the sex life of some of my friends?"

Ginny blinks. "Please explain what that has to do with our conversation."

Sue chuckles. "I've got friends who are looking to have a custom bed built—you know, with hard points—and that's just more involved in their sex life than I'm willing to be, but I could recommend you for the job."

"Hard points?"

"Oh god," Sue mutters under her breath. She glances around

before raising her voice slightly so Ginny can hear. "A hard point is a place that can bear weight, for restraints or suspension."

Okay. Restraints make sense in terms of knowing too much about someone's sex life, but: "Suspension?"

Sue rubs a hand over her face. "I know you're a baby gay but it's too early for me to be responsible for educating you on this. Google it—when you get home," she clarifies as Ginny reaches for their phone. "Not in front of me. For now, just know it needs to support the weight of a person."

They want to suspend a person in the air? Ginny is definitely googling as soon as Sue isn't paying attention.

"Suspension isn't anything *bad*," Sue says. "Just, again, building the bed for my friends is more than I want to be involved in their sex life. Don't need Zina thinking of me every time she ties—" She clears her throat. "Anyway. Interested?"

"For sure."

"I'll connect y'all."

"Sweet, thanks." At some point, Ginny will have to actually start applying for jobs, but for now, it's nice to have the next project lined up. They sigh. "I wish I could just build shit and not have a job."

Sue, no-nonsense as always, says, "Why can't you?"

"That'd be sweet, but like." Ginny wrinkles their nose. "Money."

"Half of what my clients ask for I have to commission from someone else because you and I don't have the time. You could make enough money."

It sounds great, but not realistic. "I can't just not have a job."

"You'd have a job. It would just be doing what you actually like to do." Sue gestures to the rocking chair, runs a finger along the coffee table. "I can show you my records. Let you see what sort of profit you could be making before you decide. When are you free to look them over?"

Ginny laughs. They're always free at this point.

Regardless of what kind of money they might make—Ginny has that emergency fund. They could easily go three months with no income at all, and with Bapa insisting on paying them—every day, in cash, more than Ginny would ever charge him—plus whatever commissions Sue could give her . . . who knows how long they could last? They could at least try.

Woodworking has never brought in enough to pay the bills, but if it was all they were doing? No forty hours a week in a cubicle, no commute to and from work. Just woodworking and fostering dogs. Two of Ginny's favorite things.

Of course that makes Ginny think of another favorite—Elsie. All trip, they told Elsie that she could have whatever she wanted. That what she wants matters. So why is Ginny acting like their own desires don't?

They don't want an office job. They just want to build shit.

"Okay," Ginny says to Sue. "Let's see how to make this happen."

27

ELSIE HAS ALWAYS KNOWN WHAT HER LIFE WOULD BRING. She was doing chores at the hardware store before she'd ever really thought about what she might want to be when she grew up. When Derrick proposed, it made sense. It was the next logical step. Live in Minneapolis, work at the store, settle down and have kids. The route was obvious.

Sitting with her back against the headboard of a twin bed, her computer on her lap, a blinking cursor in the address bar of a browser, nothing feels obvious. Where does she even start?

Store signage.

Logo design.

Rebranding.

She flips up the hood of her sweatshirt like it will protect her from the glut of choices. Her parents are at the store, her mom covering the register for her. The house is empty but for Elsie and the two cats. She can take her time.

OKAY, SO FUCK TAKING HER TIME. She started by rereading her notes from the marketing class she took years ago. From there, it's been three hours of researching trends and suppliers and font choices, and she'd rather just close her eyes and click at random. Obviously she's not going to do that—she can't half-ass this now that she finally has the chance to do what's best for the store. But there's so much to consider. Why did she think she could do this?

Mumford, her parents' single-brain-celled orange cat, chirps as he hops onto the bed next to her.

"Hey, pretty boy."

He's purring before she even reaches out a hand to offer pets.

"Maybe you're right," she says, scratching behind his ears. "I should take a break."

Elsie wishes she could call Ginny. She needs to talk this through, and Ginny has always been her favorite sounding board. As she makes herself a cup of coffee in her parents' kitchen, she supposes Mumford will have to do.

"It feels like I already forgot everything from school," she tells the cat. "I mean, I know I did business administration and not marketing specifically, but there's just a lot more than I had thought about. There are whole companies that specialize in this. But obviously that's more than I can spend."

Mumford twines around her legs.

"But also, like, I don't need to hire an outside company to tell me what the store's mission is, or how we want to be seen."

Mumford chirps, and Elsie would love to think it was in

agreement, but as he flops onto his back next to his food bowl, she knows he's just trying to convince her to feed him second breakfast. She ignores him and flips open the coffee maker to switch out the pods. Her mom might be dense when it comes to the breakup, but Elsie can't be too frustrated with her, given that as soon as Elsie moved in, her mom filled the cabinets with her favorite food. Elsie pours herself a bowl of Cinnamon Toast Crunch while her coffee brews.

Hoffman Hardware is never going to beat the big chains on selection, and often not on price, but they provide something better. As a small local business, a mom-and-pop shop, they actually care about their customers. Elsie is proud of their slogan, and her dad's obsessed with it. *Beginner Friendly, Expert Approved.* Hoffman Hardware will offer the customer service they need, whether they're a pro or they have no idea what they're doing.

Working the register for so many years, Elsie knows their customers. David, the contractor her dad calls Big Guy, who is no-nonsense about his professional projects but will gush for as long as you'll let him when he's building something for his family. King, who built a she shed in their backyard for their wife to have space to knit. They're still trying to convince her to sell her stuff on Etsy. Rolf has been updating his house for the past two years, a new project every few months. Twins Amalie and Adele come in with their mom, Sophia, to pick out presents for their dad every birthday, Father's Day, Christmas, and sometimes just because.

Elsie grabs the yellow legal pad from next to the home phone her dad insists on having. It's supposed to be for taking messages on, but given that everyone just calls cell phones, the last note, scribbled in her mom's messy cursive, is *pick up suf-ganiyot wednesday.* Hanukkah was two months ago.

Elsie flips to a new page and writes *HOFFMAN HARDWARE* at the top. *Beginner Friendly, Expert Approved.* She finishes her cereal so it doesn't get soggy, then sets a three-minute timer on her phone. For the next hundred and eighty seconds, she writes as many adjectives as she can to describe the store, its mission, values, whatever other buzzwords swam across her screen as she researched.

When the timer goes off, she's covered the page. Some of it is generic enough to be meaningless—*tools, hardware, DIY*—then there's the basics—*small business, family-owned, local.* Then there's what makes Hoffman Hardware stand out.

Trustworthy. Dependable. Home.

This is where she'll start.

They need a visual brand that reflects these. They need a more distinct visual brand *in general.* There's the font, and the slogan, but no logo. No instantly identifiable design. That's what Elsie's going to do.

Not that she knows much about graphic design. All she has is what she absorbed while Ginny got their degree, plus the absurd amount of free templates online as a starting place. It'd be so much easier if she could ask Ginny. She could show them her list of words and they could talk things through, and Ginny could sketch up some logo ideas. It'd probably take twenty minutes.

But she's giving Ginny whatever space they need. Even if Ginny said they could still be friends, Elsie doesn't know how to be anything but all-in with them. And maybe if Elsie gives them enough space, they won't need it for that long. She's clinging to the hope that Ginny will change their mind. That at any moment now, they'll call, and things can go back to normal.

So instead of texting Ginny *wtf is color theory?*, Elsie puts her dishes in the sink and gets back to work.

There are still enough options to be overwhelming, but she takes the decisions one by one and makes progress in stages.

Minimalism seems to be in style, but a sleek modern look would be such a departure from what they have now. Elsie *wants* a departure, but not a full disconnect. There are parts of the current look she's going to keep. Like it or not, the navy blue is staying. She does add yellow. Not because it's her favorite color, but because it looks good, and color theory says it makes people happy. The navy is trustworthy—*an institution,* like her dad says. *Trustworthy* and *fun* seem like good things for a logo to convey.

She tries all kinds of different logo templates and so many different fonts, eventually she's not sure *Hoffman* and *Hardware* are words anymore.

According to her research, they need a visual element that isn't text based. It's not like Elsie's going to come up with the Nike swoosh, but there needs to be something. Whatever she creates won't even necessarily be the final logo. She just needs something to show her dad—a picture's worth a thousand words, right? She needs him to actually *see* the potential in a refresh. They can hire a graphic designer to tighten up her design later. Maybe by the time they get to that, she can ask Ginny for help.

Elsie looks at the two *H*s. As much as she'd rather not think about Nazi sympathizer Coco Chanel, she ran across the double-*C* Chanel logo more than once in her research. Connecting the bottom of one H to the top of the other makes it look like a railroad track; connecting their sides looks a bit like a fence, which could be worse. She's onto something.

It takes another hour of tinkering before she's satisfied.

Two navy-blue *H*s, the bottom right of one forming the top left of the other, and a yellow caret sitting above the top *H*, like a roof. It's a simple, identifiable element, and if Elsie squints, she can imagine it looks like a house with a deck attached. Plus, it scales easily into a full logo—add *offman* and *ardware* to each *H*. The main font is sans serif, but the cursive script is still there, *Beginner Friendly, Expert Approved* like a curved path underneath everything.

She's probably been looking at it for too long to be objective, but whatever. She fucking loves it.

She texts a picture to Danielle.

> Gonna sleep on it, but what do you think?

Before her sister can respond, Elsie notices the time.

"Fuck."

She didn't get the chicken out of the freezer to defrost. Her mom's gonna kill her.

28

GINNY IS GOING TO TRY.

Sue's interior design business is an LLC, and Ginny looks into starting one of her own. The Minnesota state website about starting a business is not super encouraging; it brings up all the ways you could fail, tells you that about half of new businesses in the state do indeed fail within five years.

But whatever. Ginny's not doing this for five years. They're doing it for six months, and if it's not working, they'll find a "real" job.

It's different than they expected, adjusting to not having a day job. They keep thinking they need to check their email, or randomly worrying they've missed a deadline. Their days feel endless without a nine-to-five to fill them. That's a lie—their days feel endless without Elsie. No good-morning or good-night texts. No lunches. No middle-of-the-afternoon memes about naps or coffee or quitting your job and walking into the forest.

The days aren't actually endless, of course. The thing about starting your own business is it's a lot of fucking work. Research and forms and all the worrying they try to keep a lid on. Will they make enough to support themself? Is turning a hobby they love into their sole source of income a terrible idea? Will it ruin their love for the work?

Beyond more abstract questions, there are practical ones, too. Finding health insurance without an employer was a nightmare. And if they're going to register an LLC, it needs a name. What the fuck are they gonna call this thing?

All of this is on top of finishing up their grandpa's bathroom, and fixing the gate latch, and building him a new table for the breakfast nook. Ginny is bone tired at the end of the day, muscles achy and knees worse, and still each morning they get up to take Rufus to the dog park.

Maybe it's not healthy, working so hard they barely have time to think about Elsie. Maybe they need to, like, *process their feelings* or some shit. But that's not right—Ginny has known her feelings for years. Being in love with Elsie wasn't the problem; putting Elsie first was the problem.

The whole point of this . . . *trial separation* thing is that they need to figure out what they want their life to be like, regardless of Elsie.

Whether Elsie is in their life or not, they want to keep fostering dogs.

Whether Elsie is in their life or not, they want to build shit.

So no matter how much Ginny fucking misses their best friend, they keep doing what they're doing.

When they finish at Bapa's, they reach out to Sue's friends about the bed. Ginny meets Zina and Shea at a coffee shop in Loring Park. Shea is one of the most beautiful women Ginny has ever seen. She's all perfectly straight glossy black hair and flawless brown skin.

"Are you a hugger?" she says, and Ginny wants to say no just because they're afraid they'll mess up part of her perfect ensemble.

But Ginny says yes, and fuck, Shea even *smells* amazing.

Ginny blinks as they pull back, and Zina's laughter makes her curly hair bounce.

"That's how everybody responds to Shea," she says.

Ginny's face flushes.

"Don't be embarrassed, babe—I'm obsessed with her, too!" Zina hugs them next, and smells different, like fresh linen instead of lilacs, but just as good.

Ginny was there early, is already set up in a corner booth with coffee and their notebook. They watch the other two as they order. Even though Shea's in heels that would break Ginny's ankles, the top of her head barely reaches Zina's chin. Zina keeps a hand at the small of Shea's back the whole time, and Shea leans into them. It's so . . . simple. Easy.

They join Ginny at the table, sliding into one side of the booth next to each other. Ginny picks up their pen, all business.

"I've made beds before," they say, "but nothing like this. I've done my research and I'm confident I can create something perfect for you, but I'll need your input. Anything custom-made requires a lot of communication. I promise I won't be offended if you hate something I sketch up. This is about *you*—my feelings will only be hurt if you're not honest with me."

There's a momentary ache in Ginny's chest. They weren't honest with Elsie. They let out the feeling with their breath. They can't think about her.

Except it's hard for them not to. Zina and Shea remind Ginny of Elsie and themself, of how they used to be. They're completely at ease and in sync with each other, sharing a muffin and finishing each other's sentences.

"We have a couple of play partners who sometimes join us," Zina is saying. "We'd like enough hard points so I can suspend this one and a second person at the same time."

Shea giggles. "She likes to have everyone at her mercy at once."

"As though we only do this for me," Zina says. She picks a muffin crumb off Shea's chest and pops it in her mouth.

"I never said I didn't like it, too!" Shea looks at Ginny. "You ever try suspension, sweetheart?"

"I haven't," Ginny says. "But don't worry. I've done my research."

That made them think of Elsie, too, of all the things they hadn't been interested in before, but they're interested in with her. This is why they have to overwork themself; any moment of peace, and their traitorous brain thinks of Elsie.

29

ON TUESDAY, ELSIE GOES TO HER SISTER'S FOR DINNER. She doesn't do that enough. They do family dinners, but that's everyone, busy and loud. It's nice sitting with Danielle and Matthew and Declan, who's two and a half and so freakin' cute Elsie could die.

After dinner, Matthew gets Declan ready for bed and Danielle cleans the kitchen and Elsie connects her laptop to the TV in the living room. When the other two are ready, she's got a presentation to practice.

With the amount of eggplant lasagna Elsie shoveled into her stomach, there's no room for anxious butterflies. And again, this is practice. She doesn't have to be perfect. Still, she breathes a sigh of relief at the end, when her sister and brother-in-law applaud. Danielle even lets out a little squeal.

"That was great," Matthew says.

"Seriously, Elsie, it's *so* good," Danielle says. "I knew it was going to be good, but you exceeded my expectations."

Danielle isn't one to bullshit, so she must mean it.

"Lemme see the logo again."

Elsie takes a seat on the sofa—she felt like she should stand for the presentation itself—and clicks BACK on her laptop, balanced on the arm of the couch.

"I really love it," Danielle says of the logo. "I assume Ginny helped, yeah?"

Elsie wasn't ready for that question.

"Oh, uh." She swallows. "No."

"Well, what do they think? They're the graphic design major, after all."

"I, uh—I don't know." Elsie tucks her hair behind her ear. "I haven't shown it to them."

Danielle narrows her eyes. "What do you mean?"

"Exactly what I said. I haven't shown it to them."

"Why not?"

Elsie shrugs. "No particular reason."

"Bullshit. Neither of you does anything without the other knowing. What's going on?"

"Nothing!" Elsie insists, though this is clearly a losing battle.

"I'm, uh, gonna go check on Declan," Matthew says, rising from the sofa. "It was a great presentation, Elsie. I don't know how your dad could say no."

Elsie's smile feels wobbly. "Thanks, Matthew."

He flees the room. Danielle is still looking expectantly at Elsie.

"Explain," she says.

No one else knows what happened on the trip.

Or—maybe Ginny told someone. Elsie doesn't know. Elsie doesn't know about anything Ginny has done in weeks. Most of the time, she can convince herself that's fine. That Ginny is taking their time and will reach out when they're ready. But under Danielle's suspicious but kind eyes, Elsie crumbles.

"We basically haven't talked since the trip." She barely gets the words out, her voice cracking around a sudden lump in her throat.

"Els," Danielle says, moving to sit next to her on the couch.

It's supposed to be comforting, but that's what Ginny calls her, what they used to call her anyway, and the tears welling in her eyes overflow down her cheeks.

Danielle rubs her back. "What happened?"

Elsie sniffles. She hates crying in front of people. She focuses on Danielle's hand, moving in small gentle circles, and doesn't respond until she's managed to stop her tears.

"We hooked up on the trip."

It sounds so trivial when she puts it like that, but that's what happened.

"Finally," Danielle says, so quietly Elsie doesn't know if she was meant to hear it.

"What?" Elsie rubs at her eyes. "What do you mean, *finally*?"

"Nothing. Why haven't you talked since the trip?"

"No," Elsie says. "What did you mean?"

Danielle's hand stills. She tilts her head like she's weighing what to say, but when she finally speaks her tone is no-nonsense. "Elsie, come on. The two of you have been in love for like as long as you've known each other."

Elsie swallows. Danielle raises her eyebrows like she's daring Elsie to deny it.

Elsie's not sure she can, though. Maybe they *have* been in love this whole time. Elsie wanted to kiss Ginny before their first kiss. She wanted to kiss Ginny after. She wanted to go to the dance with them in tenth grade. But they were best friends, and that was more than enough. She tried not to think about what she wanted. The possibility of messing up their friendship was too scary.

And then that was exactly what happened. Elsie overcame her fear, convinced herself not to be so scared. Elsie got what she wanted. And now everything is ruined.

"I think you're right," she tells her sister. "But it doesn't matter."

"Of course it matters."

"No, listen," Elsie says.

She explains everything. The pact to speak up for what she wanted. The promise nothing would ruin their friendship. The sex—not in explicit detail, but enough to make it clear that it was *different,* somehow. That it felt bigger than anything Elsie had ever done before. And then she explains the email. The lie. The fight.

Danielle interrupts, then. "Can I say something you might not like?"

"Well, now you have to because I need to know what it is."

"I just . . . I feel like maybe you overreacted about the job thing?" She says it like a question. "I can understand why Ginny wouldn't tell you about it."

"I can now, too," Elsie admits.

It's easier to understand, explaining it to Danielle. It's easier to understand, outside of the moment. Outside of the terror that they'd just agreed to flip their relationship upside down, and it'd been based on a lie.

"But at the time it felt like what Derrick had done," Elsie continues. "Like someone I loved doing something they thought was right on my behalf."

"But it was their job, not yours."

"No, I know. But I was nervous about dating—excited, yeah, but it was this huge new change, and I was afraid it wasn't going to work. And Ginny had spent the whole week telling me that what I wanted mattered. That I shouldn't automatically put other people first. But then it felt like they did that." Elsie shouldn't have admitted any of this. It's embarrassing, and painful, and she doesn't want to talk about it. More words come out anyway. "And it just—the trip didn't feel like real life. And Ginny quitting their job reminded me of all the obstacles in real life. And even if now I can understand why they didn't tell me—they lied to me. For a week. More, even—I don't know exactly when they quit. How could we start a relationship like that? All my fears came back."

"So you lashed out."

"I lashed out." Elsie looks at the floor. She tries to swallow the rock in her throat. The fight itself was bad enough, but the next part is worse. "But I apologized. I apologized and tried to be friends again and Ginny said no."

"What?"

"They said I was right. And we needed time apart. And we haven't talked since."

It hurts to say. It hurts to think about.

"Talk to them," Danielle says, like it's that simple. Like it doesn't feel like fifteen years of friendship have gone up in smoke. "Tell them you want to be together."

Elsie shakes her head. She can't do this right now.

"Let's talk about this later." Her voice sounds sure, even while the words feel more like a plea. "What do you think about the presentation? What questions should I be prepared for from Dad? I don't want to fuck this up."

"Elsie."

"Please, Danielle."

Her sister sighs, but they go back to the brand refresh.

Danielle asks questions, tries to poke holes, find weaknesses in Elsie's arguments. But unlike everything with Ginny, Elsie has all the answers.

~~~~~

AS THEY SAY GOODBYE, DANIELLE HUGS ELSIE, LONG AND HARD.

"I just want to make sure you know what you're doing," she says quietly.

"Thanks for dinner," Elsie says.

But she thinks about that on the way back to their parents' house. What *is* she doing?

She's doing what Ginny wants by giving them space. But it's not just that—she's taking the space, too.

Elsie had been comfortable. Before the trip, she didn't think much about what she wanted. Her life was fine. Her relationship was fine. Her job was fine. She liked her life well enough. She loved her lunches with Ginny. Loved any time she got to spend with Ginny.

But Ginny can't be the only thing in Elsie's life that makes her happy. That's not healthy, for either of them. So this space is for Elsie, too. They're both taking time to learn how to be themselves without each other. And Elsie *is* figuring it out. She's doing things she's never done before, all by herself. She's focusing on herself right now, and that's important. What she wants matters. Both separate from Ginny and when they're involved.

Because yes, she has wanted to be with them. For years, she wanted to, but she was scared. Now, it's not fear that holds her back; it's knowledge. The knowledge that if they try for a romantic relationship and it doesn't work, they'll lose their friendship, too. Because that's what happened. Romance, sex, all that—it ruined the friendship. The trip was amazing. It was everything Elsie thought it could be. Holding Ginny's hand in public. Kissing them. Just getting to *be* with them. It was wonderful. But it wasn't worth it. Nothing would ever be worth losing Ginny as a friend.

So Elsie doesn't want to be with Ginny. She just wants her friend back.

30

Except it's two days before Valentine's Day—which means
it's one day before Palentine's Day, the holiday Ginny has cele-
brated every year since getting their license by going out somewhere fancy with Elsie. This does not help their stress level.

But Ginny is determined to be fine. She doesn't get to spend
time with Sue outside of woodworking stuff very often. She's not
wasting the opportunity.

Zina is already at the table when Sue and Ginny arrive, but
she holds up her hand the moment Ginny starts an update on
their bed.

"No work talk," Zina says. "We're here for a good time."

"I have a good time with my work," Ginny says over music
that's a touch too loud. "That's the whole point of this LLC I still
need a name for."

"This one hasn't helped you?" Zina asks, smacking the back of her hand lightly into Sue's shoulder. "She's the one who came up with our trivia team name."

"Somehow I don't think Ginny wants to name their company something like Dykes on Bikes," Sue says.

"That's the team name?" Ginny asks.

"We've been playing since before any of us could afford cars."

"The same group?"

"Other folks have come and gone but it's always been me and Sue," Zina says. "There's Shea and Brian and Aadi and Neena, who come when they can. The years Sue was dating Chloe we never lost, but the breakup ruined that."

"At least I brought in someone good instead of that ginger you and Shea invited who kept insisting her wrong answers were right."

"That was *one* time."

"Yeah, and Chloe only left the team for a couple of months."

"Are you talking about me again?" a round white woman asks, slinging an arm over Sue's shoulders.

"Always," Sue says.

The woman kisses both of Sue's cheeks, then takes off her coat and drapes it over the next chair.

"Chloe," she says, taking a seat and extending a hand to Ginny.

"Ginny." They shake her hand. "You're . . . the ex?"

Chloe cackles. "Almost a decade ago, sure. Now I prefer to go by my own name."

Ginny's cheeks flush, but Chloe doesn't seem the least bit offended.

"We were just telling them the team history," Zina says. She leans over to air-kiss Chloe hello as well.

"A rich and storied history, for certain," Chloe says. "Did we get out the chart of who all has dated, fucked, or had a situationship?"

"Didn't wanna overwhelm the kid," Sue says. "How's wedding planning?"

"June has been a lifesaver," Chloe says. "She's the most organized person I've ever met."

"Grumpy June?" Sue asks. To Ginny, she says, "The florist from the market who's always scowling."

"I'll be sure not to tell her you call her that," Chloe says. "She may not believe in love, but her spreadsheets work just fine."

They order drinks and talk wedding planning. Ginny tries not to think about Elsie.

"Ginny just went on a honeymoon," Sue says, and Ginny wonders why God hates her.

There's a chorus of *congratulations*!

"No, no, it wasn't mine." That gets a smirk from Sue and eyebrow raises from both Chloe and Zina. "It was my best friend's." Can they even still call Elsie that? "Or, well—it was *supposed* to be a honeymoon. The marriage didn't actually happen."

"Oof," Zina says.

"Tell me about it," Ginny says, for completely different reasons. "Anyway. Will you have a honeymoon?"

That sends Chloe into a long explanation of the decision

process when she wanted to go somewhere they could lie on a beach and her fiancée wanted to go on a bike trip through the UK.

"Dykes on bikes," Sue says, and it doesn't slow Chloe down at all.

Her story only ends once "Say My Name" by Destiny's Child begins, which is apparently the start to trivia.

"So, anyway, we're going to Greece and taking a day trip around Crete on bikes!" she says in a rush, just as the curtain to the back opens and three drag queens emerge to lip-sync.

Ginny does a double take at the last queen to appear: it's Shea. She looks even better than the last time Ginny saw her—makeup more exaggerated but still flawless. Her hair is in a high pony that she swings around her head during the chorus. The end hits a patron in the face, and they look thrilled. Thank god Ginny remembered to get cash for tips. There's a QR code on each table, too, but it's much more satisfying to hand a queen a bill while she sings to you than to tip through your phone.

All three queens end the song in splits, to raucous applause. After, Shea joins their table, squeezing in next to Zina while the other two queens greet the crowd. They're the hosts for trivia.

"Perfect, as always," Zina says, dropping a kiss on Shea's mouth.

"Thank you, baby."

"That was amazing!" Ginny says. "I didn't know you did drag."

"Gotta pay the bills, sweetheart." Shea waves her wad of tips. "And how could I deny the people a face like this?"

"You give and you give," Chloe says.

Shea puts a hand over her heart, faux sincere. "I really do."

"You got another performance or are you gonna be able to focus on winning this week?" Sue asks.

"Excuse that sass," Shea says. "I remember carrying the team on my back last week."

"Only because one of the categories was fashion history."

"Yes"—Shea sips from the straw in Zina's gin and tonic—"and you get all of your clothes from Duluth Trading Company."

"They have nice flannels!"

"You're such a dyke," Shea says, voice laced with affection. "And to answer your question, no more performances. They just needed a third for the intro."

Zina presses a kiss to the side of her head. "And you're always up for being a third."

"Obviously." Shea turns her body completely toward Ginny. "Darling. How are you?"

"Uh," Ginny says, the intensity of attention from such a beautiful woman overwhelming. "Good. I'm good."

Shea puts her hand on Ginny's. "I'm so glad. What have you been—"

"Excuse me, Miss Mouth Almighty," one of the other queens says into their microphone. "Are you here to socialize or for trivia?"

"Oh, I thought I was just here to lip-sync better than you," Shea calls back, and the crowd laughs.

Ginny is grateful for the distraction of trivia. They're not interested in talking about themself. And anyway, if they can't talk about work, there's not much to talk about. But trivia lets them become a part of this well-established group. Lets them soak in the queerness and community. Without a day job, they don't see people very often. Apparently, even introverts need company sometimes.

Between rounds one and two, with Sue and Zina in the bathroom and Chloe off chatting at another table, Shea asks Ginny about the bed. "Sue very explicitly said we weren't supposed to let you talk about work, but I can't help it. I'm so excited."

Apparently Sue was serious about this whole *all work and no play* thing, but Ginny is glad to get to talk woodworking. Work is *fun,* now. Sure, there's the underlying worry about not making enough money and having to find a "real" job again, but in general, Ginny likes what they're doing.

"The software I'm sketching plans in lets me do something called finite element analysis to determine the effects of different forces on the lumber and joints," Ginny explains. "FEA is normally used for, like, making airplanes and stuff—it's a bit overkill for most furniture, but it's perfect for ensuring hard points can hold someone, whether they be your size or mine."

"You're brilliant," Shea says.

Ginny's insides go warm at the compliment. Admittedly that's also probably from the alcohol, but either way, it's nice.

"And you know, if *you* are ever interested in suspension . . ."

Zina and Sue return at that moment, and Shea clamps her mouth closed, barely suppressing a giggle.

Sue glares. "Leave you alone for two minutes and you're *hitting* on Ginny."

Ginny blinks. Is that what was happening?

Shea shrugs, all insouciance. "You're the one who said they needed a little fun in their life."

"Not that kind of fun," Sue says.

Ginny stares at the ice cubes melting in their cup and pretends they're not blushing bright red.

"They work for us right now, darling," Zina says. "Maybe let's wait until after they finish the bed to hit on them?"

"Speaking of the bed," Ginny says, desperate for a subject change, "I really could use help naming my LLC. I want to, like, honor my grandpa with it, since he's the one who got me into woodworking. But his name's *Ralph*."

Even Shea's laugh seems to sparkle.

"Ralph's probably not the best business name," Zina says. "What's something your grandpa loves?"

"Me," Ginny says with no hesitation.

"That's the cutest shit I've ever heard," Sue says.

The music starts for the next lip sync before they can brainstorm further.

By the end of the night, Ginny has run out of cash and tipped even more through the QR code, and the team has won a forty-dollar gift certificate to the bar for getting first place. Ginny's thrilled, but this is apparently a common occurrence, given that the rest of them use a gift certificate from last week to cover half their bill.

"What do you think of Skylark?" Ginny asks Sue while she drives them home.

Sue glances over at them. "I don't know what that is."

"For my LLC. Skylark Furniture. Or Skylark Furniture and Carpentry."

If the *and* was an ampersand, that could look really cute.

"Got a nice ring to it," Sue says. "Does it have to do with your grandpa?"

"It's his car."

"Your grandpa still drives?"

Ginny furrows her brow. "Yeah? He's only sixty-seven."

"God, you're an infant."

31

THE LAST TIME ELSIE MET WITH HER DAD ABOUT THE STORE'S MARKET-
ING, IT WAS ADMITTEDLY A BIT OF AN AMBUSH. That had seemed like
the only way to make him listen, and it still didn't work. This time,
she told him what the meeting was going to be about and didn't
back down when he sighed at her.

This time, she doesn't bring sandwiches; she brings a slide
deck.

She does it first thing in the morning, as soon as the store
opens. Any later would give nerves too much time to eat her
alive. There's no office or conference room or anything where
she could project a slideshow, so even though they're in the same
room, she shares her laptop screen to her dad's computer so they
can look at the slides at the same time.

Her presentation starts with the basics. Danielle swore Elsie
had done a good job distilling her old notes and research into
easily digestible bits of info. Her dad needs to understand the

marketing principles and theory before Elsie tries to sell him on her actual ideas. She encourages him to ask questions as she goes, and he actually does—not even in a *gotcha* way, but in a way where he genuinely seems interested.

"Now, if we were a big chain store, we would've hired another company to figure everything out for us," Elsie says. "They would've done staff and customer interviews. There would've been anonymous surveys. I'm sure we could learn something from that. But we also already know the most important stuff."

Her next slide is a picture of the legal pad she brainstormed on last week. Her dad smiles as he reads her handwriting, perfectly straight even though she was writing as fast as she could. Ms. Bern had really emphasized penmanship in third grade.

"This list was my starting point." She's already explained the highlights of brand identity and logo design. "The next slide is a potential logo. I'll explain the elements and my reasoning behind them. Obviously we can use an actual graphic designer to tinker with it. This is not anything final. But first, I just want you to sit with it for a while."

Elsie clicks to the next slide, then sets a timer on her phone. She gives her dad an entire minute to look at the logo. Sixty seconds doesn't sound like that long, but silently watching your dad, who is also your boss, look at something you did for work? It's all Elsie can do to sit still. She doesn't even let herself tap her foot.

Her brain searches for distraction and lands on Ginny.

It's Palentine's Day. Their holiday. Elsie always texts Ginny on Palentine's Day. Even though they're taking space, Ginny said that didn't mean they couldn't be friends. Sure, neither of them has texted since, but maybe Elsie could. It wouldn't be crossing any boundaries. If they can still be friends, Elsie can text. And after talking it through with Danielle earlier this week, that's what Elsie wants: to be friends.

It's scary not to know if Ginny wants that. Maybe time apart made Ginny realize they don't need her, don't miss her, are better off without her. That would be okay. Or—it'd be horrible, actually. Even having not talked in weeks, Elsie has never accepted the possibility of never again having Ginny in her life. But she would be okay. She knows that now. She can figure things out on her own.

Elsie's phone buzzes on her thigh, the timer going off. She blinks away thoughts of Ginny and looks at her dad, who's smiling at her. Elsie holds up a hand.

"Don't say anything yet," she instructs him. "I want you to write down your initial thoughts. Just for yourself—nothing you're going to have to show anyone else, so don't worry about complete sentences or being nice or anything."

She resets the timer.

Her dad only writes for thirty seconds. "Can't I just tell you I like it instead of writing this down?"

Elsie sucks in a breath. "Really?"

"I'm not saying it's perfect," he says, "and I want to hear your explanation of the elements or whatever. But I do like it."

That's about the best reaction Elsie could've hoped for.

She explains her process. Keeping some history while embracing change. She shows him the versatility of the new look— how the navy blue and yellow work on a white background, but they could also do it solely in navy, or yellow on a navy background. That the two *H*s with the yellow roof on top work as their own element. He nods along as she talks.

"This is just the first step," she says. "We'd need to refresh our visual brand everywhere and make things consistent throughout the store."

She shows him aisle markers in the sans serif font that matches the logo, as well as options for temporary displays in the original cursive.

"How much is this all going to cost me?" he asks.

Elsie was prepared for this question. Not with numbers, but with attitude.

"I considered using the budget that's been growing since I graduated," she says. "I wasn't sure you'd listen, so I thought about buying the new signage before telling you. But remember this?" She clicks back to the slide with the legal pad and reads one of her brainstormed attributes of the store. "*Family.* We are family owned and operated. I don't care about this stuff because brands and marketing and hardware stores are important to me. I care about this because Hoffman Hardware is important to me. I wanted this to be something we decide together."

It's the right answer, like she knew it would be. Not that that's the only reason she said it—she's being honest, not manipulative. But the way her dad tries to hide his smile shows her she's won.

"Okay, well," he says, "get me some quotes. We'll go from there."

She did it. She made her dad see reason when it came to a brand refresh. He actually listened to her. If she can do that, she can do anything.

As Elsie heads to the register to replace her mom, she gets her phone out.

32

GINNY SLEEPS TILL TEN THE MORNING AFTER DRAG TRIVIA. Not having a regular day job is really working for them.

There's an unread text on their phone when they wake up. It's from Elsie.

Happy Palentine's Day! ♡

Okay.

That's fine.

That's normal.

It *is* normal, really. On February 13, Ginny always wakes up to a text from Elsie. Usually it's much more effusive, talking about how great they are and how honored Elsie is to be their best friend. Palentine's has always been Ginny and Elsie's holiday. They dress up, go out somewhere fancy, alternate who pays each year. This year it's Ginny's turn.

Ginny doesn't know how to respond. They feed Rufus and let him out to play in the freshly fallen snow in the backyard. Then they register their business name online with the state and pay the fee.

Sue called them an infant last night, but they feel like a goddamn adult.

The heat of coffee in their mug warms Ginny's hands as they stand at the sliding door, watching Rufus bury his head in the snow. They haven't told Hearts of Hope yet, but Rufus is going to be a foster fail. Not because there's a single thing wrong with him, but because Ginny is too attached. He's been good company the last three weeks.

Last night was good company, too. Ginny was surrounded by people who were the exact type of queer they want to be—authentic, genuine, real. *Happy.*

And Ginny *is* happy about a lot of things. The whole point of taking space from Elsie was to live life for themself, and they are. They're doing what *they* want, not building a life around her. But fuck, they miss her.

They miss the big stuff, but the little stuff, too. Taking dumb pictures. Elsie reading a book in the garage while Ginny works. Elsie sneaking treats to their foster dogs, even though that also annoys the fuck out of Ginny. Elsie doing full recaps of *Real Housewives* episodes Ginny has never had an iota of interest in watching. When Elsie loves a book so much she steals Ginny's phone to borrow the audiobook from the library so they can listen while they build.

Maybe they don't have to miss it all. They needed space after the trip, but now? Elsie has reached out. They can reconnect. They can be okay. This isolation was self-inflicted. It was important and it was necessary, but Ginny's done with it now.

> Happy Palentine's Day. Can I take you to lunch?

~~~

GINNY IDLES THEIR TRUCK OUTSIDE THE BACK OF THE STORE LIKE THE LAST MONTH NEVER HAPPENED. It could be mid-January—when Elsie emerges, she's in the same red hat and mittens she wore the day Ginny quit their job.

But everything else is different. The way Ginny's chest clenches at the sight of her. The timidness in Elsie's smile once she climbs into the truck.

"Hi." Her voice is soft.

Ginny breathes. "Hi."

"It's good to see you."

"You too."

They look at each other for a moment, before Ginny clears their throat and shifts the truck into drive. The long-term silence between them is a hurdle they need to leap over as quickly as possible, but it's a lot easier to do without having to hold eye contact.

"Thanks for giving me space," Ginny says once they're on the road. "I needed to stand on my own two feet and all that. Which I've done. And now I, uh, I miss you."

"The second we get out of this car I'm hugging you so hard," Elsie says.

Ginny's face breaks open in a grin. They couldn't hold it back if they tried. But they have more to say.

"I told you nothing was going to ruin our friendship, and then I kind of abandoned you for a while there. I'm sorry. Can you forgive me?"

"There's nothing to forgive," Elsie says, waving a mittened hand. "You needed time. It was good. For both of us."

Even only seeing it out of the corner of their eye, Ginny is bowled over by how beautiful Elsie's smile is. Their heart feels lighter than it has in weeks.

"I have so much to tell you—" they both say at the same time, then laugh.

"We have so much to catch up on. Tell me the most important thing that's happened since we—" Elsie trips over the sentence. "Since the trip."

This, Ginny thinks. They've been shaping their life into what they want it to be, all on their own, but still, the most important thing that's happened is making up with Elsie.

"I created an LLC for woodworking," they say instead.

"No shit!" Elsie smacks their arm. "That's so fucking cool!"

Ginny grins, a little sheepish. "It is, yeah."

"So you're going for it? All woodworking, no day job?"

"I am."

They tell her about doing Bapa's bathroom and looking at finances with Sue. They tell her about building the bed for Zina and Shea—leaving out the suspension part of it. They're not ready to talk about sex with Elsie. Not yet. They tell her about Rufus, too, and Elsie plucks their phone from the cup holder to scroll through pictures.

She asks so many questions, Ginny talks about themself all the way to the restaurant. They want to know what she's been up to, too, but it's nice, how much they have going on.

Elsie sticks to her word. As soon as they're parked, she leaps out of the truck, meets Ginny at the driver's-side door, and wraps them in a hug. It's tight enough they lose their breath.

"I missed you so fucking much," she says.

Ginny's face presses into Elsie's shoulder. She feels so good in their arms. She smells like the perfume she's worn since middle school, and it almost makes Ginny cry. They know they needed the space, but fuck. They need this. They need Elsie.

"You're stuck with me for life, Holtz," Elsie says, right into Ginny's ear.

"For life, Hoffman," Ginny says back.

Elsie releases the hug and beams. "C'mon. I'm *starving.*"

When they're seated, food on trays in front of them, Ginny finally asks after Elsie.

"What about you?"

Elsie's already got three fries in her mouth.

"What's the most important thing that's happened since the trip?"

"This," Elsie says.

Immediately, she laughs, but it's not sincere. Ginny knows Elsie's normal laugh, and this isn't it. This is her fake, embarrassed laugh. Ginny doesn't think they've ever heard it directed at them.

"No, but seriously," Elsie says, like her first answer was a joke, "I designed a new logo for the store, and this morning I showed it to my dad, and he actually liked it!"

Ginny lets it go. They don't need to know every feeling Elsie is having. They can focus on the good and let the awkward shake itself out.

"This morning?" they say. "This just happened, and you let me talk about myself the whole ride here?"

"I wanted to know what you were doing!"

Ginny puts their burger down and holds out a hand. "Lemme see!"

"Okay, but please recognize I do not have a graphic design degree and go easy on me."

Elsie opens a photo and slides her phone across the table, then hides her face in her hands. It's a decent logo—clean, modern, unique. Not busy, like their current sign.

"It's good!"

Elsie parts her fingers to peek at Ginny. "Really?"

"Really! Of course your dad liked it. I know he's been a dick about branding, but how could he not like this?"

Elsie finally drops her hands from her face, which is the cutest shade of pink. Ginny's chest feels warm. They missed this.

"Yeah, so, like, I did a whole presentation," Elsie says. "And he actually listened and asked good questions and—yeah. It felt good."

"I'm proud of you."

Elsie goes even pinker. "Shut up."

"I am! I know it's not always easy, talking with your family—especially your dad—about store stuff."

"Yeah, well. Someone taught me to speak up for myself recently." She shoves another fry in her mouth, then talks while chewing, like she's trying to pretend she didn't say that. "So anyway, I've got other ideas that go along with that, but I started with the visual stuff to ease my dad into it."

Was this what it was like for Elsie, back in high school? Ignoring the awkwardness, pretending it wasn't there and powering through? At least Ginny knows they can do it. The two of them have gotten through everything so far; they'll get through this, too.

"That's smart to ease him into it," Ginny says. "Tell me all these other ideas, though."

Elsie smiles, grateful Ginny's trying to be normal, maybe. Or excited to talk about her ideas. It doesn't matter why, just that it's her real smile. Ginny knows.

"Well, so, this refresh of our visual brand should come with a rededication to our ideals." She sounds so fucking smart. "We say we're beginner friendly, but the only beginners we're reaching are the ones willing to come to a hardware store and ask questions. There are so many potential customers who are too overwhelmed to get started. I want to do DIY classes. Beginner ones. So people who don't know that much don't feel intimidated or laughed at or whatever. I was even thinking you could teach one. Or Sue. Or—I don't know, even your grandpa with the spinny thing."

"Lathe," Ginny provides. "And he would absolutely love that."

"We could do one a month, and that's three months right there. Plus, we could get plumbers, electricians. Any sort of tradesperson. I'm not actually interested in tools, and I've never *had* to learn about them, because my dad or brothers or you have always handled stuff for me. But what about people who don't have those connections? If we help teach them, we can create a customer from someone who isn't currently one."

Ginny loves listening to Elsie talk about something she cares about.

"And, like, you know how my dad loves to feel super smart helping people who don't know stuff? This is gonna be a hard sell but . . . I want to put him on TikTok."

Ginny bursts out laughing, and Elsie's face falls.

"No—" They put a comforting hand on her arm across the table, still chuckling. "I'm not laughing at the idea. It's a great idea. I'm just imagining the videos. They're gonna be hilarious."

Elsie looks at Ginny's hand. Ginny takes it back. Apparently they're going to have to relearn how to touch each other, just like sophomore year.

Ginny wanted things to go back to normal. They feel normal, some of the time, but Elsie seems . . . unsure. She keeps looking at them—not with pity, but with *something*. There's just something *off*. Probably it's that they haven't talked in weeks. Ginny themself isn't completely certain how to act, how to be normal, after the time apart. And if there's a bigger reason for Elsie's awkwardness, Ginny doesn't ask. Whatever Elsie feels is not Ginny's responsibility. If she wants to talk about something, she can bring it up.

33

IT'S SO NICE TO HAVE LUNCH WITH GINNY AGAIN. To hear their voice and see their smile. To make them laugh.

This is what Elsie wanted.

She wanted to be friends with Ginny.

Obviously, everything they did on the honeymoon messed up their friendship. So they're doing exactly what Elsie suggested three weeks ago: pretending the trip never happened and going back to being friends. They're both stronger now, more sure of themselves, so the friendship will be better, too.

They make plans to do lunch again. Not until Monday, which is fine. They don't have to do lunch every day to be best friends. It's fine. It's great. It's what Elsie wanted.

So it's a little harder than she expected to pretend the trip didn't happen, but that's fine. So she has to hold back the feelings that want to burst out of her, the way her heart skips a beat when Ginny touches her. She can handle that. It's worth it.

Valentine's Day comes and goes—unsurprisingly, it's not a busy day for the store—and by Saturday morning, the brand refresh is an official project. They might not get to do everything Elsie wants—shit's expensive, after all—but her dad has at least committed to changing the sign out front. He's been remarkably easygoing about everything. When Danielle revealed she'd been budgeting more for a brand refresh than he'd agreed to when Elsie graduated, he didn't even glower—he *chuckled*.

Elsie and Danielle shared a look of bafflement, but neither voiced it. You don't look a gift horse in the mouth.

Which is why Elsie doesn't say anything but *thank you* when her dad clears a tiny corner of his desk. For her. The rest of the office is a disaster, as always, but there's just enough room on the desk for Elsie to set up her laptop and work. Because this is part of her job now, working on her laptop in her dad's office instead of staffing the register. It makes her want to scream with joy, but she holds back. Stays professional. Does her job.

She's gathering quotes for now. Potential costs for tinkering with her logo, updating their signage, redesigning the website. She makes spreadsheets. Color-codes them. Feels like she's back in school again, but in a good way.

"Elsie to the register, please. Elsie to the register."

Elsie sighs at her mom's voice over the intercom. Of course she can't have even an hour to focus.

It turns out she's not actually needed at the register.

No. It's worse. Or if not *worse,* much stranger.

Derrick is standing in the checkout lane chatting with Elsie's mother. Elsie hasn't seen him since before Santa Lupita. He made himself scarce when she moved her things from the apartment to her parents' house and left her key on the kitchen counter.

"Here she is," Elsie's mom says, and Derrick looks up at her.

His smile still makes Elsie's heart flutter. "Hey."

"Hey," Elsie says.

"He wondered if you could take a break and get coffee," Elsie's mom says for him. "I said that was fine."

That's not exactly her decision to make, but Elsie is too baffled by Derrick's random appearance to complain.

"Sure," she says. "But I don't have long."

They go to the coffee shop across the street. Elsie has always wished she could up her queer cred by drinking only iced coffee, even in winter, but while it's an unseasonably warm day for mid-February, she still orders a hot red velvet mocha, their Valentine's special. She takes the cardboard sleeve off the cup so her chronically cold fingers can benefit from direct heat.

The conversation is surface level—*Hi, how have you been? Crazy weather, huh? Damn climate change*—until they sit at a table in the corner with their drinks. Derrick clears his throat, then, and looks at his hands, big enough to make the cup in them look small.

"I've done a lot of thinking since you broke things off, which you were totally right to do, by the way. I did not give you enough consideration when I planned the wedding. Or when I proposed, for that matter. Your graduation should've been about *you*. I'm sorry I fucked that up."

It's so unexpected, Elsie's brain lags in processing. This is more reflection than Derrick did the entire time they were together.

"Thanks?" Elsie says, and it comes out like a question.

Derrick chuckles sheepishly. "Sorry, that's not even what I wanted to say, just something I figured out in therapy recently."

"Therapy?"

"Yeah, it's super helpful. Cash totally calls me on my shit, and it's like—I'm not even doing this stuff intentionally, I just need someone to point it out. Like when they asked about the proposal, it took me a while to understand what they were getting at, but now that I figured it out I feel so stupid."

They? Does her ex somehow have a nonbinary therapist? Elsie has no idea what's happening.

"I know intent isn't as important as impact," Derrick says, "but I do want you to know I never meant to steal your spotlight. I was thinking it was a great time to propose because I wanted all your family and friends to be there and share in the joy, but obviously it should have been about you, not us. I'm sorry."

What. The. Fuck. (Complimentary.)

"Okay," Elsie says. "Thank you." It's not a question this time. She does have one, though. "You figured out all of this in like three weeks of therapy?"

Derrick laughs. "Yeah. I told Cash I needed tough love and, uh, they sort of shoved me off the deep end." He takes a sip of his coffee. "But anyway, that's not what I wanted to talk about. Or, like, it's part of it, I guess. But yeah. The reason I asked you to coffee is—I totally understand if you don't want to. No hard feelings either way."

Elsie has no idea what he's talking about. He makes eye contact, holds it.

"I want to give us another shot. Like, as a couple."

"Oh," Elsie says.

Derrick keeps going. "Not like let's be engaged again, but even just dating. I love you, Elsie. And I can see a lot of things I did wrong. Probably not everything, because I'm still learning, obviously. But I want to learn with you. I want to be better with you. If that's something you'd be open to."

Elsie has barely thought about Derrick since she ended things.

"Sorry," he says when she doesn't respond immediately. "Maybe I shouldn't have put you on the spot like this. But it felt like something I had to ask in person."

He's showing more emotional intelligence in one conversation than he ever has before. But his emotional intelligence, or lack thereof, wasn't what made her end things.

Last month, Elsie thought life was simple. She thought she knew how things were going to go. How they were supposed to go. Simple seemed nice. And she could still have it, if she wanted. She could say yes. It'd be easy.

Simple and easy isn't particularly romantic.

"I know you aren't sure what you want." His voice isn't quite as strong as usual, like he's realized he's fighting a losing battle. "But I thought maybe we could figure it out together."

"I *am* sure what I want," Elsie says. She didn't know until right now, but she is. "I'm sorry, really. But I'm not interested in getting back together. I have to go."

She should explain more. She should let him down gently. She should go back to the store, at least to tell someone she's taking a longer break.

But Elsie doesn't care about *should*.

34

WITH THE SUN OUT AND THE TEMPERATURE ABOVE FREEZING, THERE ARE ENOUGH PEOPLE AT THE MARKET THAT ELSIE CAN MAKE SURE GINNY DOESN'T SEE HER UNTIL SHE'S READY FOR THEM TO. Her stomach is in knots. She knows what she wants, and she knows what she has to do, but that doesn't mean it's not scary as hell.

It's not that Elsie has changed her mind. It's not that she wants to kiss Ginny so much it's worth risking the friendship. It's that romance didn't ruin anything.

Nothing was ruined. They both needed time apart and they took it. But they came back to each other. They'll always come back to each other.

Just like in high school. Elsie worked *hard* to stay friends with Ginny after turning them down. And she'll do that again, if she needs to. Their friendship can only be ruined if they let it be, and Elsie refuses to allow that. She won't let Ginny slip through her fingers.

But the only way to get what she wants most is to ask for it. So she's going to ask.

Elsie goes to the florist's stall—she's not sure if it's more about procrastinating or about having something beautiful to offer Ginny. The stall is all flowers too bright for February in Minneapolis, but the scowl on the face of the brunette who's running it is perfectly right for the season.

After spending an inordinate amount of time choosing between two bouquets of roses, Elsie finally picks one, holding it out to the florist with water dripping from the stems.

"Fifteen bucks," the florist says. Then, with enthusiasm that seems forced: "It's a great choice. For someone special?"

Elsie hands over her credit card. She can't handle small talk right now. "I'm about to go tell my best friend I'm in love with them."

The florist blinks. "Oh. Nice." She runs the credit card. "Let me wrap these. I'll be quick."

Elsie's stomach flip-flops. She's really doing this.

She hovers near the entrance of the market with the flowers. Sue is talking to a customer at her and Ginny's stall, and Elsie doesn't want to interrupt. She wants to talk to Ginny alone. When Sue is done with the customer—who doesn't buy anything—she says something to Ginny, then heads toward the bathroom.

It's now or never.

When Ginny's eyes land on Elsie as she approaches, their brow furrows. Maybe the dozen red roses are too much.

No.

Elsie refuses to second-guess herself. She knows what she wants.

"Els," Ginny says. It feels so good to hear the nickname. "What are you doing here?"

"I want to thank you," Elsie says. "Everything I've done while we weren't talking—like all the stuff at the store—it's because of you."

Ginny's smile is so fucking sweet. "Nah, that's all you. I'm proud of you."

They're not getting it. The adrenaline in Elsie's veins has her heart thundering like she's in fight or flight.

"No, like—it's what I want," she says. "It's what's best for the store. But it's because of you. You finally made me realize that what I want matters, that good things are worth fighting for. And that's not—I don't mean to give you all the credit, because I do know this is me. These are my ideas. I'm the one fighting for them. But what I'm saying is I wouldn't be who I am if it weren't for you. You make me better."

That smile goes even bigger. Elsie's not done.

"And in realizing that what I want matters—that what I want is worth fighting for . . ." She takes a deep breath. "I don't want to be your friend."

Ginny flinches like they've been slapped.

"No, not like that," Elsie rushes to say. "Of course I want to be your friend. You're my best friend. But I don't want to go back to being friends and pretending like I'm not in love with you."

I'm in love with you. She said it. She said it in public. She said it, and Ginny is just looking at her, shocked into silence.

Elsie thrusts the flowers out at them. "These are for you. If you want them."

Ginny's eyes are as gray as the Minnesota winter sky. Their mouth turns up at the corners, and hope springs in Elsie's chest.

"Say it again."

"These are for you?"

Ginny raises their eyebrows. Elsie knows that's not what they wanted her to say.

She's not sure she's ever been this brave in her entire life, but the words come easy. "I'm in love with you. And maybe it would've been smarter not to say anything. Maybe I've just made everything that was already kind of weird and awkward even more weird and awkward. We're rebuilding our friendship, and I'm thrilled about that. But if I could have anything I want?" She shrugs, because it's so obvious. "I want to kiss you every day for the rest of my life."

Ginny's smile goes full-blown grin. That means—they want—Elsie needs them to say something. She can't be *sure* until they say something. Ginny takes the flowers and sets them on the coffee table in their stall.

"Why don't you start now?" they say.

Elsie swallows. "With the kissing?"

Ginny laughs, and it's the best sound in the world. "Yeah. With the kissing."

Elsie takes a step forward. Ginny stands there, waiting for her. Elsie's hands find their way to Ginny's face, pink cheeks and gray eyes and that perfect mouth just begging for a kiss, so Elsie gives it one.

It feels like that first kiss in Santa Lupita, like *relief* and *thank*

fuck. It feels better. Feels less like something Elsie has been waiting for and more like the start of something new. Feels like *forever*, and it's not scary at all.

Ginny breaks the kiss to squeeze Elsie in a hug. Elsie wants
to bury her face in Ginny's neck, but the height difference makes
that impossible when they're not in bed. She wants to be in bed
with Ginny. She wants to be anywhere with Ginny.

"You bought me flowers," Ginny whispers.

"Do you like them?"

"I love them." They stretch up to press a kiss against her
cheek. "I love *you*."

Elsie's whole body feels like butterflies.

"Wait a minute," Ginny says, pulling back but not letting go.
"Why aren't you at work?"

Elsie shrugs. "I figured out what I wanted, and I didn't wanna
wait."

Ginny's smile is all soft. "I love you."

"I love you."

It feels like the first time they've ever said it.

They stare into each other's eyes. In the back of her mind, Elsie knows they're in public. She knows they're being kind of gross
and obsessed with each other. She doesn't care one bit.

"I love you," Ginny says, tapping one finger against Elsie's
nose, "but you should go back to work."

Elsie sticks her bottom lip out. "Why?"

Ginny kisses her. It's a good fifteen seconds before they break
apart.

"Because if you're here I'm gonna keep doing that and no

one wants to buy furniture from someone who can't stop kissing their girlfriend."

"I'm your *girlfriend*." She kisses them again, shorter this time. "What if we just closed up shop for the day and you took me home?"

Now that she's allowed to kiss Ginny again, she never wants to stop.

"What if I just took you to my truck in the parking lot?" Ginny murmurs, clearly on the same page.

The rumble of their voice goes straight to Elsie's center. She would very much like some make-up sex, thank you.

"Love that you two have finally made up," Sue says, returning from wherever she was to ruin the moment. "But your PDA is scaring off the customers."

"You told her we were fighting?" Elsie asks Ginny. She likes the idea of them talking about her.

"I actually didn't," Ginny says. They haven't let go of Elsie.

Sue rolls her eyes. "Please. You never shut up about this girl normally, but I haven't heard a peep since the honeymoon. That, plus the hangdog, brokenhearted look on your face sometimes? Wasn't hard to figure out."

"I'm not brokenhearted," Ginny says, a little gruff, their cheeks even pinker.

"Not anymore," Sue says.

"Never again," Elsie says.

"Sue," Ginny says, still looking at Elsie. "Would you mind if I took off? I want to—"

"I'm pretty sure I know exactly what you want to do."

Elsie giggles.

Ginny finally looks at Sue instead. "Is that a yes?"

"Get out of here," Sue says. "Don't worry about loading up. I'll deal with it."

"You sure?"

"Go."

They abandon Elsie's parents' car at the market—Elsie doesn't care. She doesn't care about anything but Ginny's hand in hers on the center console.

"Rufus still pees when he's excited. Consider yourself warned."

"I thought we established I wasn't into water sports."

Ginny's laugh is loud. "God, I love you."

"I love you."

The sky is perfectly clear, perfectly blue. Like it's springtime. Like there should be buds on the trees instead of snow on the ground. Elsie certainly feels like she's blooming. The sun feels stronger, shafts of light through the truck's windshield making the whole world brighter than it was a few minutes ago. Ginny's hand keeps Elsie's warm.

When they get to Ginny's, Elsie puts the roses in a vase while Ginny takes Rufus out in the backyard. They haven't kissed since they left the farmers' market, like they both know that once they start, they won't be able to stop.

"Perfect timing," Elsie says when Ginny returns to the kitchen.

Rufus has done his business and is back in his crate, and the flowers are in water.

Ginny doesn't even look at the roses. They only have eyes for Elsie, crowding into her space until the counter digs into her back. Ginny bumps their nose gently against Elsie's. They still don't kiss her.

"What do you want?" they ask.

"You," Elsie says.

Elsie always gets what she wants.

ACKNOWLEDGMENTS

The usual suspects: Patrice Caldwell, Trinica Sampson-Vera, and the rest of the New Leaf team; Vicki Lame, Vanessa Aguirre, Meghan Harrington, and the rest of the Griffin team; Ashley Herring Blake and Emma Patricia and Tash McAdam and Zabe Doyle; my perfect wife.

Emma Veach and Jenna Miller and Mary Roach for answering my Twin Cities questions. Alyssa and Gus for doing the same and also carting me around town on my visit.

Jeff Spencer for answering my woodworking questions, even when I was asking about building a bed for BDSM play. Also for my dining room table and the name of Ginny's business. Beth Spencer for answering my "what's it like to be the significant other of a woodworker" questions.

Ashley again for beta services, and also for, you know, everything.

And Brooke and Brooke and Brooke. There are no words, because it's bigger than words.

CREDITS

PRAISE FOR MERYL WILSNER

'Wilsner is one of the hottest contemporary F/F romance writers right now'
Electric Literature on *Cleat Cute*

'Wilsner proves their serious romance range with a sophomore that laughs in the slow-burning face of their debut by kicking off with a hookup that'll have you fanning your face for days'   *BuzzFeed* on *Mistakes Were Made*

'A sexy and empowering romance'   *Kirkus Reviews* on *Mistakes Were Made*

'This upcoming romance by Meryl Wilsner is everything I've ever wanted in a love story.... Do not miss this book!'   *Book Riot* on *Cleat Cute*

'Meryl Wilsner is a go-to author for sapphic reads'   *Culturess* on *Cleat Cute*

'Wilsner is such a fun author to follow because their debut was the slowest of the slow burns, and then bam, their follow-up was the spiciest of the spicy (within trad pub contemporary romance), and so *Cleat Cute* really could've gone either way ... and gives a great compromise by making you think it's gonna be the former and then. Whew. You will know it when you see it, and you will like it'   *Smart Bitches, Trashy Books* on *Cleat Cute*

'This one struck just right.... Real enough to relate to but escapist enough to enjoy'   *The New York Times* on *Mistakes Were Made*

'Wilsner's steamy, fast-paced secret-lovers contemporary romance features fully realized queer protagonists and secondary characters.... It's not a romantic comedy but definitely has humor, as well as great dialogue and hot sex scenes'   *Library Journal* on *Mistakes Were Made*

'A hilarious, high-heat rom-com ... By coupling raunchy humor and genuine connection, Wilsner's sophomore outing offers plenty to love'
Publishers Weekly on *Mistakes Were Made*

'A vibrant, intoxicating romance' Ashley Herring Blake, author of *Delilah Green Doesn't Care*, on *Mistakes Were Made*

'Wilsner is a storyteller who gently and perfectly steals your heart and hands it back a little fuller. I can't wait to recommend this book to everyone I know!'
Denise Williams, author of
The Fastest Way to Fall, on *Mistakes Were Made*

'Wilsner makes this sports romance a winner'
Publishers Weekly on *Cleat Cute*